MAKE BELIEVE

Cory Wolfe

Copyright © 2020 Cory Wolfe

All rights reserved

eBook ISBN: 978-0-578-69631-7
ISBN: 978-0-578-75048-4

Publication Date: 11/28/2020

Cover design by: Canva/LucidPress
Library of Congress Registration Number: TXu 2-214-604
Printed in the United States of America

CONTENTS

Title Page

Copyright

Dedication

Epigraph

Part One: The Kids Are Not Alright   1

Tyler Tuckerman   2

Jennifer hall   20

Tyler Tuckerman   47

Jennifer hall   68

Tyler Tuckerman   82

Jennifer Hall   102

Tyler Tuckerman   109

Jennifer Hall   119

Tyler Tuckerman   125

Jennifer Hall   135

Tyler Tuckerman   141

Jennifer hall   146

Part Two: A Kid Is Not Alright   158

Tyler Tuckerman   159

Jennifer Hall	174
Tyler Tuckerman	187
Jennifer hall	211
Tyler Tuckerman	233
Jennifer Hall	234
Tyler Tuckerman	248
Jennifer hall	256
Tyler Tuckerman	263
Jennifer hall	271
Tyler Tuckerman	293
Jennifer hall	296
Part Three: Will The Kids Be Alright	305
Tyler Tuckerman	306
Jennifer hall	316
Tyler Tuckerman	321
Jennifer Hall	333
Tyler Tuckerman	341
Praise For Author	345
Acknowledgement	347
Crisis Hotlines	349
Upcoming book by Cory Wolfe	351

This one's for you, yes you, the one reading this,
this very moment.

You have a story, you have a past, and you have a
future.

Hoping our storylines someday meet and/or
continue to intertwine.

Cheers, to your imagination!

Beauty is bought by judgement of the eye.

-WILLIAM SHAKESPEARE, LOVE'S LABOUR'S LOST

PART ONE: THE KIDS ARE NOT ALRIGHT

TYLER TUCKERMAN

I find myself staring off into space, a deep stare where the world's sounds fade away, submerging myself underwater to an eerie, death-like silence. I routinely find myself zoning off every time Mrs. Johnson, our sixty-year-old junior English teacher, goes on a tangent about the importance of literature and how our generation doesn't care. I looked down and read a few lines from my favorite play, read, daydream, read, daydream up the scene like a creative director then stare at the white walls with purple stripes. Our prison cell drips in our high school's mighty colors of pride, integrity, and passion. The colors of Teamwork. Honesty. Friendship. I've drowned seeing and hearing that propaganda for three years now, on every wall on campus, and every cheer shouted. Mrs. Johnson clears her throat and pulls her bifocals down to around her neck, folds both hands on her hips, and lets out a huge sigh. Like clockwork. "Now you listen, back when I was a young girl, we understood and cherished the importance of books and imagination." Just as the class clown yelled out, interrupting her.

"No books were written when you were young!" The class erupted into laughter. Mrs. Johnson rolled her eyes, used to that sort of interruption, and surprisingly accepting of it. I'm still zoning off, deep in a daydream about a summer blue sky and warm blue eyes. My favorite eyes. My favorite color, blue. SMACK. A paper ball hit me in the back of the head.

"Wake up, faggot!"

I slowly close my eyes, then slowly reopen them. I hate football players. Anyone would assume that having had, our first black president, a growing number of gender-neutral bathrooms, and a surprising amount of LGBTQ aired T.V. shows that people would be more accepting. Not in Lincoln, Arizona. The devil's asshole. Probably one of the smallest towns in the entire state. No traffic lights, one bar, and a high school of 150 students. And me, the token gay.

Lincoln was prone to despair, the type of town that sucks you in and never lets you escape. Families never leave generation after generation just making their way during the day and then drinking themselves to sleep every night. Lincoln did make the state-wide news once. A train that goes through the town derailed, slicing the water tower leaving all 1,500 thirsty and frustrated. The National Guard had to supply water for a month until they got the water tower fixed. That was my first volunteer experience. The summers in Lincoln exceed 110 degrees. Not the ideal place to be when you have no water. Again, the devil's asshole.

Mrs. Johnson began to lose control of the class as side conversations started, and no one was paying attention.

"Now class, listen up, stop the talking!" she let out but was interrupted by a knock at the door. Principal Miller opened the screechy door and walked in, followed by an unfamiliar face.

"Students listen up, we have a new student joining us, this is Nicole Clark. Mrs. Johnson, will you see to it that Nicole is settled in?"

"Oh yes, of course, welcome Nicole, welcome to Lincoln High."

Mrs. Johnson is too cheery, I thought. Nicole stood there awkwardly, placing her left arm across her stomach, grabbing her right. Being judged by all twenty students simultaneously, from the style of her flip-flops, her black Jansport backpack, and straight brunette hair.

"Hi y'all," Nicole said in a soft Texas accent followed by a beautiful smile. She took a seat in the first open chair she saw, next to me. Principal Miller left, and Mrs. Johnson resumed the lecture. I slightly glanced over at Nicole, she seemed a little nervous but tried not to let it show. She opened her backpack and got out standard classroom materials to take notes right as the class bell went off. She jumped by the sudden loud ring. I leaned over.

"Yeah, that bell is the worst, they just recently changed it to be more alerting I guess." Nicole let out a laugh.

"Whoever approved that should be fired," Nicole replied.

"Right? I'm Tyler, by the way." I said, reaching my hand out, so professional.

"Nice to meet you, Tyler, I'm Nicole."

"I know," I said sarcastically.

She seemed down to earth, casual, and the Texas version of the girl next door. As we walked out of class entering the sun's rays, she began to tell me a little about herself. She was from Texas, a small town as well but not nearly as small as Lincoln. She explained how her dad got the job as the town sheriff, and she was a little homesick. I couldn't imagine having to move to a new school, a new town, a fresh hell. She started a month late, as school started in August, so she shouldn't be too far behind. Just as we were approaching the junior lockers, Principal Miller's voice echoed over the intercom system.

"All students report to the gymnasium for an assembly, I repeat all students report to the gymnasium."

Nicole and I both looked at each other, she looked confused, but I had a hunch what the assembly was about. The high school was built fifty years ago, classrooms in the shape of a 'U' with the combined gymnasium and auditorium at the top. The chairs were slightly comfortable, movie theatre style with worn-out blue cloth seats and wooden back support. Nicole and I were among the last to arrive, scanning the crowd for two empty seats. I could feel the entire student body glaring at Nicole, fresh meat.

"There, two in the back!" I pointed.

The gymnasium was buzzing with side conversations, few laughs, and paper airplanes. Finally, Nicole asked, "Do you know what this is about? Who is that in the picture in the center of the basketball court?" Confused but slightly aware of why a giant picture was in the center of the court surrounded by flowers and a microphone stand.

"His name is Cameron Fulton, he started here about a month ago when school first started, umm... but he died by suicide last week."

Nicole's eyes expanded in surprise then soft with remorse.

"Oh my god," she let out.

Principal Miller walked to the microphone stand, tapped the top "Test, 1, 2." He's so awkward, I thought.

"Okay, everyone, thanks for attending today's assembly. We have a few items we want to go over before you are all released for lunch, so please pay attention. As all of you know, we lost a fellow student last week. He had a kind soul, and all of our thoughts and prayers go to his family. Now I would like to bring up Mrs. Wilson and the school choir to sing a beautiful tribute song." This school is so small the choir is always made of the same eight people, the Glee obsessed band nerds that are surprisingly in tune. Cameron signed up for the choir club when he joined Lincoln High.

"Ready, one, two, three," Mrs. Wilson counted, followed by hums, guitar strums, and biblical lyrics. You could tell the students were sad, shaken, but not too worried as they only knew Cameron for a month. They would all be discussing the next big rumor or party by the next period. I looked over at Nicole, and she looked genuinely upset, like she could feel what the family was going through, the level of pain Cameron must have felt to take his own life. The choir finished their tribute song, it seemed vaguely familiar, but I couldn't place my finger on its name. Principal Miller returned to the microphone stand.

"Thank you, Mrs. Wilson, for that beautiful song. We all know Cameron would have fit right in with your choir group. Now, students, we are going to bring in a professional counselor from now until the end of the school year for any students who wish to talk to her. It is completely confidential, so please use the resources and don't fear your parents finding out what you both discuss; it's to help you, not get you in trouble. Given the recent set of events that took place over the summer, we want to make sure you are all in good mental health. Suicide is a difficult subject, especially for young adults, to carry with them, so please schedule an appointment with Ms. Jennifer Hall." I knew Nicole would ask.

"What happened over the summer?"
I pondered my thoughts, wanted to make sure I said the correct thing. Nicole just started at this school and will look at it with much kinder eyes.

"Umm, so over the summer... this couple, Greg and Lizzie, also died by suicide, together.... They were found holding each other in his dad's vintage Mustang in his parents' garage with the engine running. It was graduation night."
Nicole placed her hand over her mouth.

"That's terrible, oh my gosh. Does anyone know why?"

"No. Greg and Lizzie were an interesting pair. Did everything together. Never with anyone else. They didn't play sports or join any clubs or activities. I remember Greg when I was in middle school; he was a little bit of a comic nerd who wore those weird tails the comic con kidswear. He was picked on because of it." I described, Nicole nor I paying any attention to the assembly.

"I recently read an article about Lincoln," I continued, "saying we have surpassed the national average suicide rate by 23%, given the number of suicides, time frame, and population."

Nicole looked perplexed, like what in the hell kind of town did she just move to? The assembly was over pretty quickly, and all the students dashed to lunch. Nicole and I took our time, still sitting in the gymnasium.

"Thank you for sitting with me and showing me around," Nicole said as she adjusted her hair, a little tick I noticed she does right before she makes a forward statement.

"Yeah, no problem. I don't have the biggest friend group. I know the feeling of not knowing anyone."

"Well, I'll be your friend!" Nicole said, followed by that beautiful smile. "Can I grab your number?"

"I don't really have a phone at the moment. I had one that broke. It was a pre-paid that always had credits on it because I didn't text or call anyone," I said, hoping Nicole wouldn't think less of me for not being a traditional millennial.

"Oh no problem, so I take it you don't have an Insta or Snap account?"

"No, I don't..." Now, this is the part where Nicole thinks I'm weird, and we part ways forever. Just then, Nicole took out a small piece of paper and wrote down her number.

"Here's mine. I hope you have a landline at home?" She said jokingly.

Haha. "Yeah, I do."

Before I knew it, lunchtime was almost

over. The loud, shocking bell was about to ring, meaning Nicole and I had to part ways, but the school is small enough we didn't have to travel very far. As I walked to the next period class, I couldn't stop thinking about how she genuinely listened to what I had to say, attentive, she wasn't Lincoln raised. Had she not come today, I probably would have sat with a few choir kids, or Mark, he's pretty cool, but he's always with the jocks, and I already see them enough.

The afternoon flew by, and before I knew it, the final bell rang, the school was dismissed for the day. Three large buses lined up at the front of the school. I began walking to the middle bus when I saw Nicole. She was standing off to the side, probably waiting for a ride to pick her up. I ran over.

"Hey stranger, is someone picking you up?"

"Yeah, my dad said he would before he goes into work. He works nights usually."

"So I know you didn't really know Cameron, but his funeral service this Saturday at the Eastside Church. Would you want to come with me?"

"Yes, of course." She said encouragingly.

"I have to arrive a little early to set up, so we can just meet there?"

"I can go early with you. What do you have to set up?"

"Are you sure? I love sleeping on weekends, but the family asked if I would film the service for them and burn it to a DVD."

"That's so nice of you! And yeah, it's fine, I usually wake up early anyway, mostly because my dad makes breakfast and if I want food I better be up and at the table. Do you do a lot of filming?" Nicole joked.

"Film is kind of my hobby. The football coach has me film all their games for him; in exchange, he gives me P.E. credit," I said in a sigh of relief.

The football team is okay for a small school. Since I film all their games, that means I travel with the team when they have away games, the part I dislike the most. Trapped on a bus for three hours with immature football players. The smell doesn't bother me. It's kind of hot. Almost like being in a locker room, but the harassing side is a bitch.

The worst of them all is Jason Brophy, a junior that always reminds me that I'm gay and useless. He was the one who threw the paper ball at my head in Mrs. Johnson's English class. All of his harassings is usually subtle name-calling, writing slurs on my locker, and paper ball throwing. He is a teenage living example of Trump's America. Cowboy boots, cheap beer, and shotguns usually consisted of his weekend activities; he's so cool he doesn't even have a girlfriend. To everyone, he is *Jason Brophy*. My coming out to my peers' story wasn't this grand spectacle full of celebratory hugs and laughs. I actually didn't control it. Jason started telling people that I was gay in eight grade. It spread like wildfire. It seemed like the entire class ran up to tell me the rumor and ask if it was true. Well, it's not not true was my response. Nicole's dad arrived, and I ran to my bus before it left me again.

I arrived home to an empty house again. My dad is a CDL owning truck driver and has been since the day I was born. A few years ago, he bought himself an engine red semi-trailer truck, with living quarters and everything. Right behind the driver's seat. A coffee pot table next to a twin bed. He's a strategic planner. He knew what was brewing and hatched himself an exit strategy. When I was younger, it wasn't bad, his routes were always just a few hour drives here and there, but recently, those hour-long drives turn into days. His parents, my grandparents, lived in the town their entire lives, and their parents before them. My grandfather lives alone now attending to his many birdbaths and feeders, his newfound hobby. My grandmother passed away years ago when I was younger, and I don't think my dad has deep down been the same since. Numbing reality just enough, while chasing the past at the bottom of every bottle.

Our house with wheels is your typical single-wide mobile home that is not very well insulated. My mother does all the decorating in the house. Bright yellow daffodil ornaments filled the kitchen, her favorite flower. A few family pictures scattered across the refrigerator door and plant succulents on the window ledge.

My mother doesn't usually get home until a little later. She is a second-grade school teacher and is often stuck at work. I'm assuming grading the quality of the painted pictures or dried noodle necklaces? She and my dad dated in high school had me and never left town. I always wondered if they blamed me or viewed me as a reason for them not making it out of Lincoln, running off to the big city, the same dream that everyone in Lincoln has.

I plopped down back on my twin bed. Looking up at the ceiling, counting all the glue-balls that have lost their glow in the dark star. I closed my eyes and immediately saw those *warm blue eyes* looking back at me. I could smell the fresh pine from the forest and the water running in the small creek. Birds chirping as the sun's rays moved in and out from behind the tree branches. My heart began to pick up.

He had his arms around me, my head leaning into him, the safest place I've ever felt.

◆ ◆ ◆

Nicole's room was cute, blue soft bed sheets on an old school wooden bed frame. She was ruffling through her room, trying to find a pair of clean black leggings to wear with her dark navy dress, she had other black dresses, but they were still boxed up. She didn't want to go through the hassle she kept saying, beginning to get frustrated. Not with her jeans, not with her shirts, not under the bed? Finally, she tried the small dresser she keeps in her closet, jackpot!

"Finally! Thank heavens. Okay, I'm going to change quickly, then we can head out," Nicole said as she ran to the bathroom to change.

"Okay, cool." I got up and looked around her room, admiring the beat-up metal softball bat leaning against her dark brown desk, all her sports awards and trophies from junior beauty pageants. Second place medal for butterfly and backstroke. Seventh grade Outstanding Player for softball. The employee of the month from lifeguarding at a public pool in Texas. She must have had an exciting life back there, I wonder what it must feel like to completely change your life, leave all of that behind. I saw a picture, well many pictures scattered about her bedroom with the same blonde lady in them. She must be Nicole's mom. I wonder what happened to her? Nicole never mentioned her. I could hear Nicole's phone camera going off in the bathroom. She must be taking a few selfies. I slowly opened a drawer on her desk, inside was a silver flask with an outline of Texas, there seemed to be a little bit of juice left there, whatever it was.

A few pictures with her friends from back wherever she is from, and an assortment of colorful hair ties. The bathroom sink came on, she must be almost done as I slowly closed the drawer and went back and sat on her bed. She seemed normal, teenage reasonable.

Nicole then began looking for her purse, ruffling through her belongings to find that one small black purse she knows she has, and then she remembered it was downstairs. We walked down the stairs into the kitchen. The crispy, oily smell of bacon and the sizzling sound made my mouth water, Sheriff Clark was making breakfast.

"Morning there, would you care for some eggs? I just made a bucket of bacon." Nicole's dad asked while trying to flip the eggs without breaking the yoke. He was right about the bacon, though, a mountaintop sitting on the kitchen table center.

"I'll grab one piece for the road, I can't stay Pops. Tyler and I are going to Cameron Fulton's funeral service. I'm sure you have heard what happened?" Nicole explained as she searched the living room for her little black purse, still unable to find it. Sheriff Clark began to shake his head and let out a sigh.

"Nicole, should you really be going? This is a very private service. You didn't know the boy."

"I don't have to know him to show him

respect, Dad. And Tyler wants me there for support," Nicole replied as I awkwardly stood next to her. Sheriff Clark began cleaning his hands on his blue cooking apron.

"Tyler? Hi, very nice to meet you," he shook my hand as I leaned in, adjusting my camera bag.

"Nice to meet you, Sheriff."

"Alrighty, we are going to head out. I love you." Nicole said as she found her little black purse. We grabbed a few pieces of bacon and headed out the door, paying little attention to what he had just said, a typical teenager. Nicole and her dad moved into a two-story ranch-style home near the center of town, close to the Eastside Church. As we got closer, we could see the church parking lot was full. Cameron's relatives must have come from out of town as some of the cars had California and Nevada plates. A few kids played outside in the dirt with trucks and dinosaurs, a few others on little bikes cruising up and down the poorly built sidewalk. Just as Nicole and I were about to enter the church, we heard shouting and yelling. We froze. Only then, three men threw another man from the church.

"Get the fuck out of here Dennis you piece of shit, we told you not to come around!" One man shouted. Nicole was taken back, clutching her little black purse.

"That's my fucking son!" Dennis shouted from the ground all dusty, visibly drunk, and still wearing the same blue jeans and button-up shirt from the night before. His salt and pepper hair was a mess, and cowboy's boots extremely worn out. The three men began to quickly shut the door to the church.

"Don't you think about coming back in here, Dennis. We told you to stay away, but you couldn't fucking listen!" the second man shouted. We just stood there, still taken aback, but quickly ran to the door, as the men were about to shut it. "Come in darlin'," the third man said, greeting Nicole. Mr. Fulton continued to sit in the dirt, crying, smashing his fist to the ground.

As we entered the Eastside Church, the smell of paper and flowers overcame me. It was an old building that seats about fifty people—large stained glass on both sides of the walls in the center of each a white cross. The altar sat at the end of the building. It had five white floral arrangements, each standing four feet high. In the center of the flowers was a picture of Cameron; red-haired bob cut with bright red cheeks and blue braces. At the end of the standing sprays were toddler pictures of Cameron with even redder hair and redder cheeks.

"Tyler, I'm going to search for the bathroom before this starts," Nicole said as she tapped my shoulder and took off exploring. I looked around to determine where to set up my tripod without being in the way. The left-back corner looked sufficient. I got my camera out and attached it to the tripod when I heard a familiar voice.

"Tyler, thank you so much for doing this for the family, poor things, they could use all the help they can get," said Susan Smith. I could smell the alcohol on her breath. Susan went to school with my parents and works at the high school as the lunch lady. You can see her brunette roots growing in, as she hasn't bleached her hair in a few months.

"Hi Susan, yes, of course, this is just so sad. Anything to help out."
Susan leaned over. "I heard they found him in the bathtub... with his wrist cut down his entire forearm and the shower still on."

My face turned white with shock. "Wow that's intense, please no more details, but umm...who found Cameron?"

"His mama," she said, looking around the room. "I don't see her here yet, the poor thing is probably a wreck, I know I would be. I also heard his dad was abusive, and that's why they moved out here to escape him. I wonder if he will come to the service?" Susan kept on. The one thing people in Lincoln are good at is talking about each other. I kept setting up my camera, nodding.

"Is your mama coming, Tyler?"

"Umm, I believe so... the last time I asked, she was."

"Alright, well if you see her tell her I'm looking for her." Susan replied, jetting off to gossip with the next person she saw. I wonder if my mom was coming. She didn't know Cameron. But it's something you do within the community as a sign of respect. More and more people came in, all dressed in black, all silent. Among them was Cameron's mother; she had on a pair of big dark sunglasses, a black hat, and tiny heels. She was on the bigger side, so she complimented her skirt with a black blazer. She slowly greeted and thanked each person for coming, tears rolling down her cheek, and landing on her arm's bare skin. I quickly turned my camera and got some snapshots of people entering the flowers they brought, and a few of Cameron portraits. I changed the setting on my camera to capture those in black and white. As Nicole began to walk toward me, the pastor walked up to the podium and started reading Matthew 11:28: "Come to me, all you who are weary and burdened, and I will give you rest..." I've witnessed many emotional events through the eye of my camera: weddings, sporting events, lunar eclipses, funeral services, and my favorite, *those warm blue eyes*.

JENNIFER HALL

P apers were scattered across my small Ikea like cheap desk that faced a small window that was home to a small indoor cactus. My school appointed laptop sat in the middle with my cellphone and charger to the right, notepad, and pen to the left. I was settling into my new office at Lincoln High. What a drive, I researched the school before moving, and the location, but it seemed farther and more isolated than I had imagined. I traveled from Phoenix, where I used to live. I was contacted by the State of Arizona about a case developing in the small town of Lincoln, serial teen suicides, and if I was interested in helping. The school applied for a grant that was approved, providing funds to bring me in to help, as a mental health counselor. The county even allocated enough funds to support the police department, part-time, counsel some of the parents, and assist where I can with the police work. This level of activity would be so different I couldn't wait to get started. I left my position as a school counselor for the top private school in Phoenix because it wasn't rewarding. Each over-privileged student complained about the same nonsense, not having a big enough allowance or why they weren't invited to so and so's house party. The case in Lincoln seemed likethe opportunity I was craving. I needed a chance to help real troubled kids, help their parents, and really make an impact on this community.

There was a knock at the door, "Howdy, Ms. Hall!" Sheriff Clark said as he poked his head inside my small office.

"Sheriff Clark, please call me Jennifer. How has your morning been?" I asked, shaking his hand.

"Shitty... my daughter is off at that poor boy's funeral service. I told her I didn't think it was a good idea. She didn't know him. You know that was the first call I got when I started out here, I thought the night shift would have been a lot quieter."

"Oh that is terrible. I am going to meet with Cameron's mother sometime next week to see how she is doing, offer my services, be of any help. But Sheriff, why do you think it was not a good idea that Nicole went to that service?"

"She didn't know him. She didn't know any of the three deaths that occurred within the last few months," Sheriff Clark said, scratching the back of his head.

"Sheriff, I'm sorry, don't mean to decide what you think your daughter should or shouldn't do, but she is a part of this school now, the LSH community, and the town of Lincoln. Everyone is mourning, and with grief comes a process that is not all the same; those emotions could be felt, and she is being a good neighbor. It must be the Texas side," I let out a little joke to ease the tension. Sheriff Clark just nodded and agreed, taking a sip of his coffee.

I began searching through some papers.

"So I was reading the file, and it appears two students also took their lives together the night of graduation. Just three months ago. Now Cameron."

"That is correct. Found the couple in the boy's old man's Mustang in the garage with the engine running," Sheriff Clark described as he took a sip of his coffee mug.

"Now, three months before that, another student in Berza County, about two hours from here, also took his own life. Also, from a small town, not nearly as small as Lincoln, but small. Sheriff Clark, I know I'm not a detective by any means, but maybe these students are being influenced by an online source, a cult-like following." I said. Sheriff Clark could see the worry in my eyes, the frustration of not being able to help those kids before they made the decisions they could never take back.

"Kids these days are nothing like we were growing up. They are all connected and decisions driven by what is said or displayed on the

Internet."

"I'm going to begin seeing the students starting Monday. That's why I'm in my office this weekend. To get everything ready. Aside from today, how is your daughter doing with her new surroundings?"

"She's a fighter after losing her mother last year. Well, I'll say she is strong. She's been clinging to me a lot. I don't mind it, I'm just excited for her to finally be settled and comfortable. I got her a part-time job already tutoring," Office Clark said. You could hear his voice weaken slightly. The pain still lingers about his wife.

"Oh that is great! It will be good for her to stay busy and be socially active. While also allowing her to grieve in her own way."

"The one thing Nicole isn't is shy. Well, I won't hold you up, I know you have a million things you have to get done, figured I'd stop by and see how things were going."

"Thank you, yes I have a lot of prep work ahead of me, but it's going to be good," I replied. Just as Sheriff Clark was just about to leave he stopped and turned back around into my office,

"A boy you said in Berza County killed himself... how?"

"Sheriff, sorry, but please refer to it as died by suicide." I had to correct him, pass it forward. I stopped sorting papers and froze, and took off my glasses and looked at Sheriff Clark,

"He shot himself."

◆ ◆ ◆

The walls were bare white with typical rental style decor and lighting. There was a small television in the living room that was so old the screen was made of glass. The wood in the kitchen was light brown with off-white vinyl titles that were beginning to peel off. Each of the teachers' housing that Lincoln High offered looked alike, the house that I would be staying in for the remainder of the year.

The first thing I did was wash the bed-sheets, vacuum meticulously, and wash each glassware piece. You could tell this house has not had a visitor in a while as I was scrubbing the cooking pans. Lincoln High had about four of these little homes, all within close proximity to the school. After the cleaning, I began to put away my clothes and display a few picture frames I brought with.

I set up a little office in the dining room with my laptop and files. At the corner of my desk is where I kept my pothos houseplant my parents got me when I first started my career a few years back. They said it symbolizes perseverance, Ideal good luck for anyone starting a new job or adventure. I named her, Ruby.

Her vines were almost touching the ground, just inches away dangling midair. I kept a small spray bottle close to make sure she stayed hydrated, especially in this Arizona heat. It was only recently that I discovered Ruby has a variety of common names, such as, silver vine, marble queen, golden pothos, and lastly - *devil's ivy*. As I waited for my dirty clothes to get done washing, I sat in my new small office staring at the blank screen on my laptop, overtaken with flashbacks of those poor kids. I got goosebumps. Sheriff Clark showed me pictures of Cameron's crime scene to drill down the intensity of his self-mutilation.

I went into the kitchen and poured myself a glass of wine. The first sip was a big gulp I held in my mouth and then swallowed. What could have possibly been going through those kids' minds to lead them to such brutal suicides? Could all three cases be connected? Cameron was so new to the school, and he didn't even know Greg and Lizzie, but I'm sure he heard what happened. I knew that to understand the kids at Lincoln High, I must first understand their parents. I finished my glass of wine, threw on some jeans, and headed to the only bar in town, The Saguaro.

The building was old, like every building in Lincoln. As I pulled up I could see a few bikers parked out front, they must have stopped on their way through town. Next to them were beat up old Fords, a Chevy, and a cute Jeep. I got out of my car and walked by a few locals sitting on the patio. The sun had just gone down, so the temperature was perfect. I could feel them staring at my ass. I walked in the door to a dim-lit bar; it had one pool table, a jukebox, one bartender, and a full row of patrons sitting at the bar top. The odor of cigarette smoke from outside lingered inside. The floor is cold bare cement.

"Hi darling, what can I get for you?" The cute young blonde bartender asked as she grabbed cash from the man sitting in front of her. She had short shorts and a black tank top with a long bottle opener peeking out from her back pocket.

"Hi there, I'll just take a whiskey on the rocks, no preference, house whiskey is fine," I said, pulling out my wallet from my purse, still scanning the room. I found an open chair near the door, so I wouldn't have to venture too far. Up above were wadded up single, ten, and twenty-dollar bills thumbtacked to the ceiling. At the center of the bar was a six-point elk head taxidermy, surrounded by the barebones of a saguaro. The iconic 1976 Farrah Fawcett red swimsuit poster, signed and framed. Antique trinkets scattered about. Historic beer steins from Prohibition neatly displayed along the shelves above the assorted liquor. The red banner caught my eye almost immediately, Make America Great Again. Behind me, blue light with the words ATM sat in the corner, this was a cash-only bar.

"Here you go darling, five-fifty," the bartender said, sliding over my bourbon, but with no ice.

"Umm sorry, but could I get a few ice cubes in here?"

"Oh I'm sorry, yes, of course." She replied. Had she not been flirting with the guy at the end, she probably would have remembered. Just as the bartender handed me my correct drink, this older short, delicate lady walked by and sat next to me. Her chair was custom, a classic salon chair with blankets and a cup holder. She immediately continued her conversation with the gentleman next to her. Her voice was raspy as she took a sip of her bourbon and cola through a straw. Everyone seems to be well acquainted with each other. The wood door then creaked open, a man walked in. He was instantly greeted by four patrons, the bartender, and the bar dog. His hair was short, brunette with a tool belt around his hip. He had on working boots, calloused hands, and a t-shirt he cut the short sleeves off of. He sat next to me; I took a sip of my bourbon.

"Why hello there, I don't believe I have seen you around here. Is that a 1980 *Back In Black* AC/DC shirt you're wearing?" He asked as the bartender slid him his usual beer. I blushed.

"Yes it is. I loved that album," I said, taking another sip of my whiskey.

"That was a great album."

"Was? Still is!" I demanded. He laughed, exposing cute dimples on both sides of his cheeks. He took a sip of his beer.

"You're absolutely right. My name's Ricky, by the way, Ricky Tuckerman."

"Nice to meet you, Ricky. I'm Jennifer Hall, I recently moved into town. I'm working up at Lincoln High," I said and, for some strange reason pointing in the direction of the school as if he didn't already know.

"My son goes there, Tyler Tuckerman."

"How exciting, I haven't met any students yet, I start Monday," I explained. Just then, a man comes over.

"Ricky!" he shouted, patting the man next to me on the back; they then taped bottles in cheers and drank at the same time. Tyler's dad was definitely a popular one around here, I thought, sending a friendly smile to the man who just appeared.

"Martin, this is Jennifer Hall, she works up at the school," Ricky introduced us.

"Jennifer Hall, what a pleasure to meet you. Why haven't I seen you here before? Someone that beautiful needs to come around every night," Martin slurred then busted into laughter as if it was a joke, "My son, Erik, goes to Lincoln

High. Dumb ass, probably failing every class. He didn't even get to play in the last football game because his grades were so fucking bad." Martin went on, taking a drink of his beer.

"Well at least your son tries to play football," Ricky said. "My son films it, he must have gotten that from his mother." Ricky mentioned, taking a drink of his beer. The two men went on exchanging small anecdotes about their sons; some were good, while some had a bitter undertone attached. The group on the other side of me were discussing Cameron and his dad, Dennis. One of the girls mentioned how she had almost slept with Dennis one night after the two of them were partying. The other lady commented on how she didn't find Dennis attractive and that her friend must have been blacked out to almost sleep with him. The two then laughed.

Overcome with water, wine, and whiskey, I looked around for the restroom. Just like Lincoln, it was small. As I sat in the stall, two girls stumbled in and walked up to the mirror. They sounded late twenties.

"Oh my god we have to go next weekend, that concert sounds amazing, I'll ask my mom if she could watch our girls. If she's too busy, we can ask one of the kids at the high school if they want to earn a quick twenty bucks."

"They would totally do it for twenty bucks. Who is watching your little girl now?" the one friend asked as she took a sip of her vodka cranberry. I could see them through the slit in the stall. The priorities those girls shared was definitely themselves and then their kids. Before her friend could answer, *Back In Black* by AC/DC began blasting from the jukebox, the girls gasped and then hurried out of the restroom. I emerged from the bathroom to find those girls dancing along, and a fresh bourbon over ice waiting for me with Ricky smiling. "I had to play that song. You can't wear a shirt like that and not listen to it," he suggested, taking a sip of his beer.

"You're absolutely right," I laughed, walking over to thank him for buying my whiskey-cola.

"This is a welcome to town drink, High West!" Ricky said

"High West? Who knew Utah could brew such good whiskey" I replied, taking a small sip then closing my lips.

"So, where are you from, Jennifer?" Ricky asked

"I was born and raised here in Arizona. My folks still live back home in Holbrook. Small town, the population of about five thousand."

"Yeah I know Holbrook."

"I moved to Phoenix for school and work. Now here I am."

"What do you do at school? You, a teacher?" Ricky asked.

"I am a counselor. Given the events that have been going on, these kids could use someone to talk to, you know?" I said, giving Ricky my full attention. His eyes were glossy, a little bloodshot.

"Oh right on. Yeah, we don't need any more funeral services around here, so please help away," Ricky said, taking a sip of his beer. I then decided to call it a night. I thanked Ricky for buying me a welcome to town drink then headed out the door onto the patio, walking into a cloud of cigarette smoke mixed with blueberry vape smoke. I sat in my car and began to think about back home and how tomorrow my mom and I have our one-hour Sunday talk ritual. She tells me all about the new hobbies my dad is starting, the various craft projects she is working on, some new books she is reading, and how all her church friends are doing. My parents are very religious Christians, church every Sunday, volunteering around town and making sure there is a Bible in every room of the house. My mom is a retired dental hygienist, and my dad, a retired accountant. They aren't your typical retirees. They don't travel or own a large RV that they use to travel around America. They keep it simple, keep themselves busy with various projects around the community while staying active in the church. I play along because it makes her feel good, and what is the harm, right? We always end our Sunday talk with a prayer, asking the Lord to watch over me, the two dogs, my parents, and to give Emily a big hug for us, my forever eight-year-old little sister.

◆ ◆ ◆

The first day on the job at Lincoln High has started off well. Primarily because of all the prep work I did the weekend before. My office sat in one of the rooms within the larger front office of the school. Principal Miller's office just feet away, followed by the school treasurer, and a large board meeting room. I usually leave my office door open, unless I'm meeting with a student.

"Good Morning, are you settling in well?"

"Good Morning, Principal Miller. Why, yes, I am. I stopped in over the weekend to get ahead so we can hit the ground running," I replied.

"Okay great. I just emailed you a list of sensitive students, who I think you should start with," Principal Miller said as he went back into his office. I turned around to my laptop and opened Outlook. The sensitive student list included four students. Next to their names, the Principal's reason for why each is on the list. It is a justification of listing them as sensitive.

•Tyler Tuckerman – *Gay?*
•Bobby (Robert) Jones – *Choir club and knew Cameron*
•Mark Watson – *Adopted*

The list was helpful since most students would probably never schedule an appointment to see me. Instead, I will reach out and recommend they see me and try and make it recurring. If they ask why I will mention that I am making every student have one mandatory session. I decided to go in list-order. Two names on this list stand out because I've already met a parent of each. Timely coincidence? Or is this town as small as they say? Knowing that I should be mindful about where and when I am seen outside of school, especially since there aren't too many places to go. Casual run-ins are inevitable. The positive and negative judgment was unavoidable.

   I pulled up Tyler Tuckerman's file in the school database system. I figured I would start with the two students I have some background information on. He was sixteen-years-old. The record included last year's class photo. He had short brown hair with brown eyes with long eyelashes, pretty thin-looking while wearing a light blue button-up shirt. The profile detailed his class schedule, and his current grades: All 'A's'. Good for him. According to his file, he had already passed all three Arizona's Instrument to Measure Standards tests with "exceeds" status. I should prioritize Tyler. Begin a gay teenager he is more at risk of being bullied, picked on, and have suicidal thoughts. I wrote down his class schedule.

I then looked up Nicole's profile. She, too, was sixteen-years-old. Her photo was just uploaded a few days ago. I noticed, she looks a little like her father. Her transcripts from her previous high school show she was a good student and very active in sports.

According to his schedule, Tyler would be in math class. Before heading off, I stopped by the teachers' lounge and refilled my coffee mug. The lounge coffee was burnt. Just as I got to the math class door, the bell went off, and students began to emerge from various classrooms. I looked around for Tyler, but I didn't spot him. I only saw one familiar face. I recognized Nicole. She was putting on her backpack and slowly walking toward me.

"Nicole! Hi, I'm Jennifer Hall, the new school counselor."

"Hello Ms. Hall, how's your day going?" Nicole asked, displaying that Texas hospitality.

"My day is going great. How's yours?" I replied.

"Oh just another glorious Monday," Nicole said.

"I met your dad, Sheriff Clark. He's a nice man. Can we schedule a meeting? I want to get to know you. I know you're new to town, so I want to see how you're adjusting."

"Yeah he's nice until the Cowboys lose,

which is pretty frequent," Nicole joked. "Yeah sure. When should we have it?"

"Okay great. My session hours today are all open, come by anytime. I'll email your teacher when you do to excuse you from class."

"Okay cool"

"Alrighty. Well, I won't hold you up. Don't want you to be late on your first week at school," I joked back. I thought she was a sweet girl, glad that my first meeting would be with her and get an outside perspective. The day was pretty gloomy, puffy thunderclouds forming in the distance. It set a mood for all the students the first day back to school after Cameron's funeral service. The wind began to pick up; I pulled up a weather app on my phone, a 95% chance of rain and thunder, lovely.

I got back to my office and decided to continue my research. I pulled up Bobby Jones' profile. He was fourteen-years-old and has been tardy to school in the last few weeks. I wonder if Bobby and Cameron shared the same class schedule? Principal Miller noted they were friends, but how close? They must have been close for it to be flagged. I printed out his class schedule.

I then pulled up Cameron's school profile. My heart instantly melted when I saw his brown eyes, red hair, and blue braces smiling toward me. He looked confident, brave, and happy. As humans, we have to know the answers to things. We have to understand why. And when there aren't any answers, we conjure up our own reasons, we make ourselves believe in the answers. Cameron never told us why. No letter or note directing us to the reasons. A lost ship in the dead of night with no lighthouse. Why Cameron? Why? I cross-referenced Cameron's class schedule with Bobby's. They matched exactly.

I sat in my office, pondering how I would begin this online investigation. Should I create an online alias? Be among the students from the shadows? I needed a way to figure out what was being discussed in these chat rooms/forums/blogs. It was just then my phone rang. It was Mrs. Johnson, she's such a sweet lady. She informed me that Nicole was about to come to my office, and then she started going on about the upcoming weather. Just as I hung up, there was a knock at my door. It was from Nicole. Damn, this school is small, I thought.

"Hello, Ms. Hall, I hope I am not interrupting."

"Oh, of course not, never, please have a seat," I said, standing up to shut the door behind her. She took a seat on my comfortable, brown leather recliner; I reached for my notebook and pen. Nicole was squeezing her hands together, she seemed a bit nervous.

"Would you like some water?" I asked walking over to the mini-fridge I had installed for refreshments to the students,

"Yes, please."

"So Nicole, tell me about yourself, where are you from?"

Nicole took a sip of her water. Sheriff Clark already told me where they came from, but I wanted her to describe it.

"I'm originally from Texas, a good-sized town close to Austin. A cute town. I didn't really want to move, I didn't want to leave my friends and family, I liked my part-time job, a lifeguard at the community pool."

"How has the transition been for you?" I asked, slightly tilted my head, giving Nicole my full attention.

"It has been okay, my dad already got me a part-time job, I swear he is more social than I am."

"What is your part-time job?"

"Tutoring. I tutored a little back in Texas. Since there is no community pool in Lincoln, I figured why not. But, this whole move would have been easier if my mom was still around," Nicole said, looking down at her feet, breaking eye contact.

"Tell me about your mom."

"She was beautiful, such a fun free spirit. She owned a nail salon back in Texas, she always made sure my nails were on point. I would usually just go for natural colors, but they still looked great. We lost her last year to breast cancer... fuck cancer," Nicole said, still looking down at her feet. I extended my hand, comfortingly on Nicole's knee.

"I'm not sure what your religious beliefs are, but I do believe that the people we lose will remain alive through our love and memories of them. You are so incredibly brave to have traveled across states to a new school, a new town. You got her bravery," I explained.

"Thanks, Ms. Hall."

"Would you ever want to return to Texas? Like for college, or?"

"Yeah, I've thought about it. I was looking at the nursing program at Texas A&M. A few of my relatives went there, and I love their football team," Nicole joked, taking a sip of her water. Nursing would be a great career for her, her wanting to help people could really make an impact.

"That is awesome, Nicole, and let me know where I can be of any help. Maybe work to schedule a campus tour? I actually thought about going into nursing when I was at ASU."

"I'm already starting to prepare. I got this anatomy book to familiarize myself with the inner human working for now. Did you know, the sound of the heart is generated by the opening and closing of the heart valves, they are described as a *lub* and a *dub*."

"Any preparations you do now will only benefit you in the future. I'm proud of you that you are focused on your future."

"Thanks, Ms. Hall." Nicole said softly as she began to look around the room. She noticed a collection of picture frames I had sitting on my desk.

"Do you have a daughter?" Nicole asked, referring to a picture I had of Emily. She was swinging on a wooden swing set, her long blonde hair flowing in the wind with a huge bright smile. I remember that day as if it were yesterday—Christmas morning.

"No, no, I am not a mother, that is my little sister, Emily. She passed away when I was twelve-years-old... She was eight-years-old."

"Was it cancer too?" Nicole asked, looking genuinely concerned and curious. But before I could answer, I heard loud crying erupting from the main large front office. I slowly stood up,

"Nicole, wait here one second."

I opened my door to find Principal Miller walking with a male student. I recognized Bobby Jones from the photo in his file. He had his hand around Bobby's thin arm. Bobby was distraught and seemed slightly drunk.

"My best friend!" He cried. Gasping for air as he stumbled to walk. I immediately walked to him, placed both my hands on the sides of his warm red face.

"Bobby, look at me, you're going to be okay, come into my office and let's talk." I took

Bobby by the hand and walked him to my office, looking back at Principal Miller, who held up a phone symbol with his hands, indicating he would call his parents to come to get him.

"Nicole, I am so sorry, can we reschedule?" I asked, setting Bobby in my chair, he was still crying.

"Yes, of course! I'll head back to Mrs. Johnson's class," Nicole said, grabbing her water bottle and giving me a friendly smile as she headed out the door. She understood the severity of this situation. Bobby slowly began to calm down, he was swaying a little in his chair, I wondered where he got the alcohol?

"Bobby what is going on? What happened today?" I asked, sitting on my knees, looking up at Bobby's tear face and messy hair.

"It's Cam...Cameron." Bobby stuttered while using his long sleeve shirt to wipe the tears from both his eyes.

"I know you miss him, It's okay to feel the way you're feeling, but you can't hurt yourself with alcohol," I said. Bobby just sat there, still wiping the tears from his eyes. I noticed little scratches on his arm, they were red lines. They didn't appear to break the skin, more like cat scratches.

"Bobby, what is this on your arm?" I asked, pointing slightly.

"Isn't that what you do when you're sad? That's what they do on TV, and I know that's what Cameron did," Bobby said, feeling guilty and shy. I can't believe what I just heard. The kids honestly believe that when they are sad, they hurt themselves as a way of dealing or coping.

"Bobby, listen to me, it is never, ever, okay for you to hurt yourself. I know you didn't mean to, you were sad and confused. But, promise me that you will never attempt to hurt yourself again, promise me!" I demanded as I ran my hands through his messy hair. He was an innocent kid, just lost. He seemed younger than his age.

"I know you and Cameron were good friends when he moved here, I heard you both were in the choir club together, you both would practice band instruments? Play some video games, maybe?" I asked.

"Yeah, we became good friends. He taught me this new online battle game, it was cool we could play together from our own rooms online, battle people together, go on quests to earn as many diamonds as possible so we could purchase new armor and shields, it was so fun," Bobby described, giving me a slight smile.

"That does sound like a lot of fun, you should show me how to play sometime," I said.

"I would just watch Cameron sometimes play because he was so good. Some of the chat rooms were weird, the people in there, what they would talk about." Bobby said, looking confused.

"What would they talk about?" I asked.

"They were so angry that anytime you beat their character, they would yell at you to go die and go 'f' off," Bobby said, looking sad again, "They reminded me of Jason Brophy."

"Who is Jason Brophy?" I asked.

"He's a football player and a total jerk. He was always picking on Cameron and me, call us gay for always hanging around each other. He told the whole school we jack off together after school," Bobby said, tears beginning to form from his soft brown eyes.

"Bobby, I promise you Jason will never tease or be mean to you again, I promise," I said, giving him a hug. He began to cry again. If things couldn't get any more gloomy, raindrops began to slide down my office window, and the tree branches began to sway. I just continued to hold Bobby, probably the first real long hug he has gotten in a while.

◆ ◆ ◆

I sat on my couch in my warm gray sweatpants and long sleeve nightshirt, wine in hand, laptop on my lap, and the sounds of the rain and thunder crack across the sky. Today's session with Bobby really upset me. I really got me thinking about the well-being of these kids, and had I come sooner, they could have probably saved three lives. I was surfing the Internet, trying to find clues or hints to an online cult.

"The Momo Challenge?" I said to myself, stumbling across some potentially useful clues to my theory of an online perpetrator. It tells the challenge that appeared to be a hoax. Momo was an urban legend about a disturbing looking creature with big bulging eyes, a grim smile, long black stringy hair with chicken legs. Appearing on the screens of kids and adolescents while surfing YouTube or Facebook. Instructing them to perform violent acts against themselves and others.

The challenge got worldwide coverage when an Indonesian newspaper reported that Momo was the cause of suicide to a twelve-year-old girl, but nothing was ever verified by authorities. I wonder if Lincoln has its own version of Momo? Only targeting kids in the general area, after all a kid two hours from here shot himself last March, no social connection to the students at Lincoln High. I grabbed a pen and pad.

- February 28th – *Student in Berza County*
- May 31st – *Greg Norris and Lizzie Chapelton*
- August 30th – *Cameron Fulton*

This cannot be a coincidence, each suicide three months apart almost to the day. Today is Monday, September 30th. If the pattern I just drew continues, then in the next two months, this online cult perpetrator will try to strike if I am on the right path, and these suicides are connected. It was then that I came across another terrible online challenge.

"Blue Whale Challenge?" I said again to myself. The game consisted of a series of tasks assigned to the players by some administrator, a puppet-like master pulling strings. The administrator would assign the players an assignment a day for fifty days. Each day getting more intense until the final fiftieth day, where they were instructed to die by suicide. This Blue Whale Challenge got worldwide coverage when a Russian outlet reported the linking of several unrelated child suicides. The linking was their involvement in an online social network, a site that is now banned. My jaw dropped, how could humans be so cruel to one other, especially to young children. My wine glass was empty, in need of a refill.

I stood in the poorly lit kitchen, pouring myself a glass of ice-cold chardonnay until the last drop dripped from the bottle. I tossed the bottle and closed the fridge, seeing the bright young smile of Emily radiating toward me. I loved that picture. I had a few images magnet pinned to my fridge; One of my parents, one of Emily, and two of my best friends from college. I try not to think of that day, the day she slipped away. Guilt overcomes me to the point where I can't breathe and end up breaking down, 'what if' scenarios play over and over. I was supposed to look after her, be her big sister, and protect her. Being a professional counselor, I understand the grieving process, but understanding the process doesn't make it any less hurtful.

We were camping as a family. The day we lost her. My mother shouted at me, falling to the ground as tears rolled down her face, my dad trying to hold her. I knew it was my fault. I told her to follow me on an adventure where we would play make-believe in the woods. Magical princesses fighting off the evil sorcerers with our trusted beagle, Frank, as our dragon howled toward the warlocks. She was dressed as a princess, and I was a wizard, shouting spells and hiding behind tree trunks. I told her we should split up and circle around the make-believe sorcerers we were fighting in the woods. I ran down a hill, still shouting spells.Frank following behind me.

It began to rain, massive pelting raindrops. My wizard costume was soaked, and the hills got muddy, making it difficult to climb back up. More and more rain pouring down, increasingly tempestuous. I finally made it back up, and Emily was nowhere in sight. I could barely hear except the rain sputtering. Shouting her name but got no response. Frank was next to me, panting. I yelled out her name some more and still no response. I took off running, slipping in the mud as the rain continued to downpour. It was then I saw her pointy purple princess hat soaked in the distance. I ran over to pick up the cap, but still no Emily. I looked around until then I saw Emily. Her faint princess dress and blonde hair. She slipped off the muddy ledge, fallen into the nearby lake and drown.

TYLER TUCKERMAN

My laptop was pretty old, all black Microsoft that I got for my birthday one year when I really began getting into film. I still use the same video-editing program from when I first started three years ago. I made myself a little editing area in my room, right in front of the window, a 'U' shaped desk that my mom helped snag from the elementary school. Capturing the film onto the software is probably my least favorite part. You have to play the entire video as the camera is plugged into the laptop. I usually shower, make food, or clean as the process does its thing. I've been slacking lately as I still had two previous footballs to compile as well as Cameron's funeral services for his family.

The football games are a mindless edit. The coach just wants me to burn the film onto a DVD so he can review with the players, I'm assuming to improve? Try and learn from their mistakes, as they just end up making them anyway no matter how many hours of film they watch. My plan today was to crank out those two mindless football videos and get started on Cameron's service, a task that will involve some degree of creativity. The Fulton family gave me a song list, old video footage of Cameron's first birthday, how to walk, and photos from various family vacations at the beach.

An hour and a half went by, capturing the two football games on my laptop like I said my least favorite part of the process. Burning them to DVD is usually quick, about ten to fifteen minutes in total. Before I began the burn process, I was considering adding in a background song during the football games. Maybe a song about how much the football team sucks or even better, "Bohemian Rhapsody" by Queen, but I knew the coach would kill me. After all, I am getting P.E. credit for this. It was then that I heard the front door open and close, my mom must be back, she ran into her classroom to catch up on a few things. Elementary school teachers are so overworked for the pay. I decided to head to the kitchen, I needed a snack.

"Hey Mom," I said, looking for a small bag of chips in the pantry.

"Hi Ty. You got your film magazine in the mail today," said my mom as she placed a few grocery items on the table along with some mail.

"Oh sweet! Where did you put it?" I have a few magazine subscriptions from *Videomaker* and *Digital Camera World*. Nerdy, I know.

"It should be on the table, by the groceries."

"Oh I found it," I answered as I walked over and laid on the couch, flipping through my new magazine. "How was school?"

"The sprinkler head broke in front of my room, so there was water all over. The grass flooded, I called Mario," My mom described putting a few grocery items in the fridge. "You know his daughter is having her birthday next weekend. Think they are headed into the city and going to an amusement park. You know the one with that huge roller coaster. You should ask her out?"

Here she goes again, hinting at me to try and date girls. Ignoring the fact that I came out a few years ago. She is in the worst stage of denial.

"Mom, I'm gay, remember?" I am always, always having to remind her, remind her as she purposely forgets—deaf ears. I kind of want to tell her every morning when I first wake up, with the hopes that if I say it enough, she will finally *believe* me. It got quiet. All I could hear was the sound of food being rearranged in the fridge.

"I told Ms. Johnson I would help her at the Letterman's booth next week during the homecoming football game, so if you could just stay at the school until the game because I won't be able to pick you up from the house." My mom recently started doing these 'charity' exercises, where she helped out at the high school during various events. The reason is still unknown. Still, I guess it's a good thing, for a good cause.

"Will Dad be there?" I asked

"More than likely, yes, or you'll know where to find him after."

"I have a lot of footage to put together. The coach will be expecting the games by tomorrow, so I'm going to work on that. Call me when dinner is ready," I said, getting up from the couch, grabbing a soda and heading back to my room. I don't think she could tell that her comments about trying to get a girlfriend bothered me, I should be used to it by now, every chance she gets she tries to set me up with someone.

The football games were all done. The coach would have been mad if I didn't have them ready for him by tomorrow. He kept saying how they needed the footage to prep for the homecoming game. I started working on Cameron's service, in-between all the speeches, crying, and the pastor doing some readings. It lasted for about thirty minutes. They didn't give me enough songs for that length of time, but I knew how to make it work.

I started with baby videos of Cameron his mom gave me. The first song playing in the background. He sat in a highchair with a small blue first birthday cake in front of him, looking around at all the people, unsure what to do with this thing.

His mom kept putting his little hands on the cake, trying to show him that he can eat it, and it kind of worked. Halfway through them trying to get him to eat the cake, he started crying, he was over it. Then the video cut to the funeral service beginning to start, the ones I got in black and white of people coming into the church, greeting the family.

Halfway through the service, the pastor did a moment of silence. I cut to a photo slide show of the family on vacation at the beach. The next scene was vintage footage of Cameron taking his first steps, balancing on his little feet, then gravity taking over falling to the side. Luckily his dad was there to catch him.

Footage switching to Cameron graduating kindergarten then 8th-grade promotion with the second song playing in the background. Finally, cutting back to the service where his mom and aunt gave an emotional speech. I ended the video with a current photo of Cameron with the last song playing; below his most recent portrait were birth and death dates.

Cameron J. Fulton
2005 -2019

I did similar edits for Greg and Lizzie's service videos, both separate of course for each family, but at the end, a photo of them together. Her mother didn't like that part, but I thought it was necessary as they were dating and died together. She doesn't understand the artistic lens. When I first started making films, I would play make-believe, creating little movies with my action figures. Stop motion videos of them fighting, going on quests, or horror pieces. I remember making one short film with various fruits as the main characters and tried to imagine what the personality traits would be for each one. The movie was okay.

For one eighth grade project, we had to pick a social topic and present it. I choose animal cruelty, specifically in the fashion industry. Everyone just thought, oh, here's the gay kid showing on fashion. At the end of my presentation, I put together a film piece with clips I collected online to really hit home on my topic. Sadly, we had to turn it off halfway through thanks to Wendy Mendoza, who started crying after the scene with the skinning of the red-tailed foxes, yes, who was still alive. They needed to know what really goes on in the world. Needless to say, none of the girls wore fake fur for a while.

I sat in Ms. Hall's small office, looking out her little window, wondering how long it will take for her small cactus to fry from sitting in the window ledge. Ms. Hall approached me a few days ago about setting up a meeting. I wonder if she asked other students? Of course, she set a meeting up with the school's token gay. Principal Miller must have told her, or perhaps other school staff. She had on faint colors of purple and gold, our school colors. She must have felt in the school spirit since this was spirit week for homecoming. Oh, such a jolly time considering what has happened recently.

Monday was Pajama Day, so the students were encouraged to wear their pajamas to school, so they didn't have to try too hard for some students. Tuesday was Western Day, all the rednecks went all out to dress as hick as possible, and the girls decided to dress like they just got back from a country music festival. Wednesday was Disco Day, which meant every student, asked their parents if they could borrow their clothes from the 1970s. Thursday was Opposite Day, or Gender Bender Day, encouraging students to dress as the opposite gender for the day. For some strange reason, the jocks really got into it. I still think it is insane how this school always chooses to have this day, mixed with all the other joke days. For decades most schools joined in this politically incorrect, severely insensitive day during their spirit weeks. Still, as time went on, those schools have realized the insensitivity and completely removed it. Not LHS. This school's administration and community proudly support, proudly sponsors an event that makes a joke out of gender identity, completely eliminating a sense of safety and acceptance. Gay rights are not an addressed topic in the devil's asshole, too many here, it's still a chosen act that happens only on T.V. or far far away.

Finally, Friday, today was Spirit Day, so wear the school colors purple and white. I didn't participate in any day except Monday, but that was out of pure laziness. I'm glad the week is finally over, all we have left is the pep assembly and then the day is over, but before I could fantasize what I would do when I got home.

"Tyler? Are you okay?" Ms. Hall asked.

"Oh sorry, yes, I was just admiring your cactus, what a perfect spot," I said sarcastically.

"Yeah I think so as well, it's been doing great so far. Now Tyler, how have the days been? Have you enjoyed yourself during Spirit Week?"

"Ummm yeah, this week has been fun. All the students are really getting into the school spirit, which is good. The football game tonight should be exciting." I said, knowing damn well the game will not be exciting, and I could care less about Spirit Week, I'm just making her job easy by telling her what she needs to hear. "But I do have one question, why was this meeting set up? Like, why did you approach me to meet, did you reach out to other students?"

"I am making my rounds to each student," Ms. Hall answered.

"Was I prioritized because I'm gay, and the school is fearing I could be next to do something irrational?"

"Oh no, I was given the student roster and picked students randomly. It's not because the school thinks you're gay," Ms. Hall said before I interrupted.

"But I am gay, I've survived three years at this school being gay."

"That is not an easy venture, especially for a teenager to have to go through, you're brave, Tyler. I met your father last week, he was a very nice man, and very popular," Ms. Hall said. I could tell she was changing the subject.

"Did you meet him at The Saguaro?"

"As a matter of fact, yes. I wanted to check that place out, and your father was kind enough to introduce me to everyone," said Ms. Hall.

"Did he show you his big red truck?"

"No, we just chit chatted for a bit."

"Ahh, that is nice, he's a great guy. He and my mother both went to this high school," I said, trying to make Ms. Hall feel more comfortable. Before we could go onto the next topic, Principal Miller's voice came over the intercom system, instructing all students to report to the gymnasium for the pep assembly. Thank goodness, I don't think I could take a minute more of this meeting. We both got up to go attend the pep assembly when Ms. Hall's automatic air freshener she kept hidden on a bookshelf sprayed. It was a perfect mixture of oak and pine.

"Oh, I love that smell. It reminds me of back home. Let's reschedule this meeting and pick up where we left off," Ms. Hall said as she went to grab her school lanyard and phone that was sitting on her desk. I wasn't listening. That smell, it's crazy how a scent can transport you back to a place, a scene, a moment, carrying me back to him. I froze for a second until my nose became familiar with the smell. However, the memory didn't fade. He didn't disappear, in my mind, we were still in the forest, jumping over a small creek and walking through wildflower bushes trying to find the perfect pine tree to climb. "There!" he pointed, turning around, revealing that beautiful smile and warm blue eyes. Then the memory broke when Ms. Hall handed me my backpack and opened the door to her office, I let out a gentle exhale and followed behind her.

As my mom told me to do, I stayed after school, I sat in the library reading my favorite play until the game started. I kind of have a thing for plays and musicals, gay I know. Many people think it's weird to read plays, as opposed to watching them, but I like to imagine the scene up in my head. The library was empty except for Ms. Johnson, who was doing some scanning. I could hear her getting frustrated with the machine. I grabbed my bookmark and stuck it inside the play, I couldn't concentrate with Ms. Johnson yelling at the computer. Hence, I walked mindlessly around the aisles, looking at all the various book sizes, fonts, colors, and titles. Our library wasn't extensive, and the aisles only went to shoulder height. At the end of the bookshelf, I could see one particular book lying on its side, peeking out like the red flap on an old-fashioned mailbox. I walked over to flip the book right side up, revealing the title, *The Night the Angels Cried*. I got an eerie feeling, instinctively pulling the old worn-out book from the shelf, reading the back cover. I love reading. The book was a tragedy about the murder of a little girl by someone in her own family.

"Tyler, are you going to the game?" Ms. Johnson asked from across the room.

"Hi, Ms. Johnson. Yes, I am, about the head there now to set up," I said, quickly placing the book in my backpack. I already have two books checked out, the maximum amount. I then zoomed past Ms. Johnson, "See you at the game. My mom said she was going to help you tonight at the Letterman's booth."

"Oh good. Tell Michelle we will sell a few shirts and hats tonight," Ms. Johnson replied, waving at me as I walked out the door. This book seemed too intriguing to wait and check it out through the library system. If I do nothing all weekend, I should have it back by Monday. As I walked out of the library, I could see a few students still setting up for the big Homecoming dance after the football game. Our gymnasium is too big for the number of people that actually show up to the dance. Hence, every year they host it in the cafeteria. Purple balloons lined the two entranceways into the cafeteria; above the lining of the entrance were gold streamers dangling down. Cute.

I kept walking toward the football field, thinking about how there are a surprising amount of students still around. None of them went home. I took a shortcut through the baseball field, walking past the dugout to see three trouble-making rats hiding smoking pot. Trying to be inconspicuous, but the smell was a dead giveaway. One of them pointed at me, "Don't you fucking go snitching." I just kept walking, giving them a thumbs up. He could be cute if he wasn't such an asshole.

The track circling the football field was just dirt, small gravel with a reddish tint. Other schools had a tartan track field, an all-weather material made of polyurethane that circled their football field. Lincoln High was too poor for that. The bleachers were small, probably sat about sixty people max, surrounded by patches of green and yellowish grass. In the center of the two bleachers was a twenty-foot high bird's nest, as they called it, used for better viewing of the game for the announcer, the scorekeeper, and myself. Being twenty feet above the ground, I could see the parking lot beginning to fill up. People making their way to the stands, the concession stand was forming a line, next to it, my mom and Ms. Johnson setting up the Letterman's booth. I pulled out my camera and attached it to my tripod, wishing it were already halftime.

"Look at the rack on her!" The guy next to me said, pointing down to some girl in the stands. The announcer then looked down at his microphone to make sure it was off, "Shit yeah, fucking motorboat titties, think she will be at The Saguaro after the game?" The announcer asked, followed with a laugh by himself and the scorekeeper. This is going to be a long game. The sun finally set revealing Arizona's beautiful purple and gold sky and clouds, the perfect combination of light and darkness mixed together. I looked down and saw Nicole had just arrived with her dad. He was talking to Ms. Hall while Nicole walked to the bleachers with a bag of popcorn. She seemed really into the game, even though it was just the warm-ups. I wonder if it's a Texas thing.

Nicole got up and hugged a little girl. It

looked to be Chloe Garcia, a twelve-year-old in middle school who is the little sister to Monica Garcia, the biggest cunt in the entire school as well as a Homecoming Queen nominee. She will probably get it, bitch. On the first day of school, I was walking past a group of 'cool kids' sitting at the benches. She leaned her foot out, tripping me then gasping as I fell to the ground, having the nerve to yell at me for running into her. Everyone then just laughed and agreed with her, oh yeah, and Jason Brophy was there too. Like I said, the biggest cunt in school. Her daddy has money, owning a few farms that circled Lincoln, not entirely sure what her mom does. Probably nothing.

Just as millions of dazzling stars presented themselves across the empty desert sky, it was halftime, and we were ahead 34-20. I shimmied down the latter in need of a bathroom break; the first half was way too long, and I needed a break from those pigs in the bird's nest. As I walked to the bathroom, I could see Principal Miller at the Letterman's booth talking with my mom. She let out a huge laugh I had never heard before; there is no way he could be that funny. What the?

"Tyler!" Nicole yelled as I emerged from the restroom, her bag of popcorn was empty. She had on a school shirt that read "Fighting Coyotes 2019 Homecoming," she must have just bought it at the Letterman's booth.

"Nice shirt," I said sarcastically

"Twenty bucks for this thing!"

"Steep, Ms. Johnson must be a good sales lady."

"Or just someone in charge of grading my papers got to suck up somehow," Nicole joked. "What are you doing after the game? Are you going to the homecoming dance?"

"Nah, not really my scene," I replied.

"Let's hang out after the game, the dance isn't really my scene either. My dad let me use the truck tonight; we can hang out on the tailgate or something," Nicole suggested. She opened her light brown purse, revealing inside her favorite silver flask. She let out a smile and a wink.

"Oh okay, why not," I said. I've never really drunk alcohol, let alone whatever was in that flask. I did try one of my dads' beers once when I was little. He was gone, and the fridge was full of them, I remember thinking about the curiosity of what dads' favorite juice tasted like. I didn't like it; I tried a few sips then stopped.

I could see her walking toward us, her hair perfectly curled, hair sprayed, and done up. The dress was ivory with embroidery and beads pinned to the top mesh-like fabric. On one end was a deep skirt slit revealing a portion of her left leg and nude open-toed heels. Monica Garcia. She then made a wave at Nicole and me, I didn't wave back but noticed Nicole did, followed with a huge smile and a soft "Hey!" I had to ask.

"How do you know Monica? I mean, everyone knows knows Monica."

"Oh I'm tutoring her little sister, Chloe. My dad got me the part-time job, Chloe's mom said she would pay extra if I also helped her with softball and swimming, so I was like sure. I miss working at the community pool," Nicole said. "Their house is so nice, huge backyard with a pool and a slide." Dang, Nicole has been here, what a few weeks? And is already asking to tutor and help with sporting events, to the Garcia's, I hope I don't lose her to the dark side. Nicole's generosity and empathy were rare; she genuinely liked helping people and knew who she was. I hoped some of that would rub off onto me.

Half time was about to end. Heading up the ladder back into the womanizing birds' nest pit, I could hear the announcer announce the Homecoming Queen, "Monica Garcia!" as everyone then began to cheer and cheer and whistle. I knew the bitch would win as I rolled my eyes, still climbing the ladder. It was kind of symbolic, I thought. Here I had to climb and climb to get to where I needed to go, while people like the Monica Garcias of the world would just walk onto the field and win. Can this game be over already?

◆ ◆ ◆

The night was perfect as Nicole and I sat on the tailgate of her dads' old pickup truck. We sat in an empty desert lot across from the school, vaguely hearing the blasting music from the Homecoming dance. Nicole then pulled out her phone and threw on a country playlist then taking a quick little swig from her silver flask, her reaction was priceless, a cute little head-turning while blowing air out of her mouth. Damn, I guess I'm next.

"What is this?" I asked

"Whiskey, I've had the same bottle since forever ago. I also have three beers in my back-pack I brought with," Nicole said, hinting that I might enjoy the beers over the whiskey sting. I took a quick little gulp; damn, my lips are burning. I quickly swallowed and tried not to breathe out my nose and mimicked Nicole and just kept exhaling through my mouth. Nicole laughed.

"Are you okay?"

"Oh yeah, I'm good," I said quickly, still exhaling as if I was blowing up a balloon. This was going to take some getting used to. Nicole then laid on her back, looking up at the stars, both her arms behind her head.

"Join me, let's count the shooting stars," she suggested. I took one more little swig, ex-haled, exhaled, exhaled, and then laid on my back with Nicole. The night sky in the middle of the empty desert is so much more beautiful than during the daytime. The cluster of stars, some bright, some dim, was somewhat relative. From an outside perspective, they seem perfect, peaceful dots in a sea of black. When really those peaceful dots were raging in violent chaos, colliding rocks swirling around colorful nebulas, the aftermath of a dying star. Then that got me thinking about death here on earth. When a star collapses, it releases energy and matter into the universe, but when we die, what do we release into the world, pain and grief or love and solace? I used to believe the former, but as of recently, I've been experiencing the latter.

"Oh that's five!" Nicole said as she pointed to the night sky, crap I should have been counting the shooting stars instead of experiencing them.

"You're on a roll," I said jokingly. Nicole then turned her head to face me.

"Can I ask you a question? What was it like for you to come out?"
This question, no one really asked me this question: the majority of people either don't care or are in denial that one could be gay.

"Ummm... it was hard. It was kind of a build-up until finally, I exploded. Not in anger but more for myself. I was fourteen years old, it was right before my freshman year of high school, and one night I called my mom into my room and told her. She was quiet at first, and then she told me to stop. I remember my hands were shaking, and I was so nervous," I explained and then continued to lay next to Nicole in silence.

"She then told me to not tell my dad, and then said to just stop again, you can't be like that Tyler. People make fun of people like that, just stop. Like it was something I could just switch on and off. Then she left the room and told me to go to bed." Nicole was silent as we continued to lay there.

"I never did tell my dad, but I have a feeling he knows. He's hardly ever at the house. I'm sure he is having an affair with some random lady. Everyone's favorite past time in Lincoln, adultery."

A few moments of silence filled the empty space between us, a shooting star racing across the sky. "After I came out, I thought things would be different. I thought since I was releasing this weight off my shoulders that I would be set free, I could finally be myself." Little did I know I was strapping a fifty-pound weighted vest to myself and duct tape across my mouth as no one longer cared or listened to what I had to say. Getting up every morning was the most draining part about life as I currently knew it.

"I'm so sorry it was hard, Tyler and your mother didn't understand," Nicole said softly, as she reached her arm over and grabbed my hand.

"Maybe she will come around?"

"I doubt it, she still tries to set me up with girls, still in denial," I said as I could feel my face getting warm from the whiskey, feeling as if I was floating. *Beebeep.* Just than being startled by my black wristwatch alarm going off - 11:28. I quickly pulled my hand away.

"What is that? Is that your watch alarm going off?" Nicole asked *beebeep*.

"Yeah, ummm, I set it, so I knew to make it home before midnight, so I don't get in trouble." I explained, thinking quickly on my feet.

"Well we should get you home. I'm good to drive," Nicole said as she got up and jumped down from the tailgate. I got up slowly, still feeling the whiskey. I looked down at my watch for a few seconds, running my finger over the screen, until Nicole got my attention.

"Tyler! You lightweight, are you zoning off?"

"No, I'm coming" I laughed.

It was kind of Nicole to drive me home, and just ten minutes before midnight. However, none of that really mattered as I came back to yet another empty house. My dad was, for sure, still The Saguaro and my mom, I have no idea. I'm not sure if it was because I was moving around, but that whiskey was starting to feel pleasant, relaxed, and tingly. I walked into the kitchen to grab some water for bed. I walked down our thin hallway on the way to my bed-room as I was chugging my glass of water, a slight glimpse of my black wristwatch. The walls appeared to be slanted, and the floor tilted as I quickly opened my door and sat on the floor. It was quiet, and the room dimly lit. I crawled to my closet and glanced at my neatly placed black Nike shoebox in the back corner on the floor. My memory box. I pulled it out and removed the top and glanced inside, glanced at the beauty. A few pictures scattered around, a camp whistle, and a name tag. I searched around and picked up my favorite picture of him, remembering that first day at summer camp when the photo was taken. The night was warm. The moon was bright. I heard his laugh echo off the cabin walls as my eyes slowly closed. Taking off my black wristwatch and turning it over, tracing my finger along the back, feeling the scratch of his initials, 'W.A.' itched into the silver. A few tears began to slowly run down my face as my vision became blurry, and I could feel my nose getting red. The whiskey made me think of him more than ever, making me miss his voice, smell, and warm blue eyes. I miss you, William Ackhurst.

JENNIFER HALL

My chest was burning. My heart was pounding as I put both my hands over my head. Back in college, I was an active runner. I would run before exams or late at night when I couldn't sleep. It was mindless and relaxing. Oh, have those days past and the once therapeutic ritual is now a cause for alarm, I was out of shape. Before exams, I would run super early in the morning, shower, eat breakfast then spend the whole day prepping. I remember the day of graduation for my graduate program. I was so excited, and more of a feeling of relief. After all that studying, those classes and research projects, I was finally able to apply those skills into a more impactful way. The sun hasn't come up yet, and it still feels like the high nineties as I approached The Saguaro, a few cars were even parked out front, proud for them for not driving drunk. My little schoolhouse was just a mile and a half away as I put my earphones back in, strapped my phone to my armband, and took off jogging. You got this, Jen.

I sat at my little office table, new soft

sweatpants on post-shower with a bowl of cereal. It was a beautiful Saturday morning. Ruby also had breakfast as I poured her a refreshing glass of water to start the day. My insides were telling me that I was on the right path, I could feel it in my bones, maintain this balance. That phase was probably the most important life lesson my father taught me. Him being a well-respected accountant, taught me young that everything in life is about balance. The scales must be even on both sides to prevent chaos and frustration. Credits must equal debits. I took his philosophy on balance and tried to apply where ever I could. Adding time, energy, and commitment to my professional side must also be complemented by an equal commitment to self-care and friends. I had an appointment around noon at the school with Janet Fulton, Cameron's mother. We had met previously, and I tried to keep it recurring. Still, this particular meeting was suddenly scheduled, with cause for alarm. I believe it has something to do with Cameron's final autopsy and toxicology report. They usually take four to six weeks to finalize. Or maybe she sold the house. During our last visit, Janet said she was trying to sell the house and move back to the east coast with her sister. Hopefully, she sold the house and is finally able to move on, this town is a little depressing as it is.

◆ ◆ ◆

I pulled into the parking lot at the school, and Janet was already there, sitting in her old silver van, AC blasting. The days feel like they keep getting hotter and hotter as I got out of my car and walked to Janet in her van. She got out.

"Hello, Janet, sorry to keep you waiting, how has your morning been?" I asked, placing my hand on her back as we both began to walk into the school.

"Oh, not a problem dear, I showed up a little early. Things are still rattling, thank you for meeting with me on a Saturday," Janet let out. Some of her friends have been letting her stay at their place, so she doesn't have to sleep in that house alone, just feet away from the bathtub where she found her son. Blue in the face with the shower still on. We walked into my seventy-three-degree office and sat on the couch. I handed Janet a water bottle and unlocked my filing cabinet. I keep everyone's files safely locked away with only myself and Principal Miller having access.

Janet began telling me her moods that last few days. They seem to be regular, expected for a grieving mother, until yesterday when she got in the mail the final results. Janet wasn't expecting any ad hoc items to appear on the report as her son's death was pretty explanatory. Then she explained, sad and confused.

"I just don't understand, Jennifer."

"Did you know your son was taking medication?"

"No! I had no idea he was taking medication, let alone where he would get his hands on those types of pills."

"What did the report say exactly?" I asked, pen in hand ready.

"Cameron tested positive for alprazolam and oxycodone. That just doesn't make sense. Why would Cameron take these pills?" Janet asked in a sign of frustration as tears began to shed. I handed her a tissue as she gently wiped a few tears.

"Did Cameron show signs of anxiety? I wonder if it was the pressure of moving to a new town, making new friends. That is probably why, but the how is another question," I explained, thinking about how Cameron could have got his hand on these pills, especially being so new to town. I wonder if he brought them with him from the other city he was from? I wasn't sure if I should tell her now or wait? She is still trying to process the fact that she just found out her son was taking prescription medication without Janet knowing. Alprazolam side effects are suicidal thoughts. I'll wait to go over the details with her—a lost kid living with his single mother in a small desert town with no friends or family.

"This has been a lot."

"Last time you mentioned you were try-ing to sell the house? How is that going?" I asked.

"Not good. I have had two potential buys, but they both backed out last minute, once they learned what happened," Janet said, small hic-cups as she tries to find her voice.

"Janet, I need you to say it out loud, like we talked about. Saying it out loud helps with the grieving and healing process. You cannot keep it bottled up inside you. Say the words."

"I can't! I don't want to!" Janet begged si-lence thickened the air, but just before I was about to give it one more try and have her say it aloud, she spoke. "My son is dead. The buyers backed out last minute...once they learned that my son...killed himself in the bathroom."

"Janet, words matter, saying it out loud helps, but you need to say it correctly, death by suicide, let us try it one more time."

"You're right, I'm sorry, I just..."

"Don't be sorry, Janet."

"...Buyers back out last minute once they learn.... that my son died by suicide in the bath-room." I was so proud of Janet at that moment. I got up, sat on the couch next to her, and gave her a hug. That wasn't easy, that took courage to look reality in the eyes—truth, the monster that takes shape to whatever you fear the most. Distracted minds locked away in their houses, shades drawn, door bolted, barricaded from the beast. Never understanding what it takes to conquer it, but instead living in constant fear, detached from reality.

"It has to do with the little things that you don't really think about that hurt the most," Janet said, as she played with one of her turquoise rings on her right hand. Moving the ring from side to side, distracting her mind. "Going into his room. Having to empty the water he had on his nightstand. Putting the clothes he had in the dryer away. Cleaning up the candy wrappers he had left on the couch while playing video games. It has to do those little things, keeps reminding me all over again that I lost my only son." The room felt thick. Difficult to inhale as Janet continued. "And the blood droplets stained into the bathtub..." Janet paused, taking a moment for herself. I kept my arm around her.

Cleaning up after a child, who was taken before their time. Dead silence as you enter their room. Empty. Worried that at any moment, they will barge in and yell at you for being in their bedroom without permission. The print of their body still sculpted into the bed. Their little owl night light is always on, as they never turn it off. Why does everything feel like a keepsake? The bedroom is still fresh, of Emily's scent.

"Let us try and pivot Cameron's life to what he gave us. All the memories of laughs and adventures you were all able to experience because of Cameron. Have you thought about maybe creating something in his name? Perhaps a scholarship for a specific degree, whichever Cameron had an interest in, or creating an award named after him. Through this, his memory will last forever," I suggested. Tossing around ideas, glass half full, while trying to determine what would Cameron release into the world?

We made significant strides today. Today was a good session with Janet, I again told her how brave she is as I walked her out the door. We hugged and waved goodbye. It was then I noticed the third vehicle in the parking lot. Principal Miller's Jeep was parked two down from Janet's van. I closed the door and walked back into my office. Snickering at first, but then shifted to whispers. Was someone in Principal Miller's office with him? If so, it's none of my business as I shut the door behind me and sat at my office desk.

During my graduate program, one research report I prided myself on was the study of cults and NRM (new religious movement) overshadowed by death and bloodshed. Beginning with the infamous UFO religious cult, Heaven's Gate. Spring of 1997, the San Diego police department found inside a house, thirty-nine bodies, all members of the religion. They all participated in a mass suicide to achieve access onto an extraterrestrial spacecraft as the world-famous, Great Comet, Hale-Bopp, roared by, lighting up and danced about the sky.

To then go back further in history to 1978, The Peoples Temple of the Disciples of Christ, or commonly referred to as Peoples Temple. This NRM is more horrendous than Heaven's Gate. The founder of Peoples Temple, Jim Jones, orchestrated in Jonestown, Guyana, the "Revolutionary Suicide" and in total, 901 individuals participated.

It was insane yet so psychologically intriguing how one person could control that many individuals, control to the extent of convincing them to take their own life. After our session today, and learning what the toxicology report detailed, my theory of an online cult began to shift to a drug-infested scenario. Abusing drugs, especially the ones whose side effects include suicidal thoughts. If it were the drugs that were causing these kids' minds to become so altered, they commit such horrific acts, where are they getting it?

These aren't your typical, marijuana, or cocaine type of drugs. These were prescription, lab-created medication, highly regulated, and monitored, not only physically dangerous, as your respiratory could halt, but also psychologically perilous. However, there were a few things I needed to confirm first, compare the toxicology report with Greg and Lizzie, to know if they too were taking medication. I picked up my phone, thinking of one person who could help. The phone just rang and rang until finally,

"Hello, Sheriff Clark?"

Tonight was a big night—the monthly public school board meeting. In the last board meeting, they approved my visit to the school for one entire year. One of the agenda items will be to vote on the approval of a few activities and events for the students I have requested. These kids need more exposure to the outside world, past Lincoln. More field trips to the science museum, the zoo, university tours, and compete in other school events other than sports. The high school board was made up of Lincoln citizens. Their own little political power structure.

Louie Garcia was the board president, a very nice and successful man. He owns a few of the farms that surround Lincoln I recently found out. That reminds me, I need to schedule a meeting with his daughter, Monica. The night was still with a few crickets chirping at the high school. As I sat in the middle back of the library, where they host the board meetings, I was able to see the room was starting to fill up. Facing the door I saw Sheriff Clark arrive, I gave a small wave, he walked over and sat next to me.

"Howdy Ms. Hall, how has your evening been?"

"Sheriff Clark, I told you, call me Jennifer. It has been good. What we talked about on the phone, were you able to get it?" I asked softly, looking down at the wooden floors.

"And I told you to call me Brian. Yeah, I got it. Let's chat afterward."

The board members began to walk up behind the long tables. Each taking a seat behind their respective name tent. Michelle Tuckerman, Taylor Watson, Louie Garcia, Joshua Cliff, and Martin Smith. That was the high school board. It continued with repetitive courtroom lingo of making a motion, approved, denied, I at this moment, sustained, out of line, and so on. My item was approaching. One that was also tied with an increase in local tax to fund some of the various projects. News, not many people will be excited to hear.

"Next order of business, the approval for the allocation of funds for various student engagement projects," Michelle Tuckerman said as she read the document.

"Mrs. Tuckerman, please state what item number in the document, outlining how these funds will be allocated," Joshua Cliff asked.

"That item will be C17. The funds will be allocated through the increase in state-local tax within Lincoln," Michelle read. Instantly it was met with opposition. You could hear the murmur from the crowd. The room was full of about 25 Lincoln residents, most shaking their heads to an increase in tax.

"Don't you go increase my taxes to pay for some school field trip. They are just going to kill themselves anyway," said a dirty disgruntled Lincoln resident named Billy Porter, smelly of motor oil with a few holes in his shirt. His hair is oily, not your typical natural oil, but actual oil seems caked on the sides with worn-out boots. He was sitting next to his brother, Steve Porter, not too ironically enough, looked like his older brother. They both went to Lincoln High back in the day and still live at home with their grandmother. From what I've gathered, they are not positive contributing members of society. A pessimistic demeanor on life. He reminded me a lot of my uncle, Albert. Unable to hold a stable job, relationship with women his own age. Toxicly praying on those younger with a slit slip up a skit, a predatory fiend. His younger brother chimed in.

"Yeah, they are already high enough. Are these new ideas coming from that new teacher they brought in?" I instantly looked over at him.

"Billy, the tax increase will be minuscule and adjustable to live with, I made a motion to vote to approve the allocation of funds. All in favor say, aye," Louie Garcia said.

"Aye," said all the members. Thank goodness they approved. That upsets me that these residents are not willing to help these kids instead of being stuck in their own greed and hatred. I can't believe what Billy Porter said, "they are just going to kill themselves anyway." I can't understand that guy, no empathy. I'm glad Janet wasn't there or the parents of Greg and Lizzie to hear that. A fight would have broken out for sure. The board meeting lasted about forty-five minutes, it seems. Some people are not happy for sure. Sheriff Clark and I walked out together to the parking lot. As we were crossing to the lot, the Porter brothers jumped on their four-wheelers, peeled out, and drove off into the desert. So creepy. Sheriff Clark opened his side pocket in his door and pulled a few pieces of paper. He scratched his nose and handed me the papers.

"Here you go, copies of the toxicology report for both Greg and Lizzie. The top of both read carbon monoxide, ethyl glucuronide, alprazolam, and oxycodone." I know I shouldn't be thrilled about these results, but the last two matched with Cameron's. A huge discovery. This is the first evidence of their suicides being connected.

"Almost everyone in Lincoln is on the last three: alcohol, Xanax, and oxy, aside from their favorite meth or heroin," Sheriff Clark said, hinting that tracking the source would be difficult as the supply probably outweighs demand. Well shit. Do we need to be drug testing students? Have K9 deputies come to sniff the lockers? I made a note to remind myself to schedule a meeting with Principal Miller on Monday to post him on my discovery and plan.

I drove home and pulled into my driveway, trying to remember if I had any wine in the fridge. Excited on the surprise to find half a bottle left. I got comfortable, cuddled up on the couch with my favorite throw blanket and iPad. I was stalking my parents on FaceBook. Updating myself on their world, and all the exciting news happening back home. Congratulations, my best friend growing up is having another baby. A few of my friends growing up, never left home. Similar to Lincoln, but with more charm and promises. A part of me regrets moving into the city for work years ago, leaving behind my comfort and balanced life.

I kept laughing as my mother kept posting the same picture of our two dogs back home. Frankie and Wendy. Both English bulldogs, adorable as can be, suckers for love, but they drool on everything. I kept scrolling to find a post my mom shared a week ago, it was a picture of Emily with the caption, "Always In My Heart." She was standing behind a cake, laughing mid polaroid as everyone sang Happy Birthday. She looked so happy. I liked the picture and commented, "forever" with a heart emoji. As hard of a worker my mother was, she always found time for family.

Just then, my landline phone suddenly rang. That thing never rings. It was an old bell sound vibrating throughout the living room. I could see the old telephone shaking every time it rang. I placed my iPad and wine on the table and walked across the living room. I picked up the landline phone.

"Hello, this is Jennifer."

Nothing. Just silence on the other end.

"Hello?"

Lucid stillness.

I just hung up and scratched my head, walking back to the couch. Just as I was about to grab my glass of wine, the landline phone rang again. The vibrations echoing, like from an '80s horror movie. I walked across the room. I picked up the phone.

"Hello?"

Nothing, again. This was starting to become annoying and creepy. I just hung up and disconnected the landline phone from the wall. Problem solved.

I finished the rest of my wine and crawled into bed. Doing one more scan through Facebook, a few more videos of the various gender reveal parties, wedding engagements, and university acceptance letter openings. All my friends back home, taking me away for just a moment. I turned the light off and plugged my phone in. Just to have it start ringing a moment later. I leaned over and grabbed my vibrating machine. Unknown caller it says. I usually always have my phone on silent. I just laid it back down. The vibration against my wooden end table made a distinct noise that continued for about fifteen seconds. I let it go to voicemail.

TYLER TUCKERMAN

SUMMER of 2015

I stood next to my bed with both hands on my hips, thinking what in the hell was I to pack. My empty intimidating suitcase looking back. A few shorts and t-shirts made the cut, followed by some socks and underwear in the side pockets. I then heard my mom,

"Ty! Are you almost ready?" She yelled out from the living room.

"Yes! One sec," I replied, rolling my eyes and trying to zip up my suitcase. The zipper always gets stuck. It was the beginning of the summer before my freshman year of high school. My mom thought it would be a good idea to attend this random summer camp for two weeks, probably so she doesn't have to watch or look after me, her vacation. I searched for my journal and my favorite play to read to take with me, my escape in case I don't make any friends. I walked down our thin hallway, suitcase in one hand and my new camera in the other.

"Are you sure you want to take your camera?" She asked.

"Yeah, I will need something to do up there."

"Oh, there will be plenty of activities for you to do up at the camp," My mother replied in a sound of aggravation, putting on her sunglasses and opening the front door. She was already a little upset with me as I had missed the van pick up this morning, so she now has to drive me four hours north into the mountains where the camp is being held. I probably should just stay quiet.

About halfway through the drive, I was looking out the side window. We were driving up a mountain range, back and forth, as we slowly gained elevation. The terrain was beginning to change, from greasewood and cactus to pine and aspens. My mom then handed me a brochure. What the heck? The camp is called Welcome To Earth. It showed a massive lake in the center with small cabins on one side and outside courtyard, a huge fire pit, and various games scattered across the lawn. The camp was in the middle of the forest in northern Arizona. I had never traveled that far before, so this was definitely going to be out of my comfort zone. Oh cool, it says they offer an outdoor film exploration class, sign me up. They provide this two-week camp every summer, winter, and spring for students aged fourteen to seventeen. I hope my mom didn't read that part, and this is the only time I have to go. I also wondered if her shipping me off to summer camp had anything to do with the fact that I came out a month ago to her. It didn't go over well. Then it hit me. Oh. My. God. She was sending me to a conversion camp for gay teens like in *Boy Erased*.

We turned off the main road, a small green sign saying "WTE Camp 1.5 Miles" with a right arrow. The road was a smooth dirt road, drivable for even my mom's little four-door Toyota. The trees were beautiful, so green, tall, and fresh looking. I have never seen pine trees before. As we got closer to the camp, I began to get a little nervous, social anxiety, as I knew none of the other kids, and I'm not the best at making friends. My palms were sweaty.

Finally, we passed under a huge sign made of wooden boards painted green, blue, and red that read in all caps, WELCOME TO EARTH. The first thing I saw was the lake, some kids were playing on the shore, while some were holding onto a rope as they swung into the lake from a tall beat-up pine. Not going to lie, the lake looked more significant in the brochure. My mom pulled the car up to a small wooden cabin with a few staff members standing outside, wearing green polos, tan shorts, and each holding a clipboard. We both go out of the car to be greeted by a cute redhead teenage girl.

"Hello! And Welcome to Earth Camp, my name is Lindsey, are you checking in?"

"Hi Lindsey, yes, I'm checking in Tyler Tuckerman. Sorry for the delay," My mother explained, again bringing up the fact that I missed the morning van pick up. I stood next to her and Lindsey, slowly dropping my suitcase to the ground and clutching my camera. There was the right number of campers around. I wonder if they all had come to this camp before because they all seemed pretty familiar with one another.

"Oh, that is not a problem; however, you did miss the orientation. We went over the camp in general, all the exciting classes and activities we offer, and a little networking exercise. Alright, let me check the list...ahh yes, Tyler Tuckerman," Lindsey said, and she scanned the registration list.

"Here you go, Tyler. This paper has a list of all the activities and classes you would like to sign up for each day. Look it over and return it to us today," Lindsey explained, handing me several pieces of paper, the same brochure I already had, a name tag, a whistle, and a black wristwatch.

"What is this stuff for?" I asked, trying to juggle all the items in my hand.

"The whistle and watch are for safety measures, in case you get lost or hurt you can whistle for help," Lindsey explained with a bright smile. "Alright well you are all checked in Tyler, your sleeping cabin will be Cabin C, you can take any available bed. We will make an announcement when dinner is about ready around six o'clock."

I feel like I'm in prison. What the hell? Well, worst case, I can always run away and live off the land or find a stranger on the road and ask them to bring me back home. My mom turned to me and gave me a big hug.

"Ty, you have fun and enjoy yourself. Make friends and remember to be on time when the van arrives in two weeks to bring you back. I'm not coming back up here to get you. Here is an emergency phone. Only used in case of an emergency, it's prepaid with twenty credits."

"Thanks, mom, I won't forget, and I'll call you before we leave so you know I made it on the van," I said, returning the hug. She got into her car and drove away. I stood there, hands full of things, a small suitcase, one camera, and no desire to really venture around.

I walked into Cabin C. It was pretty warm and no sign of any available beds. There were bunk beds, each with one small flat pillow and a thin red-checkered blanket. But some were different, as the majority of the campers brought their own pillow and sleeping bags. It was then someone walked into the cabin; I was a little startled and quickly turned around. He was tall, probably just a little under six feet. He had short brunette hair. His plaid button-up was tucked into his dark brown shorts, and he was wearing hiking boots. Finally, those eyes reminded me of a midmorning sunny sky, warm and blue.

"Hi, Tyler?" said the tall, handsome stranger.

"Umm, yeah. Hi," I said, trying not to blush, dropping a few of my items as we shook hands. Nice grip.

"My name is William, William Ackhurst. I was chatting with Lindsey, and she said you just got here a little late and might need a show around."

"I did miss orientation. Do you work here, William?" I asked, staring at those blue eyes.

"No, I don't work here. I came here last spring, so I'm a little familiar with the land." William explained as he scratched the back of his head, "Oh, if you are looking for an open bed, I believe there is one on the other end of the cabin. Next to me."

"Okay, cool, thanks, hope you don't snore," I said quickly, oh my god, why did I mention that.

"No, you're good, I don't snore." William laughed. He then walked me over and showed me the available bed. I put my stuff down, suitcase under the bed, my camera under the blanket and pinned on my nametag, wasn't sure if it was required.

"Is this a conversion camp like in Boy

Erased?" I had to ask, William looked confused.

"I am sorry. I didn't understand a word you just said?" He laughed. Crap, I guess not.

"Sorry, I meant to ask if this was a specific type of camp. My mother didn't give me many details on the drive up." I replied.

"I would say the type is outdoors."

William was showing me around the campground. We had just walked by the fire pit where everyone gathers for a fire, music, and stories every night after dinner. He seemed very kind and gentle. My heart was pounding our entire interaction; it still continues to do so. I hope he can't tell. He then began showing me the sign-up sheets and going through some of the exciting courses. His favorite is the archery course. He learned to use actual bow and arrows to nail a circular target, testing your skills of patience and strength. He recommended the kayak class, teaching the campers to balance, paddle, and experience kayaking throughout the lake. It was then that William was called over by a few other campers, they must have met last spring. I thanked him for showing me around and his suggestions on the different courses, we waved goodbye and jogged off.

I went back to the cabin, it took a minute for me to remember which was mine. Cabin C, that's right. I walked in and sat on my bed. I unboxed my new phone and looked around for an outlet to charge it. I saw one next to Williams's bed. You could tell he brought his own pillow by the pillow casing. His whistle was hung up on the wall, and his name tag clipped to his bed frame. His massive backpack sat on the bed, while under was a pair of Nike tennis shoes and flip flops. So organized. I sat on my bed and tried to fill out my course list, I got to pick three courses that would alternate every day. Then realizing, I don't have a pen. Cool.

◆ ◆ ◆

The dinner announcement had just gone off just a few hours later. I was walking along the lakeshore, trying to spot a few fish swimming around. I walked over to the large outdoor pavilion. Picnic tables were scattered about, and the campers were grabbing trays and forming a line. The food seemed okay as I sat down at an empty table, chicken stew, mashed potatoes, and steamed veggies. Before I could begin eating, William sat next to me.

"Hey there," he said, laying his tray next to mine, and I immediately forgot how to breathe.

"Hey William," I replied, taking a sip of my water.

"So, did you sign up for any fun courses?"

"Yeah, I did sign up for the kayaking class

that you recommended as well as the outdoor film exploration and some random hiking/survival course. I figured why not."

"I noticed your camera, that's cool, man," William said. I have never had anyone call me

"man" or "bro" before, and he is still hanging around, so he must not know that I am gay. I wasn't going to tell him, I didn't want him to think less of me or worse, hate me after I told him, I'll just go back in the closet for the next two weeks.

"Yeah, bro," I said back. Wow, that was awkward; I just took another sip of my water, rolling my eyes at myself. I wonder if he could tell by the way I said it, that I don't call people "bro" often.

"So I am not sure if they told you yet, but we are required to go on one of the approved trails/hikes. You go in and register for whichever one. I think there is like seven to choose from," William said, taking a bite of his mashed potatoes.

"No, I didn't know that."

"Well, if you want, we can do one together? A few campers all get together and do a few."

"Okay! I mean, I am taking a hiking/survival course," I joked.

"Sweet, the wilderness prep course is required to go on *The Shepherd's Trail*, it's my favorite, I did it last spring. It's less popular because it's the longest so it won't be crowded. No one goes on it because it's a full day's hike to the top. We will have to camp and come back down the next morning. But the view at the top is worth it all," William explained.

I'm sorry, but did he just say an entire day hike, camping overnight and coming back down the next day?

"I don't have any camping gear or a tent or a sleeping bag," I said.

"You can rent them at the rental cabin," William said as he pointed to the rental cabin next to the registration cabin. Well, it looks like I'm going camping.

"Let's do it," I replied, unsure what I just got myself into.

"Cool, we can pick up the gear the day before we want to do the hike," William said as the both of us then continued to eat.

"I'll see you around Tyler," William said as he patted me on the back and took his empty tray to stack it up. Patting me on the back was our other physical interaction. Why a pat, though? Listen to me, I'm starting to sound crazy. Is boy crazy a thing? I could see him from across the lawn playing corn hole with the other campers. He was so outgoing, he did a little victory jump each time he scored points. It was cute.

◆ ◆ ◆

Four days have passed, and I was starting to get slightly homesick. Not so much the fact that I missed my parents, but I missed my bed, my room, and my sanctuary. I miss being alone when I want to be alone, eating alone, sleeping alone, and not have to shower installs, like a prison. The only thing that has me going is the chance, the opportunity to go on a hike with William. We could finally be alone, in peace, and just surrounded by each other's consciousness. Every once and a while around the campgrounds, I see him wave and gives me a big smile. I don't think he looks at other campers the way he looks at me, it's like we have something special. I'm just not quite sure what it is yet.

I found out that to go on a hike, I have to become certified, especially on the trail that William wants to do, since it is overnight. The camp requires us to take a wilderness preparation course to teach us necessary survival skills and CPR. Think of it as an accelerated boy scouts class. I second-guessed taking the class but figured this was the only thing stopping me from being with William. Every day we learned something new. Building a fire, how to tell direction by reading the stars, how to stop and bandage a bleeding flesh wound with a basic first aid kit, how to build a primitive shelter in case of a rainstorm. Finally, how to stay positive by learning the words to "I Will Survive" by Gloria Gaynor.

I tried to bring my camera with me whenever possible, taking those small opportunities to capture something magnificent—snapshots here, snapshots there. I looked down and saw this caterpillar crawling up the side of the rock I was sitting on, I'm not sure what type of caterpillar it was, but he sure was chunky. I pulled my camera around and filmed the little guy crawling up. The coloration was beautiful, all green with black and red spots that followed down the entire length of its body. In the end, a yellowish horn with a black tip. I don't recall caterpillars having horns, so I slowly and gently poked the horn to have it fold like a blade of grass.

"That's just to scare predators, the horn can't actually hurt you." While taking the course, I met this quirky young girl named Molly Fritz. She was kind of an outdoor nerd with dirt in her nails and blonde blonde hair that always appears to have forest sticks in it—this outdoor Boheme hippie. I asked Molly to take me on a few small hikes every day, so I could prepare myself for the big hike William suggested. It was short fifteen to thirty-minute adventures. It usually takes me longer because I stop and take pictures. Molly always turns around and tells me to hurry up, I think since the time we've all been at camp, she has showered once as her hands and glasses were always dirty off in the woods doing something. I kind of wished I was like a caterpillar, that one day I would transform into a beautiful butterfly and fly far far away.

"Tyler! Take a picture of this pine cone I found!" Molly asked, I was still filming the caterpillar, I was less interested in pine cones, "did you know that there are male and female pine cones?" Molly said, adjusting her dirty glasses and putting the damn pine cone right in front of my face.

"Umm, no I did not know that pine cones were neither male nor female, I thought they were just, I don't know, pine cones."

"Oh yes, the most popular one you think of when you think of a pine cone is female. The males are small and more inconspicuous, they release the pollen that dances in the wind until it finds a female, stellar right?" Molly said excitedly

"Yeah, sure, the circle of life." I was used to Molly going on these factual speeches every once and a while, I guess I could relate to her being a little socially awkward. Still, I don't go around spreading knowledge about pine cones. Instead, I stay quiet and only speak up when I need to.

"Hannah! Look at this, do you think this is a male or female pine cone?" Molly turned to ask another camper, Hannah turned around and slightly tilted her head. Also, taking this wilderness prep course was a girl named Hannah

Walker. She had long, brunette hair wrapped in a messy bun. Always wearing the same laced cowgirl boots with a camouflage shirt with the words "Cabela's" in pink written across the center. I think Cabela's is a place you go to buy all your hunting, fishing and camping essentials, she doesn't strike me as someone who's never been hunting or camping.

"Ummm, probably a male?" Hannah answered, not really paying attention.

"Nope, it's a female, everyone always thinks that I was telling Tyler that the males are smaller and don't really look like pine cones." Molly went on. Our instructor needed to hurry, we were all waiting for him, this rock was starting to get a little uncomfortable. I picked my head up to see if he was anywhere close when, there, I saw him, William. He walked toward us in his light brown shorts, mountain boots, and a red tank top. He was so gorgeous. He kept getting closer and closer as I tried not to stare, a slight smile erupting on my face. I then noticed he put his finger across his mouth, seeming like he was hinting for us to be quiet as he was walking up behind Hannah. Until finally, he placed both his hands across her eyes, surprising her.

"Oh my!" Hannah gasped quickly that turned into a smile. "Who is that? Oh my gosh, tell me!" I don't know, the way she said it seemed like she already knew who it was. William still kept his hands over her eyes, were they flirting?

"William Ackhurst, is that you?"

"You got me!" William said, releasing his hands as Hannah quickly turned around and gave him a slight gentle push as he began to laugh.

"What are you guys doing?" William asked Hannah.

"We are waiting on Mr. Lang, we have our wilderness prep course, but I don't know where he is?" Hannah answered.

"Oh, I saw him up by the cabins, they were fixing one of the doors, so your course will probably be pushed back."

"Thanks, Mr. Lang, we've been waiting here for like 20 mins. I don't know why I have to take this wilderness prep course, I already know all of this stuff. This hike better be worth it, William," Hannah said. What did she mean by this hike better be worth it? Was she coming along with us? I hope not.

"Yes, it will be, I promise! Hey, want to go jump in the lake? It will be really fast!" William asked. Hannah stood there as she adjusted her messy bun. Now that I'm looking at it, I think Hannah meant to make it look messy. Make the appearance that she completed the bun in fifteen seconds when really it probably took fifteen minutes to perfect.

"Okay, yeah let's go, I'm going to run to my cabin to change real fast." Hannah answered as they both began to walk away. William turned around and gave Molly and me a goodbye wave. Then he turned around and gave Hannah a flirtatious push. I looked down at my hands, then back up at them, walking away. I was feeling something I've never felt before, jealousy. It's produced deep in your gut, where it cooks and churns. The heat it produces rises until you feel your heartbeat inside your hands, face, and lips. You find yourself having to control your breathing as your breaths become longer and longer. Your eyes dry from the lack of blinking. All these feelings are synonymous with love and hate, compassion, and rage. Or just merely, heartbreak.

"Want to go for a quick little hike?" Molly suggested as she was picking up and tossing a few pine cones around, "Since Mr. Lang probably isn't coming anytime soon." This jealous sickness was making me in the mood to do nothing, absolutely nothing. It was as if I became paralyzed. Never In my life have I wanted to be another person more than right now. I wanted to be the one he took to the lake, gave flirtatious pushes and casual surprises from behind.

"Yeah, let's go," I said as I slowly stood up, adjusting my camera strap. I have to keep my spirits up and remind myself about our big hike!

I was laying on my little bed staring up at the ceiling, for some reason I couldn't fall asleep, my mind racing. It's probably due to seeing Hannah flirt with William. I wanted to write my feelings down inside my journal, but it was too dark, and everyone was asleep. I pulled out my little flip phone to check the time, *thirty-two minutes until midnight*. The cabin was warm as I slowly went out from under the covers, still laying on my back, staring up. I turned my head over. It appears William was also on top of his blanket, sound asleep as he would let out a few snores every once and a while, toss and turn, then back to snoring. Every night he always wears the same silver basketball shorts to bed, no shirt. His legs were pretty hairy, dark hair all the way up to his thighs. He has beautiful legs, athletic mountain man legs. A slightly hairy chest, and a few noticeable abe muscles.

SMACK! SMACK! SMACK! What in the hell is happening? I was being hit by multiple pillows over and over, SMACK! SMACK! I quickly put my hands up as I began to hear laughing.

"Stop! Stop! What the? Stop!" I yelled as the pillow smacking didn't subside, it looked to be about four and five campers around my bed, all hitting me with pillows, "Stop! Stop!" then all the commotion woke up William.

"Hey! Cut it out, what the hell are you guys doing?" William shouted as he quickly got up from the bed and grabbed a few of the pillows from the campers' hands.

"It's just a little prank, we do it every year to the new campers," one of the campers said, justifying his prank as a, well we had no choice, type response. All the other campers on our side of the cabin woke up and looked around, one of them even let out: "Oh he got the pillow prank, I'm going back to bed."

"Yeah it's not that big of a deal," another said.

"Go back to bed! Before I call Mr. Lang, the prank is over," William demanded as they all began to slowly walk back to the other end of the cabin. My hero. "How are you feeling, Tyler? I'm sorry about all of that, they do that damn prank every year," William walked over and sat next to me on my bed, his legs and mine, inches apart. He put his arm around me.

"I'm okay, it just startled me. Thank goodness it was just pillows. Thanks for making them stop."

"Yeah, of course, I'll make sure they don't bother you again," William responded, followed by a quick wink. My heart instantly melted. He then got up and went back to his bed. I could still feel the warmth and pressure of his arm around me. "Have a goodnight, buddy." I slowly laid on my back, trying to process all that happened, it was all so fast, them attacking me, William saving me and sitting next to me on my bed.

"Goodnight, William." Everything changed in an instant. I was no longer upset by the poison of jealousy. Instead, drunk on the world of William and I, I've never had someone defend me, jump into a blaze, and save me without fear. Could it be that I finally found my knight in shining armor, my one in a million prince? I turned over and admired the outline of his body as he laid on his bed, I closed my eyes and thought about how I never wanted to leave. I felt at home.

The end of the cabin was completely dark, the only light was the moon, full and mysterious as its light pierced through the window onto half of William's bed. Crickets serenading the empty woods around our cabin.

"Psst. Psst," I heard softly. I turned my head over and listened to a soft, "Ty, are you sleeping?" William whispered as he seemed to lift the side of his bedsheet up.

"Not anymore," I whispered back. I slowly got up and tiptoed into William's bed, instantly feeling the warmth of his body and bed as we began to cuddle.

"I've never done this before, I'm really nervous," William whispered into my ear, his arms tightly holding me.

"I've never done this either, you don't know how badly I've wanted this," I said as I turned my head over, I couldn't fully see him,

100

but I could feel him breathing on my lips, I slowly took a deep inhale as we kissed. William quickly turned me around to face him, as he kissed my forehead, the right side of my temple, then down my neck. I rubbed my hands through his buzzed hair as he continued to gently kiss below my ear, I could feel the vein in my neck pulsating. He softly wraps around me, totally engulfed in his arms as we finally became one. The safest places I've ever felt, cradled between his thighs. William grabbed my hand as I helped him take off his silver basketball shorts, I could feel the trail of hair on his lower stomach, warm and throbbing.

BeeBeep. BeeBeep. BeeBeep. Are you kidding me? A camper's alarm. I rubbed my eyes, removing the sand. I looked around, and the sun was up, and Williams' bed was neatly made. What time is it? I moved around in my bed and felt something wet. I looked down, and my pajama pants were soaked, great. I was feeling a wave of emotions. I quickly searched for my journal and began detailing this memory, I wanted to savor every detail. I pray one day I'll wake up to proof, other than that, it was all a dream.

JENNIFER HALL

I always get so antsy five minutes before a meeting. I've always been like that, the most punctual person in the room. That is probably one thing that gives me a genuine inability to control anxiety. That is being late for an appointment. The worst feeling, I can't think about anything else. I always think about what I could have done differently to make an appointment on time. Left sooner? Taken that other street? etc.. Sheriff Clark and I were outside Principal Miller's office, we all had a meeting to discuss the possible drug problem at the school and ways to combat it. Illegal drugs in all forms, not just pills. Two o'clock hit, and Principal Miller opened the door to his office, perfect.

"Come on in, Ms. Hall, Sheriff Clark."

"Howdy Principal Miller." Sheriff Clark said. "I hope this Thursday is treating you well."

"Living the dream." We all three took a seat. His desk was large. Stacks of paper sat next to a small paper filer. At the center, a large calendar with each day scribbled, highlighted, scratched out items, and behind Principal Miller, a large window into the parking lot.

"We wanted to escalate some issues to you, Sheriff Clark, and I believe there to be a serious drug problem. With that being said, I want to kick-start the DARE as well as SADD programs as my first flagship programs with the funds that the board just approved. Also, with the help of Sheriff Clark, we want to schedule random drug searches. Sheriff Clark will bring in his K9 deputy," I explained, adjusting my glasses and quickly scanning over my notes, I wanted to make sure I touched on all the key points. This was serious, and I'm hoping with the sound of my tone and already looping in Sheriff Clark to this meeting, we can hit the ground running.

"Okay, thank you both for bringing this to my attention. Okay, I knew drugs were common around this town, but I had no idea it would leak into the school. Okay, I can approve the random K9 drug search, Sheriff Clark can work with Ms. Hall to set up a date and time. Okay, now for the two programs, I can put in the request, we have the funds, but the board would still need to approve the programs. I'll reach out to Michelle Tuckerman, talk about putting this on the agenda for next month," Principal Miller said. He seemed flustered but surprisingly aware of the severity of this ordeal.

"Thank you. I'll keep you posted when we set a date for the random drug search," I said, and Sheriff Clark and I both got up from the chairs, leaving Principal Miller's office.

"That was quick," Sheriff Clark let out.

"Yeah, I told you. Since you were there, Miller couldn't say no," I said, handing Sheriff Clark a bottle of water from my mini-fridge. I wonder if when Sheriff Clark was a little boy, he dreamed about becoming a police Sheriff, I only ever see him in his uniform. I wonder what regular clothes Brian wears? What does he do for fun? I'm not going to lie, he is pretty good looking for his age, early forties, I would assume. Soft Texas accent, his face is clean-shaven, with a little bit of salt and pepper hair. He's tall, about 6'1" with not a sizeable protruding beer belly or dad bod. He probably has an athletic body. Oh my gosh, why am I thinking this way at work? Stop. Stop. Stop.

When I was a sophomore in college, I almost had a misstep with one of my professors. I caught myself and stopped. I didn't realize that by the end of the semester, I was staying after class and walking with him to his office. Where I still didn't leave. My friend noticed it at first, pulled me aside, and asked. I denied then looked at reality in the eyes and confirmed. I stopped taking his classes. After leaving my strict high school to attend college, my first two years were pretty wild, for your average ex-Christian. Getting drunk for the first time on Mikes Hard Lemonade in the dorms at 3AM. My girlfriends and I stuffing our faces with pizza after the bars closed. Casual sex. Over caffeinated. Altogether abandoning my father's wise, balanced lifestyle philosophy.

"I will say, the pills are going to be hardest to find. These dogs weren't trained to sniff out pills. These will take some digging to find. But if we crack one student who knows who's all taking them, they're onto something."

"Yes, I want to send a message. Maybe we can schedule a mandatory assembly where we talk about the drug crackdown, and while the students are at the assembly, the K9 deputy can search the lockers," I suggested. That was a brilliant plan. Let all the students know we are no longer tolerating the use of illegal drugs, on or off-campus. We are starting to see the color of change, it is in the works. I just can't stop thinking about how if we began these programs months ago, three students might still be here. Then that got me thinking about the student in Berza County. Was his death the result of medication as well?

"Sheriff Clark, how can we inquire about the details regarding the death of the student in Berza County?" I asked, he looked a little confused, taken aback.

"You mean like his autopsy and tox report?"

"Yes, do you think that the student was also taking medication? The same medication as the Lincoln students?"

"That might be more difficult to obtain as it's a different county, jurisdiction."

"Well, what if I made a visit to the family?"

"Be careful with that, but you might get some answers."

That was the one underlier I wasn't considering, the student in Berza County, and if he is connected to Lincoln's deaths. Is this something siloed to only Lincoln, or is there a more substantial answer? I was considering driving to Berza County two hours away to see if I could find something about him. Connect these deaths, find anything, even just a name, and know his story. Sheriff Clark began talking me away from making a trip to Berza County, insisting it's not worth the time for the depth of answers I would find. I walked him to the front of the office. We chatted about setting up a time for the project and how he would be in touch.

Damn, the outside feels good. I got out of my small cool office and took a walk around campus. Getting some sun and fresh air. It helps rejuvenate. Back at ASU, I would love to just walk around the university, admiring the massive stone buildings. The beautiful architectural details edged at the top—the surprisingly fascinating clash between historic and modern. I would get such a great workout in, ASU is one of the largest public universities. When I didn't want to run on the sidewalk or treadmill at night, I would jog around campus. I knew I was safe with the campus police, and the walkways were lit up, plus the dorms were so close.

I had my hands in my pocket, and for a rare lapse in time, I was thinking about nothing at the moment. Meditation relaxed. Just as I was about to hear zen, Ms. Johnson approached me.

"Hi, Ms. Hall. You soaking in some rays?" Ms. Johnson asked, taking her glasses off.

"Yes, those offices get pretty chilly."

"Oh yes, darling, I have my classroom sweater. Knitted it three years ago." She is the best, knitting her own little classroom sweaters. I should ask her to make me one. "But I wanted to talk to you about something. For one assignment, I had the students write their thoughts on, *Romeo and Juliet*, we just finished it." She then had my full attention. What did a student write that was so alarming to Ms. Johnson. "It was Tyler Tuckerman", Ms. Johnson reached into her pocket and pulled out a folded piece of paper. I unfolded to see an assignment by Tyler. It was a poem.

He sat on the ledge
about to betoss
trying to find
his Will *that he had lost*

down on the ground
warm and blue
his Will *waited*
content and true

into his arms
enter his dome
where I must land
to finally be home

"Does this sound like he is writing about jumping off a building?" Ms. Johnson asked. She put her glasses back on and reached for the paper to re-read it. Jumping off a building? I don't know or Juliet talking down to Romeo from her balcony? It was interestingly beautiful and has some underlying meaning. But what, though?

"Can I take this? I'll reach out to him today. Thank you for bringing this to my attention."

"He used the word beautiful to describe it," Ms. Johnson let out just as I was folding the paper to place in my pocket. "When asked to describe in one word, the acts of Romeo and Juliet. He used the word beautiful. Please reach out to him."

"I will thank you again."

TYLER TUCKERMAN

Journal Entry: SUMMER of 2015

I t was the morning of our big hike. Finally, with only two days left at camp and the day was here. My long-awaited alone time with William, just us two. All those wilderness prep courses, learning the words to "I Will Survive" and practicing CPR on a doll would all finally be put to the test. William wanted to wake up early and get started before the sun came up. I'm not a morning person, as I was getting up and dressed, William was already outside getting everything together. We went the day before to rent all the necessary equipment. I met him at the outside pavilion, the sky was barely starting to lighten up, but the sun had yet to break across the mountaintop. William pulled out a map of the hike.

"So the trailhead is just west of the lake, we will cross here and take this path until we get to a small creek, we will get wet crossing. After the creek, we will walk along this ridge until we come to this massive rock where we can stop and have lunch. After that, it will be climbing uphill a little, some switchbacks until we hit this bend, and we will be at the top," William said, pointing to different parts of the trail. I probably understood fifty percent of what he just said. Thank goodness I had Molly take me on a few smaller hikes to prepare myself, as this was the ultimate test.

"Will I be good enough to climb in these tennis shoes?" I asked.

"Yeah you will be fine." William replied. Just then, remembering. "Crap, I forgot my black wristwatch."

"It's okay, here you can use mine," William said as he quickly took off his watch and handed it to me. I slowly reached out and grabbed it from his hand, our fingers touching. I don't wear watches, so it was a little challenging putting it on. Almost there, nope. Just a little closer to the strap, nope. One more time, nope. Until William leaned over and buckled my watch. He didn't say a word, just gave a smile. I gave a smile back as I put my red whistle around my neck.

❖ ❖ ❖

At the beginning of the trail, there was a sign

that read The Shepherd's Trail. Below are details of the hike, such as the overall time one way, some tips, and the intensity level: moderate/advanced, cool. We both had on a backpack supplied with our gear, essentials, and food. William talked to Lindsey, and she snagged us some granola bars, fruit, and water. They sold pre-packaged meals for overnight hikes. William took charge leading the way. All I could see was his backpack, beautiful legs, hiking boots, and a white baseball cap. The trail was easy so far, just a flat dirt trail. The air was so fresh as I inhaled the smell of pine. I'm not in Lincoln anymore.

It was then that the sun began to rise, the light piercing through and the rays warming our backs. William stopped and turned to face the sunrise.

"Wow, how beautiful."

Birds began chirping and flying around, trees were becoming visible, the forest was coming to life. It appeared to expand forever—a few logs on the ground, a few on the trail that we had to step over. The path was slowly beginning to change, from flat dirty to rocky with a few log obstacles. William started asking me questions about myself. Where am I from? Did I have any siblings? It was weird to talk about myself, detailing the town I live in out loud. William was also an only child. We began noticing small commonalities between us. His favorite number is *twenty-eight* because that's the day he was born. I tried not to overthink all the questions he was asking, trying not to mistake his friendliness as flirting.

"What happened to that tree?" I asked, pointing to an all-black tree, no branches or leaves, and it appeared to be cracked down the middle at the top.

"It looks like it got struck by lightning," William replied.

"Oh damn, what are the chances?"

"Did you know that there are both male and female pine cones?" I asked him. Thanks, Molly, I guess some of those factual speeches could come in handy, I sounded outdoorsy.

"What? I didn't think pine cones had a gender, I just thought they were seeds, that's pretty cool."

"Yeah, all these pine cones around us are female, the males are smaller and don't really look like pine cones. Little fun fact for ya." We kept walking forward, little pockets of silence.

"Tyler, can I ask you a question?" William asked. Oh no, hope he's not going to ask the question I think he might ask. Can we just continue to admire the green, prickly forest and not get into my past? Two truths and a lie. I spy. Anything but a blank check direct injection question. "Feel free to tell me to shut up or tell me to mind my own business, but are you gay?" William asked. I slowly closed my eyes. Gradually the forest went dark. I was at a fork in the road, in a position to make a choice, live from a Hollywood game show where I must answer correctly to win the big prize. I could lie and continue to stay in my closet until the camp was over and maintain this friendship we have, or I can tell him the truth if he is, in fact, a friend.

"I'm gay. I came out to my mom about a month ago. It didn't go well," I said, biting my lip and counting the number of seconds until he responded. Anxiously at the starting line waiting for the gun to go off. Waiting to burst out of the gates with everything I have, or like the shy kid on every team, do nothing. I was silent, he didn't hear me—next question. Every second felt like a minute as we were approaching five seconds.

"I'm sorry, Tyler, and thanks for telling me. It's not easy to open up to people. To be honest, I've been a little confused myself. I haven't told anybody," William said. There was a pause. Again, back at the starting line, waiting for the sound of the gun. Did he just respond to what I think he just said? He has been a little confused himself? Is this really happening? My heartbeat began to pick up, my palms getting sweaty. What do I say?

"Well hopefully, things fall into place for you soon," I said, looking at his shadow in front of me, double his height size, then looking at him. He wasn't an illusion. He was real.

"Yeah I hope so too. It's just so hard, people don't understand, at least not where I'm from," William replied. I'm glad he opened up to

113

me. Felt like he could trust me to tell me that. The feeling a kid in school gets while scouring the audience for his parents, to finally, after so many shows, sees them sitting in the front row ready to cheer on his performance. It was then that I felt like I was seen for the first time like someone understood me. I couldn't help but smile as I stared down at the dark brown dirt. William continued to lead the way.

I felt like there was something invisible between us. An unforeseeable being pulling and twisting us together as the conversation seamlessly continued. Having now become more comfortable with each other, I asked Will a simple favor, if we could take a quick ten-minute break, let the horses rest, cool the engine. He just laughed and agreed.

We were a good way through the beginning part of the trail, so I figured it was justifiable. Damn, I was tired, even with all those practice hikes. Bright red homegrown tomato face as I tried to lower my breathing, the fundamental trick, just look away, admire the surroundings. I don't think William could tell that this hike was literally killing me. It was okay if he didn't, he'd be worth it.

The rippling was constant—a faint

stream sound with no intention of stopping as we approached the creek. I like the sounds of water, it was peaceful and different. The only time I hear the sound of running water comes from a faucet. Tallgrass began to appear on the lips of the trail. The air started to get slightly more relaxed as the trail thinned, the pine trees stormed closer, and the branches began to hug. The creek wasn't as big as I had initially thought. This creek is manageable, the stubborn pre-teen throwing a fit, I first thought the stream was going to be more like a raging alcoholic throwing a fit.

I was hoping I wouldn't have to get wet, but that doesn't look possible. Damn. I looked over to find William, and he appeared to have wandered off. Well, great, I guess I am going to die on this trial, no William. Until I could hear my name, where did he go? I walked upstream a little way, and there behind a tree growing on the creek bank was William, he found a log that tipped over across the creek, forming a bridge. Oh, thank heavens. William began shaking and wiggling the trunk, trying to determine how well situated the beam of wood was. Looked good enough. William decided to go first, placing both hands out as one foot stepped up on the log. He placed one foot in front of the other, slow balancing as he did the tight walk—the most adorable circus performer.

"Don't fall!" I kept yelling, a playful flirt.

William would just look back at me and point a finger, indicating if I yelled that I would be in trouble again. But to any of my luck wanting to see him wet after he fell in, I was next to cross, I was next to waltz across this dead tree. I took a deep breath, put both my hands out flat, and began. I kept looking down, I don't know why this log appeared more full from the side. I was taking my time.

"The longer you take, the higher your chances of being on the log when it moves!" William shouted, well fuck, I thought, he's right, I have to get off this log. I then began to shuffle a little faster. Both arms straight out as William began to tap on his watch. I'M COMING! As I got closer, I asked for Williams' hand. He walked over and reach out. Faster than a heartbeat, my foot slipped as I leaned forward. Gravity was quick to react, but William was more rapid as I still had a hold of his hand as he pulled me up. A milli-second lapse in time, I was in his arms, and precisely three heartbeats later, we kissed. I think I now understand where that phrase, "Take My Breath Away" stemmed from. All of this happened so fast I haven't had time to breathe, literally. After we kissed, which lasted, I don't know, about six seconds, I unintentionally let out a loud exhale. William looked a little confused.

"Sorry, I was literally holding my breath through my entire attempt to cross that dead tree," I explained, wanting to make sure he knew it was because of the log. It was not because I was out of shape, or worse that I thought our kiss was weird. Then the awkward silence came as I kind of just stood there, and William turned around and began marching the trail, a quick little pit-stop. And just like that, my face was a bright red homegrown tomato again.

◆ ◆ ◆

We finally made it to the ridge. The trail was mostly rocked on the edge of the mountains east side. A quick wrap around on the edge of death until we got to the massive rock where we could take a break and enjoy some pre-packaged camp food. William was walking a little faster than usual. I noticed a few instances where I had to actually jog a little to catch up and then continue walking. Was it the kiss? Maybe I wasn't a good kisser, and now he's over it? Very likely actually. I hate not knowing what people are thinking. Why was he in such a hurry? Why did he pick up speed right after we kissed? I should just stay quiet for the rest of the hike.

"This ridge part isn't very long. It should be wrapping up soon," Wiliam said as he pointed forward, still walking a little faster than usual.

"Okay." I said, still trying to figure out his sudden change in intensity. My legs were definitely tired. I felt like climbing the rest of this section on my hands and knees. I wonder if he would carry me if I asked? Maybe later, I can't right now, I think we're fighting.

Just like that, you could see the side of the massive rock, the end was near. Just as we were about to make it to solid ground and no longer walk on stones on top of other stones, I had to ask him.

"Hey, did I do something? You seem to be in a hurry all of a sudden?"

"Yeah, I want to get this ridge part of the hike over with so we can relax and eat," William laughed as he picked up speed a little more, his backpack beginning to bounce. I smiled and thought about how I might be overthinking things.

JENNIFER HALL

There was one more hour left in the school day, and I had one last student appointment. It was with Mark Watson, a junior. I quickly scanned through his file that the school had. It wasn't much. His current school portrait. Dirty blonde hair that was long enough to comb back. He must be outside often because he was tan. His grades are good, a B average. He played all sports, and if my memory serves me right, Mark Watson was on the list that Principal Miller gave me when I first started. The sensitive student list. Let's hope that Principal Miller was just overreacting and he's a good kid, per his file he's excellent. I recall every time I walk around campus, or at various events, Mark Watson is always smiling and laughing. The social butterfly bringing light to every conversation. There was then a knock at my door, he had on a gray graphic t-shirt that displayed red bolded words, "Empire State Of Mind" with black basketball shorts.

"Hey, Ms. Hall. What's up? I think I'm a little early for our meeting today."

"No you're good, come on in." I said. In the

middle, Mark sat on the couch and placed both arms across the back of the sofa. He seemed very confident but polite. I turned my chair around and grabbed my pen and pad.

"Your office smells good," Mark said, looking around at all my books, framed pictures, and this glass ball award sitting on my desk. I was awarded by the first school I worked at, student engagement achievements plus my five-year mark.

"Thanks. It reminds me of back home. So Mark, how have your days been?"

"They have been good. It sucks that football season is almost over, but I am excited for basketball to start up. My three-point shot needs work." I noticed Mark had traces of red and purple marks around his left eye.

"What happened to your eye? It seems to be a little red and purple."

"Ah that," Mark put his hand and touched the side of his left eye. "I don't want to snitch, but Jason Brophy and I got into a little scuffle at practice the other day, none of the couches were around. It's not that big of a deal, it doesn't hurt."

"What caused this scuffle?"

"I don't let people push me around. He was teasing me and having me do crazy things at practice, so I finally said no." I'm glad to hear that he stood up for himself. Jason's name is one that comes up quite often at these meetings. I'll have to put him on my priority list.

"Please don't get him in trouble, It happens, I don't want people thinking I snitched or whatever."

"I'll have a talk with him. I won't say your name, but that other students have brought it to my attention."

"Thanks, Ms. Hall. Yeah, he's just a bully. He is always picking on Tyler, especially at our away games."

"Tuckerman?"

"Yeah, he seems like a cool dude—kind of reserved and keeps to himself. We actually hung out a little up at Welcome to Earth Camp. I got so good at archery while I was up there."

"Oh, you and Tyler went camping together?"

"Well kind of, I went one winter and this past spring. We hung out during the winter. After camp, we hung out a little at school. Then when I went during the springtime, he seemed different. I hardly saw him, he kind of stopped talking to me. I don't know if I did something. I wondered if it had anything to do with that one camper everyone was gossiping about."

"What happened? Did a camper get hurt?"

"No, I guess a camper a lot of people knew, killed himself just a few days before camp started. His name was William, a pretty funny dude. I met him when I went in the winter, it was the only thing people were really talking about for a few days. I didn't go this last summer. I wanted to go to a more sports-focused camp and work on my game, you know."

"Yeah, I totally get that; work on your game. Well, can I ask that you continue to be polite and maybe try speaking to Tyler? Usually, people are going through more than they let on."

"For sure, he seems cool."

"How have your classes been? Did you fill out that college assessment I had passed around?"

"The grades are good, they are good. I did not take that assessment yet, Ms. Hall, I apologize. I" ll have it done by our next meeting."

"Sweet, so tomorrow?" I joked. Mark's eyes got wide in shock with a little comical grin.

After I met with Mark, I sat pondering in my chair. Was William the student from Berza County? I turned to Google. I started with keywords: "William," "teen suicide," "Berza." Nothing appeared in the search. Well hell. Let me think, let me think. Then I remembered what Mark said, that camp he went to where he met William, I adjusted some keywords: "William," "Berza," "Welcome to Earth Camp." A few links appeared as I read each line, and there, an obituary from a funeral home. I felt like I was finally on to something. There was no mention of the cause of death, and no mention of suicide, which is pretty standard as most parents won't publicly admit when the death is by suicide. I scanned the page: "On Thursday, February 28, 2019, William Ackhurst, loving son and brother, passed away at the age of seventeen." This was so heartbreaking to read. "William had a passion for hunting, hiking, and seasonal trips to Welcome to Earth Camp." Now that I learned his last name, I did a search in FaceBook, and there, the first page was his FaceBook Memorial Page. The header read, "Remembering William Ackhurst" and below was his picture. Buzzed brown hair, a charming smile, and piercing blue eyes. The page timeline consisted of people posting photos of William. Him being held by his mother the day he was born, his first time hunting with his father dressed in camouflage, him and his friends swimming in a lake, various group prom pictures, and him at the top of a snowy white mountain. Each image had a comment after comment after comment. Everyone exchanged memories about William and what they loved most about him.

Mark mentioned that Tyler got sad and extremely distant last spring when word broke about William. I wonder how close Tyler and William were? I didn't see any photos of them together on William's memorial page. I couldn't find any social media account for Tyler. I looked up Tyler's class schedule and phoned his biology teacher to tell him that I was booking a meeting with Tyler during his lecture tomorrow.

I looked back and re-read William's obituary. The remembrance, the passions, lifes delicate and unstable curiosity. With one blink, I was reading Emily's life passions detailed in her memory. A soft hand that sought mine to shelter any uncertainty. Life's precious moments are always fleeting. Constantly cherish and re-cherish the gift that is love, because, in the blink of an eye, all you could have left is a memory.

TYLER TUCKERMAN

Journal Entry: WINTER of 2017

I searched through my backpack for scissors. Small little school scissors to open this pre-packaged powdered mashed potatoes, just add water and stir. They have a salted garlic flavor, so they aren't bad. William has been obsessed with this pre-packaged teriyaki chicken bowl; just add boiling water into the bag. Let it sit and lunchtime. I usually carry the food, snacks, and pillows in my backpack with one wood log.

William carries the water, tent, sleeping bags, and two logs strapped to the top of his backpack. He promised when we got to the top, we could build a fire. We recently began taking this small foldable tray for boiling water, instead of creating a little stand with rocks.

This has been our fourth time hiking The Shepherd's Trail, and I will say that doing this hike in the wintertime is my least favorite. I can never move my hands, even with gloves. I dress as if I'm about to visit Antarctica, while William takes a more relaxed approach. Yes, believe it or not, the northern part of the state has a substantial elevation increase compared to the south, usually what people think of when Arizona is mentioned. Thus, yearly amounts of snowfall in the winter. I recall Molly Fritz saying something about northern Arizona receiving, on average, 100 inches of snow. Her favorite place during the winter is Arizona Snowbowl, a ski resort in Flagstaff. I could not imagine myself trying to ski or snowboard, sledding, on the other hand, sounds fine. Casual William has a jacket and jeans on but only one layer. The pine branches collect piles of it as it hung above us. The rocks are half visible, half-frozen. The sky today was a little overcast with no wind. Hoping there is a zero chance of snow, I guess we should have checked before we left.

So despite all the challenges of this hike. All the times I actually did fall in the creek and still the many breaks we have to take because of me, we do it because it's William's favorite hike. During our two weeks together at camp each summer, winter, spring, he gets to pick one day and plan our date, he always chooses this hike.

His knees were almost touching his face as he sat on the flattest rock, balancing his teriyaki chicken bowl with both hands. He looked adorable, trying to take bites. I pulled out my camera. He hated it when he caught me filming him. He said it was cute at first, but now he calls me a weirdo and pulls me closer, getting jealous of all the attention I gave my camera and not him. He does let me take pictures of him. He was mid teriyaki chicken bite when he glanced over and saw me, camera in hand, a big smile on my face, the red dot blinking. He just shook his head, rolled his eyes, and took a bite.

I can't recall the last time I was actually happy, or at least happy for this long. It became a flow, a routine of intertwining each other into one another. Reading the other, gentle observations fueling the ever-expanding idea of us. How am I so lucky? I beg my mom to let me go to Welcome to Earth camp just so I can see this jerkface. We are very discreet as William hasn't come out. He described his parents a little, and it doesn't sound like his dad, a member of a white supremacy group, would be supportive if he found out. A verbally abusive snake that needs to be matched with a shovel. The family's rotting spot after being discharged from the military for neonazi affiliation.

After we chatted about it for a little bit, stuff made sense, like William's beautiful head is always buzzed short. William doesn't believe in the hate his father thought in. His dad knows that, but the only requirement is a tight buzzed head. William did mention the anxiety he felt. Big-brother watching his every move considering his father's duty in the military was a Surveillance Technology Expert. His father flipped out on his mother one year after he suspected she was having an affair, secret text, and unknown phone calls. Still, it turns out she was planning his fiftieth surprise party. Since then, William is convinced his father monitors all their emails, calls, and texts. His biggest fear is his father finding out about his sexuality.

I'm glad this camp occurs three times a year. Not nearly enough, but enough for William to not be home three times out of the year. He still has his friend group at camp; they usually compete in events against each other, race across the lake, or hang out during lunch. We often have breakfast and dinner together. I have a small friend group just consisting of Molly Fritz, some campers from the film explorations course. Actually, this kid from Lincoln High, Mark Watson, has started coming here. He is an incoming freshman, and I am a high and mighty sophomore. He is probably the person I hang out with the most.

Just like that, it began to snow. The forest became silent as small white flakes raced to the ground.

"Are you serious?" I said, pulling the camera away from my face. William just laughed.

"It's not that bad, *babe*." Ugh. Babe. I love it when he calls me, babe, and it was rare. He is very stingy with the name, so I knew when he said it just now that we were having a moment.

I did get footage of William trying to eat than being invaded by snow. He got up from sitting on his little flat rock, packed away his trash teriyaki chicken bowl into his backpack, and walked over to me.

"See, it's not that bad," he said as he grabbed the back of my neck, leaning me in for a kiss.

◆ ◆ ◆

Like always, William was leading the way. The snow has slowed down to hardly any falling. This next section of the trail is all up-hill, gradual incline of twist and turns, back and forth, or as William calls them, switchbacks. I leaned down and picked up some snow. Quickly using my hands to roll this ice into a ball be-fore my hands froze. Right as the perfect shot is thrown, its chucked forward, moving through the air until - smash! Williams backpack.

"Boy!" he yelled out, quickly leaning down to form his own snowball to retaliate with. Tossing his ball through the air, I dove for-ward - miss! I played in the snow and got up, to then be hit by the second snowball, how does he build them so fast? He suggested one camp year that we should bring the cornhole boards and beanbags so we could play once we got to the top. I shut that down, I am not carrying wood boards up a mountain. So we settled on snow-balls instead of beanbags, and we just dig a snow-hole instead of boards, it works.

It was my idea, I thought of it last winter, our first winter doing this hike, that we should sync our watches. I wanted some way to stay connected with him after we leave camp. The hardest thing is the last day of camp, saying goodbye. We can't dramatically run into each other's arms out on the lawn, crying. We have to be discrete. Say our goodbyes are the night before. William's van picks him up before mine does, so I don't see him for too long in the morning of departure. I thought to sync our watches, but William suggested the time that the alarm would go off. *We combined our two favorite numbers.* Mine being eleven, I don't know if it's something about the way it sounds, ele-ven, or because it's just two one's, side by side, two in-dividuals, in love. Williams being twenty-eight, the day he was born. So every night, our watches go off at *11:28*. Sometimes i'm so tired, deep in sleep, and the alarm goes off, ugh, that's what ir-ritates me the most. But it's cute. It helps.

We can't text that often as I have a pre-paid, no job, and my mom wouldn't keep buy-ing me more credits. Emergencies only, she said. Some nights when William really missed me and felt a little sad he would call, but didn't want to get caught chatting on the phone. He had phone curfews, he would just leave the phone next to his stereo and play, "Iris" by the GooGoo Dolls. He would call, I would answer and instantly hear the strumming of the guitar.

I always underestimate this part of the trail. I was tired, and charging through some snow isn't helping. The snow isn't too deep, about half a foot in some places up to a foot. I finally got some hiking boots. They were my birthday present request last year, so much better than those tennis shoes I had.

"Sshh!" William let out, froze dead in his tracks. I did the same, quickly looking around to try and figure out why we had to freeze. I was kinda nervous. My first thought was a bear, but then I was like, no dummy they are hibernating. William pointed forward up the trail to the left, a momma deer and her fawn. His little legs were wobbling as he tried to balance and walk through the ice, he would sometimes face-plant directly into the snow. The cutest thing ever! I quickly got out my camera and took a few pictures, then some footage of the fawn trying to walk across the trail, the momma being patient as she was just a few feet ahead.

"So adorable," I said, putting my camera away and walking up to William. I grabbed his hand. William looked down at me and kept getting more and more handsome, his eyes kept getting bluer and bluer, and my heart was getting more and more full.

◆ ◆ ◆

I'm not sure if I said this yet, but I'm cold. I cannot wait for our campfire. One of the things I do like about doing this hike in the winter is William rents the two-person sleeping bag so we can cuddle. Wrapped up like a burrito. Before, I was about to complain about the cold out loud, and the sun appeared from the clouds. I knew if I did complain, William would just say, well, the sun's out now.

"Can I grab a granola bar from your back-pack?" William asked as he turned around, then he let out a shocking, "Holy sunburn, Ty, your face is red!" He began to laugh, but he also looked concerned.

"Sunburned?" I said as I took my glove off one hand, placed it on my face. "Ouch, I am sun-burnt, how could that happen?"

"The sun's rays still penetrate through the clouds and reflect off the snow," William explained, hinting that he asked me if I wanted some sunscreen before we left the hike down by the lake, but I declined. He then walked behind me and began looking through my backpack. He pulled out and handed me a small bottle of SPF 50 sunscreen. It might be a little bit too late for that, but at least I can minimize further damage.

Another cool thing about doing this hike in the winter is the calm delicate elements. The snow on the trail in front of us, clean and untouched. Casually interrupting the uninhabited parts of the forest trail. I wouldn't mind one day buying a cabin in the forest. A very long long long way from now, but it's still fun to fantasize. William and I living in this cute cabin, maybe a golden retriever or two? William was not charging ahead this time but instead slowed down as we were hiking side by side.

"Will, if you could choose anywhere in the world to live, right now, where would it be?" I asked.

"Hmm, I would say Lake Louise. It's up in Canada. My aunt went a few years ago and showed me pictures. The massive baby blue lake between large snow-capped mountains and the brightest green pines. That's where I'd love to live out my days." I loved that he already knew of a place and why. I should think of mine.

"What about you?"

"I don't really know. Somewhere by the beach, maybe?" I said. "I've never been to a beach."

"No way!" William let out, in shock. "We need to change that!"

"Do you ever think about the future?"

"The future?"

"Yeah, like, after camp. Pretty soon, we'll be too old to attend."

"Sometimes. I try not to think too much about it, but yes, the good parts."

"What do you see?" I asked as silence suffocated us both.

"I see you." William said, looking down at the snow then squeezing the back of my neck, "I see you." At that very moment, my weighted vest came off, the duct tape across my mouth, removed. He then pointed forward, yes, finally, the bend was just ahead, the final big bend, and we had arrived at the mountain top.

"Can we build that fire when we get to the top?"

"Oh definitely, first thing," William smiled.

JENNIFER HALL

L ike most of my rides home, I pondered if I still had wine left in the fridge. This time was sad to learn there was no wine left. I had to run and grab some before the store closed. As I pulled into the parking lot at the small local grocery store, the only place in town that sold wine, I could see Billy Porter on his four-wheeler, holey shirt, and oil-stained jeans. He was talking with a young blonde girl. He kept trying to bring her closer, she casually laughed off the advances as she played with her hair and looked up to the sky. Sheriff Clark told me that a mother around in town filed a restraining order against Billy. He kept making advances to her daughter, creeping on her during school functions and around town.

Luckily, she graduated this past May and moved away. Sadly, the only way a girl can stop being harassed in a town like this is to move away, run far away, and never look back. Within a blink of an eye, I saw what appeared to be Billy slip the young blonde something. He had his hand low, tried to discreetly hold something out as the girl grabbed it. What was it that he gave her? I didn't want to run over and cause a scene, that would get us nowhere, this was a slow battle, and I just got a massive tip. Then Billy appeared to wave his hand toward the street. I tried not to dramatically turn to see, then I heard a loud, HONK! I slightly turned to see a big red semi-truck cruise on by. Ricky Tuckerman? I remember Tyler mentioned his father drove a big red truck. This just reaffirmed how small this town was.

The local grocery store was just like your typical small-town mom and pop business. One payphone out front, two wooden benches that no one sits on. A travel trailer sat behind the store, that is probably where some of the store workers stay. There was always a massive rush of melon and cotton field workers every other Friday. Cashing their checks, and send a money order to their families back in Mexico. Two or three white buses filled with seasonal laborers. Under the law of the H-2A visa program, farm growers are allowed to import workers from across the Mexican border.

Businesses that participate in this program have to pay the workers minimum wage set by the government. But that is way more than what they would be making performing the same job back in their native country. In return, the employers only have to pay a minimum wage for a very labor-intensive heat stroke inducing conditions. Coleman Grocery Store is the only place in Lincoln with the capital to cash all those checks and also offers Western Union Money Order services. Luckily for me, that cash checking rush was not today as I was approaching the liquor aisle.

You could tell that Lincoln residents have a particular taste in liquor as some brands and types were covered in dust, while others only had one or two left on the shelves. Coleman Grocery didn't have a wide range of brand options on wine, so I usually stuck to the most giant bottle for the lowest price. Hasn't failed me yet.

I decided to get two bottles to stock up with. I was pushing the cart around, window shopping, looking at all the tchotchkes and wall decor. As I passed the meat aisle, I came upon a small row of books. Some new, some old, neatly shelved. Looked like no one had recently browsed the Coleman Grocery literary collection. One book on the outdoors got my attention as I need to adventure the desert mountains more. I could then hear from the next aisle over, a woman yelling and getting frustrated,

"I told you, I am not buying you that. Goddammit, go put it back right now, Bobby." I wonder if that was Bobby Jones' mom getting upset with Bobby, poor guy. I then had flashbacks to our meeting when I first started at LHS. My meeting with Nicole being cut short by Bobby being escorted in by Principal Miller, crying and drunk, and the little red scratches he had on his wrists. I should reach out to his mom again and keep her updated on his well being, maybe then she would be less aggravated with him and be more understanding. My first meeting with her was quick as she appeared distracted and summed up Bobby's attitude to teenagers being teenagers.

"Go fucking wait in the car. Here's the keys!" Bobbys' mom hissed back. I tried not to overthink it. Maybe I should schedule another meeting with him as well. I then saw at the end of the aisle, Bobby quickly walks by, then out the door. Yup, it was him.

I turned back around toward the book-shelves and began to pull the Outdoor Adventure Guide book from the shelves when a small, worn-out book a few books down, slipped, and landed on the floor. I turned the free-falling book over, *The Night the Angels Cried*. The cover art was mostly light blue with a small white teddy bear in the center. After scanning the description on the back, I got a feeling of curiosity. I quickly flipped through the pages like I was shuffling a deck of cards. The pages have a yellowish tint. When was this book published? I kept rifling through until I came across a bookmark tightly placed in the middle of the book. I scanned the page for keywords. It seemed to be saved on the scene where a little girl passed away. It was a small bookmark, a white rectangle piece of paper with writing on it. Blue pen on both sides were the numbers *11:28*. What could that mean? I got to the front cover and on the inside was a stamp, *Property of Lincoln High School Library*. I didn't want to get in the middle of whoever stole it from the library, so I put the book back and proceeded to the checkout lane.

◆ ◆ ◆

I pulled into my driveway and grabbed the paper grocery bag, hoping it wouldn't break with the weight of the two jugs of red wine. If the plastic bag did break and both bottles shattered across the sidewalk, I might just kill myself. Stop Jen, what is wrong with you, don't joke around like that, especially now. I approached the door to see a little letter, inserted into the crease from the door and frame. What is this? Was I invited to some party? Or a passive-aggressive "keep the noise down" letter. I grabbed the letter, stuck it in the paper bag with the wine, and unlocked it.

I wasted no time putting the wine in the fridge, yes I like my reds cold. I looked around the room and noticed the old living room phone was still unplugged, It should probably remain that way. I then remembered that white letter, pulling it from the paper bag and quickly ripping it open and unfolded the piece of paper.

Slowly placing my hand over my mouth. I could feel the instant sweat from my side. My heart pounding out of my chest with scenes of fear and melancholy. My guts were weightless as they seem to be floating inside me. I could feel Emily's soft, delicate hand, clutching mine as she looked up at me with those innocent Disney eyes. I instantly went back in time to a slumber party I threw, building a fort with couch cushions, dining room chairs, and a purple fitted sheet. A few of my friends circled in the middle with a camping nightlight in the center as we told each other ghost stories. Quietly hearing Emily call out my name, asking if she could join us. All she wanted was to be with her big sister, looking back, I was so unkind. Hisser her away so my friends and I could continue. I remember it got to the point where I pushed her out of my room and locked the door. I would give anything to unlock that door and let her in. My hands were shaking as I tried to swallow my dry throat. It was typed text in the center of the paper. Times New Roman read:

Do you think Emily would have killed herself?

TYLER TUCKERMAN

The air was warm and a little thick, unusually warm for March 1st. I was a little annoyed and somewhat concerned. It was probably about an hour or so after the last van arrived. William was nowhere in sight. No call and no text. All the familiar faces roaming around the campgrounds, Just not Williams.

"Hey, Ty! Want to go jump in the lake?" Molly asked; she already had her one-piece blue swimsuit on, the same blue as William's eyes.

"No, I'm good, I'm not feeling too well, my stomach is in knots."

"Okay. Well, get to feeling better. See you around for dinner?"

"Yeah, sure," I responded distractedly. Was William blowing me off? Ditching me? This was not like him to miss a seasonal trip to camp. The campgrounds were empty without his laugh, without his charismatic charm and mysterious way about him. It's like I was going through drug withdrawals. I have never been to camp without him being here, I have never slept in Cabin C without his bed next to mine. We have been to this camp *eleven* times together. 1,330 days since the first time I experienced those eyes. Little did I know, or would I even want to have known that the winter of 2018 camp season would have been our last. Maybe then I would have cherished those casual glances, with every passing season, each glance lasting a second too long. Was I entitled to be angry that he didn't show? Was I allowed to that emotion or any emotion about him missing one camp season? It wouldn't have been as bad had I not just realized that Hannah was also not around, she did not show up either. The poison of jealousy was settling inside my stomach again, my mind going to the worst-case scenario. They ran off together.

I wasn't about giving up hope. Maybe his van broke down? Blew a tire out, and they are waiting for another van to come to rescue them. Like my first time coming to camp, he missed his van ride, and now he has to get a ride from his mom. That's probably it. I pulled my camera out of its bag and decided to scroll through old pictures while I waited for William to arrive. The first smile stretched across my face since I came to camp.

I continued to wait for him by the registration cabin until they announced dinner. I was sitting next to the wall facing the lake when I heard them. Two gossiping girls who work at the camp confirmed it. They didn't say how they didn't say why all they said was that William Ackhurst of Berza County killed himself in his bedroom. Those words were strangling me. I couldn't feel anything. Paralyzed. Numb. William is dead. William died. William is no longer. I will never see William again. All those words glaring directly into my eyes, watching life fade. My eyes were dry from the lack of blinking. My stomach going ice-cold, a feeling of emptiness. And in that second was also when I became invisible, as the only person who really saw me was gone. I continued to sit on the ground as I couldn't get up, my vest was back on. I couldn't scream as the tape was again wrapped around my mouth. I was a void, an anomaly beautifully constructed to only be seen by him, those warm blue eyes. *Everything he did was beautiful.*

Journal Entry: SPRING of 2019

The tent was entirely laid out on the ground. The view was swallowed in clouds. Just as I was about to finish setting up the tent, it began to rain. Slow at first with a few drops hitting me randomly, then to a more constant flood. I grabbed the end of the flexible beam stick and put it through the hole at the bottom of the tent. Snapped the clips of the tent to the flexible beam stick so the tent would stay up. Zipped down the door, and quickly jumped in. Soaked. I laid out my sleeping bag, pulled my pillow close, turned my head over, and cried myself to sleep. This was my sixth and final hike up The Shepherd's Trial, as I was lost without *my shepherd.*

We were sitting on the ledge. We arrived at the top of the mountain, the final end of the trial, to be presented by breathtaking views of the mountain range. The sun was warm, and the sky was blue. We decided to wait to set up camp and take in the view instead. William came and sat next to me. We were under a little tree overlooking the valley. He put his arm around me. We could feel the sun's rays toasty and bright as they moved in and out from behind the tree branches. I leaned my head into his shoulder as we sat there in silence. lub-dub. Williams' arm was across the back of my neck, I reached my hand up and grabbed his fingers dangling down the side of my arm. lub-dub. Like a content-loving cat cuddled up on the couch with its passionate owner, Williams pur was thumbing from his heart I could always feel. lub-dub. I liked to imagine our heartbeats were synced, mine for his and his for mine, every time. Lub-dub. Down the side of my neck is where I would feel his warm breaths go, followed by a chain reaction of goosebumps and butterflies racing down my arm, to the tip of my fingers, and out into the world. lub-dub.

I could still hear the rain tapping against the tent as I was suddenly awakened in the middle of the night. *beebeep*. I laid there on my back, looking up at the top of the tent as it continued to sway in the wind, then turning to my side, looking at Williams' empty side of the tent where he would always sleep. *beebeep*. I could feel wet, fresh tears run down the sides of my warm red face. *beebeep*. I didn't wipe the tears away. *beebeep*. I leaned my hand over and turned it off. The alarm on William's black wristwatch he gave me was going off - *11:28*.

JENNIFER HALL

"**S**tudents please be seated. For those of you who do not know who I am, I'm Sheriff Clark. You were all brought here on this lovely Monday morning as there is some stuff we want to fill you in on. First, starting right now, we are beefing up our drug search program at the high school. Once a month, K9 Deputy, Freedom, will search the entire school for narcotics as well as during sporting events."

I was sitting in the back of the gymnasium, off to the side. I just wanted to hear Brian's intro and tone, he's doing a great job. I walked out of the gymnasium to meet and escort Deputy Gomez, Deputy Flynn, and K9 Deputy Freedom around the school to get this search started. It was perfect timing with all the students in the gymnasium. Freedom was a beautiful light brown German Shepherd, young and hyper.

You could tell she is well trained and really into her job. Sniffing high and low, locker to locker. Then she stopped and sat down, perfectly still, looking up at Deputy Gomez. I quickly took out the codebook for all the lockers and opened the locker Freedom stopped in front of. Books, pencils, pictures, and permanent marker writing covered this student's locker. A black backpack hanging from the top as Deputy Flynn put on blue latex gloves and grabbed the bag, quickly looking in each pocket. In the small front pocket, inside a metal breath, the mint container was a, or what appeared to jewels? Or clear gems? Or perhaps crystals.

"What are those?" I asked.

"Appears to be crystal meth," Gomez said. "We'll take this in to sample it, determine if it's a mixture of various narcotics or just one." He opened a small lockbox, placed the breath mint container inside, and locked it. I have a feeling he's going to be opening that little lockbox a few times today.

"Okay, let me jot this locker number down as a hit," I said

"Once we are done, we will round up the students whose lockers were positive. Flynn, make a note on what was found in each and get the paperwork going as we continue," Deputy Gomez said, reaching into his pocket and giving Freedom a "you did it!" treat.

We were making good progress, about halfway done searching all the outside lockers, we had four locker hits. The narcotics spanning from crystal meth to marijuana. But no pills. We wanted to do a thorough search of all the lockers before making arrests and approaching the students. We couldn't make it seem as if we were singling out specific students, as per the law, but instead a massive search. Also, we couldn't drug test all the students, but we were allowed to test the student's members of athletic teams.

We got a list of the male and female athletes and instructed the coaches to cascade the mandatory drug test. Lincoln has a small health clinic in town, mostly used for flu vaccines and standard check-ups. We called and had the doctor at the health clinic, Dr. Singh, stop by the high school to oversee the drug testing. All of this was done Monday morning to not give the students time to hide any of their narcotics or attempt to sneak fake pee into the drug testing.

This was all going according to plan. I felt proud of myself. Brian walked by to check the status of the search, he wasn't surprised when we told him what and how much had been found thus far. About three days ago, I ran into him at Coleman Grocery Store. He was picking up steaks for dinner, and I feminine products, I blushed. Like a shy boy asking his crush to the dance, he placed both his hands inside his dark blue wrangler jeans, looked to the ground then up at me, and asked if I would like to go to dinner with him this Friday evening. I said yes, of course. We then parted ways, and like a teenage girl, I blasted music the entire ride home.

We finally arrived toward the backend of the school buildings, some of the primary classrooms that were built in the 1950s. Some were empty as there were not enough students to fill, so no use for them. The door was locked, it was dark purple, almost black. I doubt any students have hidden drugs in here as the door was closed, but I had never been in here. The room was empty, with nothing on the walls. There were no desks, paper, or even a pencil—one large window with overgrown bushes outside covering any sort of view.

All the dust had settled in the room as if we had just unveiled a hidden tomb. As the room was completely empty, I had no interest in looking around. I was shutting the old dark purple door when I glanced over to my left, and of the corner of the room, there was another door. That other door was different, it definitely stood out after I noticed it as the door only stood about three and a half feet tall. I walked over to open the door, only to find it was locked.

The keyhole on the doorknob was old fashioned, which seemed to require some sort of skeleton key. I was beyond curious what in the world does this little door lead to? I was so caught up that I forgot about the drug search. I quickly walked out and locked the door behind me.

I caught up with the search crew who were heading back to the main office. They decided to go into the meeting room to test the narcotics found. Deputy Gomez had a test that would identify the narcotic type and purity. You place the narcotic inside, then release the first solution module and shake the bag. The solution will turn blue if positive. To no surprise, all paraphernalia tested positive. Included the bag of meth. They started mapping the locker to the student. They wrote their names down, and Deputy Gomez and Principal Miller went around the school and rounded up the students.

I talked with Sandy Bloom, the school receptionist. She's terrific at her job and is probably the most tenured employee at Lincoln High. Her short white permed hair fits perfectly alongside her all-white New Balance sneakers. She was helping gather the names of students. Every morning when I walk past her desk, she always has her little cup of oatmeal, black coffee, and knitting yarn laid across the counter. Like many people in Lincoln, Sandy's family has been here a few generations, finding that one good job and doing a great job at it, providing and making their way in the world.

"Sandy, I love that scarf you finished knitting. The yellow and orange colors look beautiful, and just in time for autumn!" reaching my hand over and feeling the scarf. Sandy had just finished knitting last night and promised to bring it into show me. So many of the ladies here are crafty, I need to take up a creative hobby, except wine. Well, maybe figure out a way to merge the two. "You and Ms. Johnson should open up a little store."

"Ms. Johnson is so much better at knitting than I am, but thank you, yes I really liked these colors, and I'm not much of an orange type." Sandy said, also reaching over and feeling the scarf, mirrored response.

"The both of you should start a collection! Yeah, you both can create your own knitted clothing line, we can call it S&J."

"Oh how cute!" Sandy laughed. "Darling, do you have any plans tonight? Eddie and I are going to Bingo up at the VFW tonight. Would you like to join us? They always have fun prizes, and it's such a good company."

"I have zero plans tonight, and I would love to join you and Eddie. I haven't visited the VFW yet. Is there any sort of buy-in?"

"Just $10 and you go for about two hours" Sandy then placed her hand to the side of her mouth and faced me, "and they serve wine."

"Oh wonderful. What time does it begin?"

"They start reading the balls at six o'clock."

"Beautiful, this will be fun!" Just as Sandy and I were finalizing our evening plans, the doors to the front office opened. Walked in were the six students with whom we found either some narcotics in their locker or their drug test came back positive. They all had their heads down. With Looks of uncertainty as to what is currently happening, and the unknown of what will happen to them. Except for the last one to walk in, Jason Brophy. He looked like he could care less. They were all told to be seated, and I was going to talk to each one, ask about where they got the drugs, the ones who helped will have fewer consequences, and vice versa. I decided to start with Jason first since out of the six students, this was the first that I recognized.

I quickly pulled up his profile before our meeting. It says here he is seventeen years old, a junior and grades barely good enough to allow him to continue to play sports. His school photo was dated last year with a smug smirk across his face while wearing just a plain white t-shirt. No drugs were found in his locker, so I scanned for his drug test results provided by Dr. Singh at the health clinic. Says here, he tested positive for Xanax and marijuana. In his school profile, his mother's number was listed, Margarette Brophy. I decided to give her a call, inform her that her son tested positive for drugs, and to confirm if he had a prescription for Xanax.

My call with Margarette was short as she had to get back to her tables, sounded like she was a waitress. She was not happy with our call, which was a relief, I could never tell if these parents would rather be their kids' friends or be actual parents. She stressed that she did not know where her son would have got his hands on Xanax as neither of them was prescribed that drug. She seemed a bit hesitant to confirm that same with marijuana.

He had his arms crossed and was chewing on some short plastic straw, looking around the room, again, he could care less. I walked up to the boys.

"Jason, do you want to come to my office?" I said, standing by the door. His hair was blonde and cut short, the back seemed to be a little longer as if he was trying to be able to eventually joke about having a mullet. His jeans were dark blue with tan working boots. He walked past me and didn't say a word, walked into my office, and sat on the couch, folding his arms and chewing on that fucking plastic straw. I gently shut the door.

"Jason, I'm sure you know why you are here. Your drug test came back positive. Do you want to explain why you were taking these drugs and where you got them?" I asked as he continued to sit there, appearing to make no intention of talking. The room became silent, as my question then turned into a staring contest. He then reached his hand up and took the straw out of his mouth.

"I didn't test positive."

"It says right here you tested positive for Xanax and marijuana," I said, handing him the test result. He made no effort to reach and grab it.

"I just found them on the road."
That's his answer? That he just found them on the road. I know he was covering for whoever sold him those drugs.

"You found them on the road. Interesting. Okay, so If you just found them on the road, why not take them to the local police department? Per your test results, you used them. So, you use random drugs you find on the side of the road?" I asked, trying to drill, get him to crack, and tell me where he got the drugs.

"Maybe."

"Maybe? Jason, do you feel strong anxiety at home or at school? Are you stressed to the point where you think you have to take drugs to feel better?"

"What are you talking about?"

"You tested positive for alprazolam, or also known as Xanax. Why are you taking anti-anxiety if you claim to not suffer from anxiety and smoking pot? That just doesn't make sense."

"If I tell you I suffer from anxiety, will you leave me alone?"

"Where did you get these drugs from? Your mother confirmed you are on no prescription medication."

"What the fuck? You told her?"

"Yes Jason, this is serious. Stop taking drugs you are not prescribed. Are you aware that Xanax side effects could cause paranoid or suicidal ideation? And mixing that with marijuana? There is enough tragedy in this town. They don't need to bury another kid. So I'm going to ask again, where did you get them from?" Damn, that was harsh, maybe I shouldn't have said that. But still, he needs to understand reality, teenagers are always in their own bubble, always angst and ready to blame the world. These small-town kids are a cakewalk compared to those rich city kids. I would prefer to help with the problems of drugs and life, not so much, drugs and narcissism. Rural America. The issues are raw and real, not fake and manufactured.

"Ms. Hall, I'm not going to tell you where I got those pills, so if we could just speed this up. I understand I'm probably going to get the harshest punishment for not telling," Jason said, placing that nasty plastic straw back in his mouth and folding both arms. Cocky little shit.

"Fine. Go to Principal Miller's office. He's expecting you."
I hope the other students cave in and tell me what I want to know—at least one. Jason got up, opened the door and left, I too stood up and called the next student into my office. That meeting left me flustered, I just had to shake it off.

"Jose Mendoza, can you step into my

office?" He seemed a bit nervous. He kept adjusting his blue hat that read L.A. across the center. His pants were a little baggy as he pulled them up before sitting on my office couch. "Jose, do you know why you are here?"

"Umm, I think so?" Jose mumbled.

"You think so?"

"Aye, Ms. Hall, I'm sorry. I was holding those for a friend. Please don't call my dad!" Jose begged. Well, that was easy. I just sat back in my chair, thinking if he was this easy to crack, he should be able to quickly tell me where he got them from.

"Where did you get the meth from, Jose?"

"No, I was holding it for a friend. I didn't buy it. He asked me to hang onto it. I'm telling the truth, Ms. Hall, you have to believe me! Aye, I would never do that crap," Jose said frantically. Since Jose was not on any sports teams, we couldn't test him, so there was no way for me to know if he was taking the drugs.

"Who were you holding them for?" I asked, again, getting more mad and annoyed.

"He doesn't go to school here. One of my buddies that works in the fields. His family is back in Puerto Penasco."

"Puerto Penasco, Mexico?"

"Yeah. Again, I'm so sorry, Ms. Hall. I'll take two weeks detention, just please don't tell my dad."

"Jose, you were found with a Schedule II

substance on school property. Do you understand how serious a Schedule II narcotic is? Under federal law, a conviction for meth possession can result in up to one year in jail. Right now, your father finding out is the least of your worries. Do you understand, this is extremely serious? Go see Principal Miller now."

I got up and opened the door. Just to be safe that Jose didn't run out the door after notifying him of how difficult it was, I asked for assistance.

"Deputy Flynn, can you escort Jose to Principal Miller's office? I'm going to phone his parents." If all that doesn't scare the shit out of him to never ever be involved with these drugs again, I don't know what will.

PART TWO: A KID IS NOT ALRIGHT

TYLER TUCKERMAN

I have never really ridden on a four-wheeler, let alone drive one myself. Nicole invited me to tag along with her and Mark Watson for the day. They have been spending a lot of time together, I was excited when I got the offer. I always liked Mark, going back to our camping days. The plan was to take Mark's four-wheelers out in the desert. I was nervous about going but figured what the hell, just do it. I didn't tell my mom what we were going to do, as she would probably freak out. When my dad was younger, he and my uncle, Jack, were involved in a pretty severe accident. My dad broke his arm, and Uncle Jack had a serious concussion. Neither of them was wearing helmets. They were going too fast around a turn, hit a little pump, and both flew off the four-wheeler. I didn't inherit my dad's thrill-seeking adventure.

I sat in my room waiting for Nicole to pick me up in her dad's old pick up truck, she loves that thing. I was sitting at my computer desk, scanning the internet trying to find pictures for this little film project I was working on. I needed to work on something other than footage of our lame high school sports team. I was plotting the short film in my head and jotting down ideas. I had my journal laying out on my desk, doodling scenes. I wanted to try something challenging, like filming water—bubbles floating fast and slow to the surface, small and big bubbles. Black and white lens view, adjusting the exposure levels, as the water flowed and shifted around. A fun two to three-minute film. I got really excited as I came across this device you add to your camera to film underwater. I had to get it. My mom has a stash of credit cards she keeps for emergencies. I snuck one out from her dresser drawer and ordered the camera attachment online. Right after I updated my desktop photo on my laptop to a stunning capture of Lake Louise.

I heard Nicole's truck pull up to take us to a little spring up in the desert mountains that Mark must have suggested. I decided to bring my camera along, figured I could get some cool footage if the spring does exist. It's been raining for the last few days, so I'm banking on the natural spring being pretty active.

◆ ◆ ◆

I picked it up four-wheeling reasonably

quickly as long as we were riding on a flat dirt road. Every once and a while, you'll see quick turnoffs, one exit to go right, drive forward, then another exit to go left, on a different trail. We have just been going one way, toward the mountain. My head compressed as the helmet Mark had for me was a perfect fit. It was near silence with the fitted helmet, the sound of your voice echoing inside. I had my own four-wheeler, a baby blue machine all to myself, while Nicole and Mark shared one. Theirs was black and silver and looked like it would be a lot faster than mine. It was then that I realized I was using Mark's eight-year-old little sister's four-wheeler.

We quickly took a left turn down a different trail. Baby blue was able to make the sudden turn intact as we continued to charge toward the tectonic plates. This was actually fun, the brakes are touchy, which could be a good thing, I need to be able to stop. The only thing that sucks is the acceleration isn't the best. Mark and Nicole keep having to turn around and wait for me.

I started to think about William and how he would wait for me when we did our hike. Walk forward yards away, turn around and wait. I would catch up, and he would continue walking again, eventually always, in front leading the way. The mountain was getting closer and closer. We finally made it within her shadow as the temperature seemed to have dropped. Up close, the mountain is beautiful and surprising green. Greasewood trees covering the hill, along with cactus, and blue palo verde. Massive random rocks all outlined the bottom of the mountain and a few scattered. Mark brought some outdoor essentials in his small ice chest, it's tied to the back of my four-wheeler.

It was hard to take my helmet off when we got to the top of the mountain. Nicole had to help. Ears bright red, the helmet fabric stitched across my cheeks.

"Catch!" Mark yelled as he tossed a can toward me from his small ice chest. I caught it just in time. Immediately opening the mystery can, to have the foam explode through the cap crease. Beer bubbles landed on my nose as my eyes were still wide with shock. Mark and Nicole busting up laughing. I just wiped the foam off my nose, opened the beer all the way, and took a sip. Well deserved.

We decided to hang out a little before adventuring around. I sat on Baby Blue with my beer between my legs, both my hands on the handles, pretending to race. Mark and Nicole were one his legs crossed as they were facing each other, *playful flirts*. I could hear them, Mark trying to kiss her as Nicole taunts him gently. I began to zone out, staring forward, the sound of them reminded me of William. That could have been us, he could have been here today, on my four-wheeler.

"Hand me another, too, please." Nicole

said to Mark as he was digging through the ice crest. They both are on beer number two. I'm slow at this. They cracked the cans open, cheered, and took a big gulp. They were perfect for each other.

"Mark, weren't you mentioning how you and Tyler went to camp a few times together?"

"Yeah, I was telling Nicole about the Welcome to Earth Camp and how she needs to go one time."

"Maybe not in the winter." I replied.

"There is a huge lake, beautiful pine trees all covered in snow, it could be your winter wonderland. I think it would be cool if we went together. I can teach you archery. We can make snow angels every day, snowball fights, and just hang out for two weeks, what do you say?"

"You're so convincing. Yes, let's do it this winter," Nicole said as she leaned in and kissed Mark. "Tyler, why don't you like the wintertime at camp?"

"Because it's cold? And the most beautiful time to go is in spring. If you want breathtaking views of new forest life, go in the spring."

"Hey Tyler, did you know that William guy everyone was talking about last spring?" Mark asked as he took a sip of his beer. I did the same, my sip was a little longer than his this time.

"We hung out a few times."

"Tyler, do you have a boyfriend?" Nicole

interrupted.

"Babe, William passed away a few months ago," Mark said, placing his hand on Nicole's side. Nicole didn't say anything, just took a sip of her beer. Mark then looked over at me, as if to finish my sentence, but I don't want to. Talking about William out loud might make me feel closer to him, finally convince his heart to speak to me, and his eyes to see me.

"No one knew we were dating." I said. "We met at camp my freshman year and went back every session to see each other."

Nicole slowly got up, placed her beer down on the dirt, and walked over to me. With both hands, she bear-hugged me, saying how sorry she was. Then Mark jumped off his four-wheeler and ran over and hugged me. I've never had two humans hug me at once, sort of uncomfortable, but sweet.

"Talk to me anytime you want." Nicole said as she continued to hug me.

"I'll do my best." Mark and Nicole then both stood up and proposed a cheer

"Cheers, to friends who are here and friends who are not." We raised our cans and finished our beers. I, of course, was last to finish then like a gang of vigilantes we threw our helmets back on, started our four-wheelers and rode off into the desert.

We made it to the springs. The hype was a little exaggerated. It was neat, don't get me wrong, but it was a small amount of water. Flowing down the side of the enormous rock, almost forming a water slide. I'm sure it's way more active and exciting when it's actually raining. I did get some impressive shots, though, quick videos of the water running down the rock in slow motion. At the bottom, a small puddle developed at the top of the brown pool was a breakaway for the water to flow downstream, nourishing the desert life.

Thank goodness for these goggles, the dust was really starting to pick up from Mark's four-wheeler in front of me. I could taste the dirt, the chalky desert. This part of the desert doesn't look familiar, it doesn't seem to be the same way we came. Some of the cactus and Palo Verdes stand out. I was just following Mark, he must know where he is going. If we weren't going back home, where are we going? After a while, your thumb starts to get sore from continually pressing the gas pedal, mine was on the brink of falling off. Come on, Mark, where are we going?

One by one, small pieces of automobile parts began to appear. Old, rustic engines, hoods, and tires scattered about. Were we riding into a junkyard? Before I knew it, entire cars began to appear. Broken, smashed, impounded, the old, wheelless collection formed isles and isles. This was definitely a junkyard. It was then Mark turned into one of the car isles and turned off his four-wheeler. We all quickly took off our helmets.

"Where the hell are we?" Nicole asked, looking around.

"This is Porter Brother's junkyard."

"What is Porter Brother's junkyard?" Nicole asked.

"This is where Billy and his brother live and work. You've never heard of the Porter brothers? I think their mom and grandma also live here," Mark said.

"Umm, no, who are they?"

"Just these crazy desert hillbillies. Sometimes a few guys and I ride in here all fast, peel out, piss them off and take off. Last time they chased us on their four-wheelers, but mine is way faster."

"Okay, we are not provoking the Porter brothers. We are going back," Nicole said as she put her helmet back on, giving Mark a look she was serious. Thank goodness too, I didn't want to be here. Mark and Nicole took off, but Baby Blue was having trouble starting. Fuck, fuck, fuck, fuck. I stopped trying for a few seconds. I remember Mark mentioned something about a choke, "turn on the choke before starting if you're having trouble," but I can't recall where he said it was. Fuck. Hopefully, they realize soon I'm not behind them, and they turn around. You could hear the cars creaking from the wind.

Parts falling over yards away. I took my helmet off and looked around. I was surrounded by cars and car parts.

Rocks moving around, slight rumbling as I heard a truck slowly driving down the central car aisle. Fuck. I just remained seated on Baby Blue, both hands on my helmet. Billy Porter pulls up in his truck.

"What that fuck is going on here?"

"Hi Billy. I'm so sorry. I was riding around and got lost. Now my four-wheeler won't start," I said, holding my helmet with both hands. His truck was old and dirty. Worse than Sheriff Clark's vehicle. Billy was wearing a black trucker hat and an oil-stained gray shirt he cut into a tank top.

"Do you think you would know what is wrong?"

"Ah, let me check." Billy got out of his truck. I've known of Billy and his brother from as far back as I can remember. All of Lincoln knows them. I sometimes would see Billy at a few of the home football games, stalking some of the high school girls. This is our first actual interaction. I was surprised that he offered to check the problem with Baby Blue. I was a little worried he might just punch me and tell me to get off his property. I stood up and hopped off, still holding my helmet with both hands.

The door was screechy as he slammed it shut. He seemed a little annoyed that he had to help me. You could see the round tobacco case stretched into his back dark blue jeans pocket.

"You're Ricky and Michelle's kid, right?"

"Yeah. My name is Tyler."

"That's right, Tyler. I remember your parents. When they were in high school, I was in grade school. Your dad was good at football, man. We hang out sometimes at The Saguaro." Of course, they do.

"That's what I hear that he was good at football," scratching the back of my head. Just then, Baby Blue was up and running.

"Billy, thank you so much!" I threw my helmet on and leaned my hand out to shake his. He wasn't this scary desert hillbilly that everyone describes. I think it was his reputation that I was afraid of.

"Welcome. Now get off my property. Make no mistake, I'll give you a beating if I see you trespassing around here again. I don't care who your parents are," Billy said as he started to pull his tobacco case from his pocket, shaking my hand with a wink. His hand was dirty, callused, and hard. I quickly took off.

How was I going to get back home? I have no idea where I am riding. I wonder how much gas I have? All these questions circling around in my helmet. A slight panic attack was due to erupt. If Billy Porter didn't show up to start Baby blue, I might still be sitting there. His hand was so rough and bad. Probably hadn't showered in a few days, or at least not with soap. I still can't believe how oil-stained and callused his hands were, and why did he wink? To show he was just joking about being stern on the whole, "get off my property" or "I'll give you a beating" thing. I just kept riding forward, away from the mountain and Porter junkyard. On the brink of giving up, I could see dust. Larger and larger, the brown cloud got as Mark emerged from behind a bend.

◆ ◆ ◆

We were all safe back at Mark's house sitting in the back of Nicole's dad's truck. I was lying in the truck bed, legs dangling down over the tailgate. While Nicole and Mark were standing in each other's arms: drunk in each other. Just a moment ago, she scolded Mark for driving so fast, leaving me behind and not checking to see if I had started Baby Blue first. I wonder when my new underwater camera attachment arrives? That would be perfect for taking to Lake Louise, coming out of the water shots, having the sharp light gray mountains slowly appear.

"Ty, when do you have to be home?" Nicole asked, popping her head out of the creature she and Mark had formed.

"I would say early, It's a school night." I could feel the letdown, she obviously wanted to stay longer. Nicole kissed Mark goodbye. I slowly got up, a little light-headed, nice.

"Alrighty, buddy, it was fun hanging out today, we should do it again sometime," Mark said as he went in for a hug.

"It was fun, minus the whole Porter junkyard incident, but we should go riding again." Nicole went in for one more kiss goodbye, which then turned into a quick makeout. Sounds fun. Okay, and now we're ready to finally leave.

You could tell she was happy. She would let out a smile randomly, laugh at everything, and listen to the same love song, over and over. Since we've been in this truck, we have heard the same country-pop love song three times in a row. It's hard to be around that version of happiness, a text in which you know, their satisfaction is stemmed from falling in love. It reminds me of how cruel the universe can be, but while also showing me how beautiful it can be. Out the window, I looked over the cotton fields. Flashbacks to when I was young, in third grade and running about the cotton fields, playing tag with old friends. Ones that have now grown to win Homecoming Queen and throw paper balls at my head. Nicole reached her hand over and lowered the volume.

"Ty, why didn't you tell me you had a boyfriend, who committed suicide?" Nicole asked.

"I'm sorry now that I said it out loud it

sounds extremely personal and private."

"Can you not describe it as 'committed suicide'? I'm sorry. That terminology is dated with an insensitive undertone. Please say 'died by suicide'. I'm just susceptible when it comes to William. And the way people talk about him and how he passed."

"No! I am sorry! I had no idea of the effects of those words. I didn't know there was a correct way to say it. Thank you for educating me," Nicole responded. She was so understanding.

"It's okay, And I haven't told anyone about William and me. He will always have a place in my heart. I'm trying to move on, but easier said than done. And the fewer people who know about us, the fewer people asking how I'm doing."

"I won't bring it up again. Unless you want to talk about it."

"Okay. Maybe when I get a cell phone," I joked. Nicole just gave me confirming eyes as she turned the volume back up, playing the song for the fourth time.

❖ ❖ ❖

My computer desk chair is so comfortable. The perfect amount of cushion, as well as curvature of the back and adjustable arm, rests. It belonged to Lincoln Elementary School, but my mom got creative one Christmas, and wah-lah. Nicole had just dropped me off. Instead of engaging in conversation with my mother, who is sitting in the living room, grading papers and watching television, I ran to my room, grabbed a towel, and hopped in the shower.

Afterward, I slowly opened the door to my bathroom. The water in the shower never gets hot enough, pretty warm, but never hot. Single wide limitations, I guess. I mentioned that to my mother a while ago. She said she would get my father to look at it. I'm assuming he never did. Just like how he never fixed the tires on my bicycle, and never replaced the window in the living room after a bird flew through it. I guess I haven't really discussed with her how as of lately, my dad hasn't been around. It was okay a month ago. But now, I don't know. My mom doesn't tell me things like that; even if I ask, she will probably give me the same line in the same motherly tone, "Oh you know, probably at The Saguaro." She forgets to include, "Oh you know, probably fucking Stacy and staying at her place, eating her fucking food, and buying her fucking drinks, at The Saguaro." That's more like it, mom, get angry. Yeah, if only.

"Ty! Will you come to take the trash out, please." She yelled from the living room floor.

"Yeah," I mumbled, slipping on my sandals. The air outside is still warm at nine o'clock. I held the leaking trash bag out and quickly walked across the front yard to the street where our garbage bin sat, nearly full. Stepping back, I noticed two lights beamed down the road. They were on for a few seconds, then turned off.

They were lights from a vehicle. I couldn't see enough to determine what type of truck it was. Then the beams appeared again. I stood like a deer literally in headlights. The vehicle was getting closer and closer, faster, and faster. Then again, the lights went off. It was a truck. I was already on the inside of our front yard fence, and walking up the patio steps when the truck drove by, the beams were still off, it was Billy Porter's truck.

JENNIFER HALL

A large slab of concrete surrounded by permanently installed benches sat out in front of the old VFW. The building was built shortly after World War II, from what Sandy had told me. The Veterans of Foreign Wars, an organization promoting patriotism, history, and education. A handful of Lincoln's older residents were all drafted into the war, so establishing this building made sense. It's the perfect spot to host events for all of Lincoln's residents to attend.

This Saturday, November 2nd, is the celebration parade and festival the town coined, "Lincoln Day." The 118th anniversary of when John Lincoln purchased a small lot of land, dug a well, opened a business, and slowly began to attract followers and aspirational investors to help build a town. The parade is held every year on the first Saturday of November while the air is still warm and the nights are cold. Perfect for the outside dinner hosted at the VFW. I noticed large cracks in the concrete dance floor as I walked passed, a few weeds and some grass growing in between. I hope they clean those up before Saturday.

I could hear the murmur from inside. I had arrived just in time. I looked around for Sandy, maybe I should have called her before I left. She sat in the middle of the room. I love how she is wearing her little pink velvet visor inside. She was sitting next to her husband, Eddie, who was wearing his black leather VFW jacket. Honorary patches covering the front and arms, the American flag being one of the largest. It was a full house as the town was recently invaded by "snowbirds." Seasonal retirees leave their northern states, like Oregon and Idaho, and flock to a mild warm climate every winter. For them, no snow means a warm winter. The town's population almost doubles by the end of December. These are the birds who took a head start and settled into town early.

"Darling! You made it," Sandy shouted and waved. I waved back and pointed to the check-in station to grab my BINGO cards and some wine. Lucky for me, no one was in line as these snowbirds are even more punctual than I am. Almost every man in the building was proudly wearing some sort of patriotic attire, even the BINGO ball announcer, who sat upon a small stage on the opposite side of the hall.

Cards in one hand, drink in the other, I shimmied to the seat next to Sandy. She was chatting with one of her snowbird friends, who did not have a pleasant look on her face. Her hand was covering her mouth, and she was really leaning into the conversation. Sandy must be filling her in on what has happened around town these last few months.

"Jennifer, so glad you could make it. This is my good friend, Eleanor," Sandy said. I took a seat and reached my hand over. Eleanor is a very adorable lady wearing a blue floral blouse and a white velvet visor. Why wasn't I sent the visor memo?

"Eleanor, it is very nice to meet you, my name is Jennifer. I recently moved into town, working up at Lincoln High."

"I recently moved into town too, about a week ago," Eleanor said. "But this is my third year here."

"Jennifer works counseling the kids. She was brought in after all that stuff I was telling you about," Sandy said to Eleanor.

"That is just awful, unthinkable. Thank you, Jennifer, for all that you do. These poor kids," Eleanor said as we were interrupted by the BINGO announcer getting the room's attention as he began to spin the large ball cage. You could hear the BINGO balls rolling around. I looked at my BINGO cards and noticed the number sequence was off, interesting. Usually, the numbers in column "B" are from 1-15, column "I" are from 16-30, and so forth, gradually increasing.

"Sandy, is it just me, or are these BINGO

cards not in the standard order?" I asked.

"B2!" The announcer said, everyone in the room stopped what they were doing, and all looked down at their cards. The announcer kept spinning the cage wheel, then stopped, and a ball rolled out, "N9!"

"Oh yes, one of the VFW members makes them on her computer and prints and cuts them out to save money. Eleanor noticed that as well, she probably doesn't know all the rules," Sandy chuckled.

"Okay that makes more sense; I was a little confused." I said.

"I30!"

"Sandy, can I ask you something? When I took the deputies around the school, I came across this room with a dark purple door, it was locked. It had nothing inside, no desks, or office furniture. I noticed a small door about three feet tall that was also locked, what room was that?" Sandy was probably the best person to ask, considering she had been at the school the longest.

"When the school was built, you have to remember corporal punishment is legal in the state of Arizona, and back in the 1950s well-practiced. That was the disciplinary office. Students were sent there when they misbehaved and received. Usually, with a wooden paddle, or they were made to stay at a desk all day writing. Now for that little door, you saw, inside that is a pitch-black closet where they would send the students who continued to misbehave. They would keep them in that room all day, without food or water, until school is over." Sandy looked sad and a little ashamed as she described to me the purpose of that room. I was at a loss for words, we were having a moment as Sandy, and I were both connecting the intentions of that room psychologically and the recent string of suicides, until our moment was interrupted by,

"Bingo!" a man shouted out, and everyone then began to clap. I wonder if we just continue with the same cards until all the prizes are gone? I love how everyone clapped for him when he won, such sportsmanship. I would have never guessed that room was used for corporal punishment, it is so barbaric. This town is so remote and isolated who knows what laws were being broken at this school.

"Now we keep playing with the same BINGO cards until we are out of prizes, the last prize is a $50 gift card!" Sandy said as she took a sip of her wine.

"O8!" said the announcer. I was quiet as I stared at my cards, thinking about the living conditions in the 1950s.

"Jennifer, how have the kids been? Has there been any light shed as to why this has recently happened?" Sandy asked. I took a big sip of my wine.

"We are making progress on narrowing down commonalities of the students who took their own lives. I have noticed differences in the overall well being of the students born and raised in Lincoln, compared to the students who recently moved here. The new students have a different outlook on life, an ambitious outlook. Mark Watson was recently adopted by a family here. A funny, light-hearted kid. Nicole Clark recently moved here from Texas with her dad. She's incredibly kind and attentive. I'm trying to get all the students exposed to life outside of Lincoln. My proposal for a field trip into Phoenix to the science museum was approved. We are finalizing dates." I try to take moments where I stop and reflect. We have made significant strides in helping these kids. I need to remind myself of that.

"BINGO!" A lady in the front corner shouted out as the room began to clap again, she quickly got up and went to claim her prize. My wine was almost in need of a refill. Eddie was kind enough to refill mine and Sandy's glass.

"I feel like I should tell you this," Sandy said. "James Scott went to Lincoln High in the 1950s, my mom remembered him and knew him. They would hang out and adventure around. If I dig through the school records, I bet I could still find his file with a school photo."

"Who is James Scott? What is his story?" I asked.

"He was rumored to be gay. My mom told me he confessed to one of his girlfriends. She then told everyone at school, and he was picked on a lot because of it. James Scott was the first reported suicide in Lincoln, back in 1955."

"What happened to the family?"

"O1!"

"The family left shortly after. The town was shaken. Suicide isn't something you heard about back then, let alone knew someone who didn't. That's why I get concerned and worried about Tyler Tuckerman. And told the principal to add his name to the list he gave you. I don't know for sure if he's gay, but I hear people talk. I hope he's doing good."

I took a sip of the rest of my wine, my mind began to race.

"James Scott went missing for a few days until they found his body up by the springs. At first, they thought he fell off the side of the mountain. but when the police went to the top, they found he had left a flower and a forgiveness note." Eddie has just arrived back in time with our full glasses of wine.

"B1!"

"That is terrible. Sheriff Clark was telling me about the desert springs, but he never mentioned a boy died out there."

"He probably doesn't know, not too many people do. Oh my, Jennifer, you have a BINGO, look you got the four corners!" Sandy said as she reached her hand over, pointing to the card. Sweet! I did get a BINGO. The excitement quickly turned into deja vu, "BINGO! We have a four corner BINGO!" Sandy shouted, but those numbers, those four numbers appearing on my card looked so familiar, then it hit me, the bookmark inside, *The Night the Angels Cried* in blue pen; *B1, O1, B2, O8*. The entire room began clapping. My ears are buzzing. Why was the world presenting me with those numbers again? I got goosebumps, quickly plastered a massive smile across my face, showed the announcer my winning card, and claimed a $15 gift card. I didn't want to stay, my superstitious mind racing.

"Sandy, I'm so sorry, I'm going to quit while I'm ahead. Please win the big prize!" I leaned over and gave her a hug.

"Okay dear, glad you could make it. Get home safe."

I was staring at my computer screen when the last school bell went off, you would think I would get used to the shrieking sound by now, but it always gets me. I cannot begin to describe how excited I am that Friday is finally here. Not only is it Friday but tonight is my date with Brian Clark. We decided to go to the cute cafe in town, The Desert Flower. When I first moved into town, I went once and got a grilled cheese and a side of fries. It was decent.

This date is exactly what I need right now. These last few days I've been having some horrible nightmares. The dark side of my mind awakening, unleashing horrible scenarios of walking into my childhood home to find both my parents, brutally murdered. Crimson red blood flooding the kitchen floor. Emily continued to stab their lifeless bodies uncontrollably, grunting, and shouting as she was doing it. Emily was soaked with a purple face, wearing the princess costume she drowned in. In every dream, Emily would eventually look up at me and whisper, "This is all your fault," right before I wake up, drenched in sweat, with tears running down my face.

Brian is the distraction I need.

Our texting habits have picked up. I wasn't much of a texter before, but it's nice to get in quick chats with Brian throughout the day. I offered to meet him at the cafe, but he wants to pick me up at my house. A few students asked if I would be attending the last games of the season tonight. I had attended every other home football and volleyball game, so I believe I was off the hook. I needed this night for me. I raced home and showered and got ready. I know Brian didn't care what I looked like, but It was more for me, I haven't done this in a while. I had Music blasting while using my hairbrush as a microphone, spinning around in the bathroom, and dancing throughout the house in just my favorite, pink floral lace bra and panties.

There was a knock at the door at 7:15PM. I heard the knock and got a huge smile, I lowered the music, put my heels on, and walked to the door.

"Howdy, Jennifer. Wow. You're so beautiful," Brian said. He was holding pink and red Transvaal daisies, gorgeous. I couldn't help but smile as he handed me the bouquet, and we both leaned in for a hug. This is starting off well. Brian was wearing a blue denim button-up, a white cowboy hat, and brown cowboy boots. Having been in the city for most of my life, I have never really been around the country type of man. I have been missing out.

"Brian, these are gorgeous. You really shouldn't have!"

We sat in a window booth, a fake cactus succulent in the middle as the server handed us both a single side menu. Our server was a young girl who didn't currently attend Lincoln High. At least she didn't seem familiar. Probably a recent grad. We spent some time looking at the menu as the conversation just kept flowing. Brian was so respectful and aware. I now understand where Nicole gets it from. This town needed a sheriff like him, someone who actually cares. I waited to see what kind of drink he ordered before I did. The second he said domestic beer, I grind internally, then asked for house cabernet.

Our food was more than halfway gone, and we were both working on our second round of drinks. Brian mentioned maybe hitting up The Saguaro after dinner for some whiskey. We both bonded over our love of bourbon. Or maybe our love for Kentucky.

"You were telling me that you had gone to BINGO Monday evening with Sandy? How was that? Did you win?" Brian asked as he took a sip of his beer.

"As a matter of fact, yes, I did. I won a $15 gift card."

"What? That's awesome!"

"I left shortly after, though. Can I ask you a question?"

"Of course."

"Are you superstitious?"

"Hmm, I mean to a certain point. Do I believe that every day we are presented with signs that impact our future? No."

"Same here. I am asking - now this is going to sound crazy - but when I was at The Coleman Grocery Store, I found a book. Inside was a handwritten bookmark with the numbers *11:28*. Monday evening at BINGO, my winning card had the four corners with the same numbers in sequence: *1-1-2-8*. What is that about?"

"That is interesting. To be honest with you, do you want to know the first thing I thought of when you said those numbers?" Brian asked.

"Yes, please!"

"*Thanksgiving.* This year Thanksgiving lands on November 28th. Maybe this is the universe's way of telling you to remain thankful, count your blessings, not your misfortunes, oh, and to eat your heart out!" he laughed. "What is your favorite Thanksgiving dish?"

Holy shit, Thanksgiving this year does land on *11/28*. This man is amazing, he is such a positive force that is just bursting with energy. I needed to hear that, I needed reassurance that I was not going crazy with everything going on. I just smiled.

"Thank you for that. We all should remain thankful. You're absolutely right. Besides turkey and cranberries, I would have to say my mom's mashed potatoes."

"Mashed potatoes are the best," he said. "That is still crazy that you got those exact numbers. After a while, being on the road and having to see so many license plates, when I was off work, I would see some of those patterns. I think we sometimes act on superstitious signs as negative when that isn't true." Brian said. He was a good man.

"What are you doing tomorrow for Lincoln Day?"

"No plans. Just attend the parade. Then the dinner and dance event at the VFW."

"My brother is coming into town in the

morning. They are flying in and grabbing a rental and heading into town for the parade and staying a few days. Would you like to join the Sheriff's float? We will have all the cop cars lit up, alarms roaring." Brian joked. "You could help Nicole toss candy to the kids. Then we could go to the event at the VFW together?" There was no way in hell I could or would say no.

"Your brother? That's great, when was the last time you saw him? And the float, that sounds like a really great time, yes, of course."

"Right before Nicole and I moved out here. It will be good to catch up with him and his wife Julia, and their two kids. Ryan is Nicole's age. Aaron is about a year old," Brain said as he finished the rest of his beer but not before I finished my wine, two seconds faster. We were both in agreement that we would walk over to The Saguaro. Have some bourbon on the rocks while listening to music on the app powered JukeBox they recently got installed.

TYLER TUCKERMAN

I have become very skillful at most useless abilities, like balancing a bowl of cereal on my knee while sitting on the couch. Halfway dressed, halfway ready to take on the day. I particularly like the mornings, watching the sky light up, feeling the warm sun shining through the living room window, which, by its looks, still has the hole where the bird flew into it. Duct tape and cardboard covered the crime scene as my dad has yet to be home to fix it. Still, with Stacy, I'm assuming. The last time he pulled this disappearing act, it only lasted a week. This time it's been several. He's like a house cat; the neighbors begin feeding, and it eventually finds a new home.

I could hear my mom getting ready, pop-country music playing from her phone. She has been taking forever getting ready today, probably because it's Lincoln Day. She will be all over town, socializing it up and pretending that everything home is peachy.

I poured the rest of my milk down the sink drain and skipped off to finish getting ready. If William and I were going to Lincoln Day, setting up lawn chairs to watch the parade, dressing up for the dinner dance, then yes, I would be over the moon about today. But he's gone, and so I'm miserable. We were meeting up with some of my mom's teacher friends and their little kids.

My mom was on the phone with Susan, discussing the location for the parade set up quickly turned into gossip. Susan claims to have seen my dad last night at The Saguaro with a girl other than Stacy. Damn, this cat is hungry. The neighbor's neighbor? My mom and Susan have been friends since kindergarten, both played sports together and dated the same guys in high school. My mom was the only one in their friend group to graduate from college. A few attended but dropped out and moved back to Lincoln. Susan is the first of them. We were about to leave, so I gathered my camera equipment and sat back on the couch.

"Are you ready to go, Ty?" My mom asked as she came walking out from her room, her hair teased, and sprayed into this massive bump.

I was sitting in a cozy lawn chair alongside the highway that runs through town, all ready for the parade, staring up at the many

188

cloud formations, thinking of William. I can never look up at the warm blue sky and not think of those eyes, or us on our favorite hike, our first kiss, our snowball fights, and those campfires. I miss you, *Will*.

I could see that Susan supplied the group with a few beverages poured from a cardboard box, maybe that's why they keep her around. Interesting. Every pickup truck had its tailgate down as they all lined the street. Kids in the back of them, jumping and playing around. Teens sitting on the end of the tailgate, on their phones, or talking about. The adults, all sitting in their personal camping chairs, all ready for the grand parade.

They always begin the parade with the fire department, with all the fire trucks blasting their horns and flashing their red and white lights. A few local businesses always opt into the parade, I'm not sure if there is a fee to attend, but it's good marketing. I got up from my lawn chair, took out my camera, and began capturing banners, signs, and excited sugar high kids jumping as the intro to the parade video. The town council always tries to make it enjoyable by offering awards for the best float, funniest, loudest. My mother, of course, is on the board of that council. She should have been a politician. Thanks to my mom volunteering me, they always ask me to film the parade for them, super exciting stuff.

I would walk up and down the street, get

up close to the floats to capture different angles. Everyone was waving and cheering into the camera. Colorful balloons tied to every vehicle with long streamers dangling behind. I captured those in black and white.

I zoomed in far to get the floats arriving on Main Street half a mile away. Float after float after float. I switched back to color and slowly zoomed out *when I saw him*. A bright white smile, tanned, muscular arms, blue eyes, and a red tank top. He was walking toward me.

William?

I could feel my heart in my chest as I pulled away from the camera lens, nearly dropping it. I couldn't hear my own thoughts as kids screaming, music blasting, and cars honking filled my mind. Why was I out of breath? I pulled my camera back up and looked through the lens again.

But I didn't see him. Dustin Hemley walked behind the last firetruck, throwing candy to both sides of the street. He was wearing a red tank top with white writing: "Lincoln Fire Department." He married the fire chief's daughter and recently moved into town. He was handsome. His smile reminded me of a lot of Williams. So did his charisma and his biceps. I restrained myself. I wanted to run-up to the road, kick those little shits aside, and collect all his candy.

Today was a pretty great day to be outside. Behind the fire trucks came some vintage cars. They appeared to be straight from the film, *Grease*. One after another, bright teal, red, white, and purple cars drove by. They must belong to a few snowbirds that recently moved into town. There is no way actual Lincoln residents could afford cars like that. I walked back to where my mom and Susan set up a base to sit in my lawn chair. I was tired of standing, and to no surprise, they were just gossiping it up.

"No, they did not; they arrested him?" One of my mother's teacher friends asked. I tried not to look over at them as they were talking.

"Yeah, for selling drugs to the kids at the high school. They brought in drug-sniffing dogs, I think about eight lockers had drugs," my mother explained. She mostly uses the information since she gets from being on the high school board to gossip.

"Crazy, right? I told my boy, they better not find drugs in your locker, or I'm going to beat you so bad you'd wish they took you away," Susan replied.

"The students who confessed to getting the drugs from Billy Porter only got a few weeks of suspension and community service. The students who did not confess to where they got the drugs got expelled for the rest of the school year as well as community service," mom said. I remember the assembly last Monday with Nicole's dad. I wasn't paying too much attention as I have never done drugs, so I had nothing to worry about.

I could hear singing and music blasting from various large speakers. It was the Lincoln Choir Club. The school truck had multiple speakers on the tailgate. The club members walked behind, singing along and tossing candy and school swag around. Cameron's mother, Janet, was wearing a school choir shirt and was walking with them to honor her son. When he first moved into town and started school, Cameron seemed so nervous. With that red hair and his blue braces. He became perfect friends with Bobby Jones. I wasn't in the choir club, nor was I an active gamer, so we really didn't have much in common.

The VFW spot of the parade was going a little slow as the veterans don't walk fast, they should have had them go last, or put them on those Wal-Mart scooters. Many of the veterans wore red MAGA hats over their bald heads. The MAGA aspect got me thinking about Texas and the ongoing Texas Black Lives Matter marches. I started wondering where Nicole was. She had to have come to the parade, everyone is here.

A few police sirens announced the entrance of the Lincoln Police Department. A few squad cars drove in front, displaying their blue and white lights. Jennifer Hall was riding in the passenger seat in one of the vehicles, with Sheriff Clark driving.

"Oh look, in the police car in the front passenger seat," I heard Susan say behind me. "I knew they were dating."

"They seemed to be getting really close every time I was at the school. Like a little too close, borderline inappropriate," my mother said.

I think this is the first time I agreed with this group of hyenas. I am not too fond of Jennifer. I don't know, it's something about her holier-than-thou bullshit. I feel like she judges everyone here. We were a step down in her social hierarchy. What has she actually done to help anyone? Besides interviewing us on how we're feeling and what we're thinking. I bet she would love to have her own television show. A sort of therapy entertainment show. I have a chip on my shoulder to call me in to her office on her first day. As if someone at the school singled me out as the gay kid, and so I MUST be the one most in need of her counseling. In reality, it's the jocks and bullies who would benefit the most from Ms. Hall's attention.

I could see Nicole's bright smile and dirty blonde hair as she was walking behind the last cop car. Like everyone else she was throwing candy on both sides of the street, we locked eyes, and she gave a huge wave, ran over with a large handful of candy and placed it on my lap.

"Tyler! Here you go, all for you," Nicole said as she then ran back to the parade. So kind of her. I could see she was walking with someone, seemed to be our age, and judging by his mannerism, he too seemed to be gay. Did Nicole find a new gay BFF? She found a new puppy to love? A feeling was starting in my gut and slowly rising up, I could feel my heartbeat in my neck. It was jealousy. This guy was also throwing candy and waving to everyone like he knew them. I continued to sit in my lawn chair, opening up a few pieces of candy with my left hand and filming with my right.

The middle of the town was packed. The parade had ended, and I looked around for my mom to give her the can we leave now look. My stomach was starting to hurt from overeating candy. Everyone was headed to The Saguaro or the Cactus Flower Cafe. I was hoping to spot my dad around but had no luck.

"Ty, I'm going to run into The Saguaro real quick to say hello to Bob and Charlotte," my mother said as she put a few things in her purse. "Are you hungry? I'll give you cash to grab some food at the cafe."

"No, I'm okay," I said, stomach still hurting. After mom walked away with Susan and two others. Nicole came up behind me, startling me with a "Boo!"
"Oh my!" I let out, placing my left hand over my chest.

"Did you enjoy the parade? We threw out so much candy, didn't we, Ryan?" Nicole said as she looked over to the guy standing next to her in a blue and white "Lincoln Police Department" t-shirt. He had on a few metal bracelets and a few silver necklaces and had a nose ring. Definitely gay.

"We must have gone through like, I don't know, twenty pounds of candy?" Ryan said.

"Tyler, this is my cousin Ryan. His family is visiting from Dallas," Nicole said as Ryan reached his hand out, we shook.

"Nice to meet you, Ryan," I said, feeling like an idiot. "My name is Tyler."

"Come with us tonight, Monica is throwing a party at her house," Nicole said to me. "Her parents are out of town. So while our parents are at the VFW dinner thingy, we will have our own party. Everyone from school is going." He had dirty blonde hair just like Nicole's, but with the sides short and the top well-groomed, gelled and slicked back. He reminded me of a preppy pretentious banker or *GQ* cover model.

"I don't know. I don't think Monica likes me very much."

"Oh stop, you're coming, she will be wasted and not even know you're there. I'm dropping my dad off at Jen's, then we're going to Mark's house. We are taking his four-wheelers to the party," Nicole explained.

"Fine I'll go. Do I have to bring anything?" I asked. I've never been invited to a house party.

"Nope. Mark has booze for us to bring

with me and I have a bottle of whiskey. Ryan, sorry I know you hate whiskey, but I know Mark has stuff you like," Nicole said.

"I don't hate hate whiskey. I hate you on whiskey," Ryan laughed. I wonder what he meant that he hates Nicole when she drinks whiskey?

"Oh stop; in my defense, everyone that night was being so rude, and you and I had to leave."

"Ty, we'll pick you up around nine?"

"Cool." Lowkey, I was kind of nervous, I hate social settings, especially with my peers. They are all so unintelligent and immature. It's grueling to interact with them. But heck, they probably think the same thing about me. Don't talk to the gay kid because you might catch the gay. That was the slogan that went around the school during my freshman year. Now I'm about to party with these people?

◆ ◆ ◆

I was at my desk writing in my journal when I heard my mom leave for the night. Clicking on the lights, the television going silent, the clanking of her heels in the kitchen as she gathers her purse. I was all dressed and ready for Nicole to pick me up. It was approaching nine o'clock, and I wasn't expecting my mother to still be here. She had asked me several times what my plans were and if I wanted to join her and her friends. I declined every offer, said I'd just stay in and watch a movie.

"Bye, Ty!" she shouted as she left. I continued to doodle in my journal. A combination of poems, sketches, and deep thinking was scattered about page by page. A lot had to do with William, and trying to process, in any way I can, the fact that he's gone. When would I ever see him again? Under what circumstances? Most people would not confess this, but I'm sure many think about suicide. At one point. The idea, the fantasy, the contemplation. The idea was never around *how* I would die, the various painful and non-painful methods. Still, instead they were always around, *who* would show up to my funeral? What would they be saying, feeling, and thinking? How long would it take for me to finally be forgotten in others' minds, and what would I release into the world? I could see it now, all of the various lies my mother would be saying around town on how happy we all were, and my dad howling his grief at The Saguaro.

I heard a knock at the door and looked down at my black wristwatch, 9:10, that must be Nicole. I recently found a slot on the wall close to my closet, so I used a kitchen knife to make a little door that I use as my hiding stop to store my journal.

♦ ♦ ♦

Nicole, Ryan, and I piled into her truck on our way to Mark's. A combination of country music and pop blasting, getting us hype for the party.

"Why are we taking Mark's four-wheelers? Why can't we just drive your truck to the party?" Ryan asked. He was sitting in the middle seat.

"Monica's parents are out of town, and her dad ensures she doesn't go anywhere by keeping the main gate to the house locked so no one can drive in or out. So we're all driving to the back of her property. There's a trail that leads to her backyard."

"Sounds like a lot of property," Ryan replied.

"Yeah their house is beautiful. Go when I tutor Chloe, Monica's little sister. I'm going to help her with softball, but before that, they want me to teach Chloe to swim. Their pool is heated. We might get in tonight," Nicole said.
I was not informed about the pool, and I am not getting in.

"They better be paying you well," Ryan joked.

"Oh yes!"
We pulled up to Mark's house, and he was waiting outside.

"So Nicole, you and Ryan can take my four-wheeler and Tyler, you can retake the little blue one. I'll go on my dirt bike. It should take us about twenty minutes to get there. I'll keep all the booze in my backpack."

As we pulled up into Monica's back yard, you could see a ton of people around the pool and walk inside and outside the house. My heart began to pick up. I was getting nervous. We pulled up next to a group of four-wheelers and dirt bikes. The second I turned off Baby Blue, I could hear the rap music bass rippling through the air. There were a lot of cowboy boots and short jean shorts everywhere. A few girls had their legs dangling into the pool and were surrounded by red solo cups. Two games of beer pong going next to the pool with a tournament schedule written out on a large piece of paper. My fellow students were shouting and yelling as they missed and made their ball into a cup. Nicole ran off to find Monica and introduce her to Ryan. I stood by Baby Blue while Mark was taking off his helmet and putting a few things away. I didn't want to venture around alone.

Large floor to ceiling windows with sliding doors, the music seems to be coming from speakers built into the house, both inside and out.

"Tyler, let's go inside and grab a drink," Mark said as he led the way, thank goodness for him and that he stayed behind so I wouldn't have to be alone while Nicole was social. He walked inside the kitchen and dining area. Even more, people were inside than out. I was trying to determine if our entire school was here. I followed Mark to the kitchen island. He placed his backpack on the counter and pulled out the booze he brought.

"I hope it's not all shaken up from the drive over," Mark joked as he opened a can of beer, instant foam erupting out. We both laughed as he handed me a beer.

"Cheers!" Mark said as we both took a drink at the same time. I was starting to get comfortable being here. I hope the alcohol would help with the nerves as I took two more sips. I was watching people but not trying to look like I was people watching. A few people kept coming up to us and greeting Mark. They do this little handshake, then hug, so choreographed. I was not sure if he could tell I was nervous, but Mark passed over a black liquid shot.

"Here you go," he said as he started to fill another shot for himself.

"What is this?"

"Liquid courage, you can use your beer to chase, if you don't like the taste of black licorice," Mark said as he picked up his shot and took it quickly, then began pouring another. I remember when Nicole and I were hanging out in the back of her truck after the Homecoming football game to exhale, exhale, exhale after taking a shot. Oh man, I am not a fan of black licorice, hope all the exhaling works. I took a sip of the beer to get rid of the taste, only to have Mark slide me another.

"I talked to Monica and told her everyone I brought with. I told her I brought you, and she didn't care, so you're all good," Nicole said as she entered the kitchen looking for her bottle of whiskey. I gave a slight smile, prepared myself for this next shot, and took it.

I was definitely tipsy on the verge of being drunk as I sat on the couch. This couple was making out on one end, and I tried to sit as far away from them as possible. Across the room, Ryan was laughing and talking to people he had just met. It then hit me that I was not a *cool gay*, that I was an inferior loser gay who only dreams about getting with guys like Ryan Clark. The world is hard enough having to find your place in the straight world, getting the girls to not stab you in the back and the jocks to not beat you up. Then you throw in the gay world, and you must find where you fit in the tier system. How many followers do you have on social media? Who can get the most likes? Take the sexiest pictures? Have the hottest straight girlfriends, and how many hot guys can you sleep with?

Ryan would quickly switch from talking to laughing to dancing to back to singing. He made himself a red drink mixed with vodka. Mark, Nicole, and a few others came over to me.

They wanted to play a drinking game. We all sat on the floor in the living room to form a circle. For a second, I thought we were about to play spin-the-bottle.

We sat in a circle and played a very crude drinking card game. It was pretty entertaining as a few of the cards' demands were quite ridiculous. To make out with the person next to you, to chug the rest of your drink, take a shot with someone, pass nothing happens, to finally, my turn again. I always get so nervous. If it's the kiss card, Mark is to my right and Tim, the guy who owns the game is to my left. If it is the chug the rest of your beer card, then I'm screwed because I cannot chug. I would prefer the card I draw to be for me to take a shot or give me the ability to demand a shot to give someone. I think it was a combination of all the beer, the black licorice shots, and inside this circle that I finally felt accepted. Everyone here is someone I go to school with, and we were all getting along so well. Laughs. I leaned over and drew my card, and got a gold mystery card. I showed the circle, not sure what that means.

"Ohhhh the gold card! The golden ticket!" Tim started shouting. A few people began to chuckle as they didn't know what that card meant.

"What does that do?" Mark asked. That doesn't sound like a good thing if Mark doesn't know what it means.

"Basically the owner, me, gets to tell you to do anything I want," Tim said. I'm sorry, but did he say I have to do whatever he says? Because I drew this damn gold card? He reached his hand into one of his pockets, "I want you to take this!" It was a blue pill. Tim handed it to me as I just stared at it.

"What is that?" Nicole asked.

"Pure 110% MDMA," Tim responded. The circle got a few eye openings from some people, and a few jealous signs. I was a little skeptical as I just continued to hold and look at the pill. People then began cheering me on as I guess they could sense my hesitation. I was finally being accepted, one of the guys. With the help of all the alcohol, I concluded that I can't let them down, and right as Nicole was about to tell me I don't have to take it, I placed the blue pill in my mouth. I took a few sips of my beer.

"Yes! Now it's a party!" Tim yelled as we then continued the game. I just sat there, trying to process what it was I just ingested. It's a happy drug, only good things can come from this, everyone said it was a feel-good drug. Don't get freaked out, it's okay. Just relax, have another sip of your beer.

❖ ❖ ❖

We were standing in the kitchen, our drinks were sitting on the island counter. I looked over, and it appeared Nicole had already drunk half her bottle of whiskey. Damn. My beer was halfway gone. It felt like a wave, a wave that started at my lower back and traveled up my spine and to the top of my head. Once at the top, it massaged around then quickly spread in all directions down the sides of my head. It was the music as I could begin to see the bass traveling throughout the kitchen. Dancing about the fluorescent bulbs, fading in and out to the beat of the music.

I couldn't help but *smile*. That turned into a *grin*. That developed into a *chuckle*. I laughed to myself as this feeling was somewhat familiar, but also so totally new, totally foreign and unexpected, and fantastic! I looked down and started rubbing my fingers against my inside palms, they were a little sweaty, and the massage was feeling great. My smile was still radiating. I couldn't help myself. It was then that I felt the best feeling I have yet to physically handle. Two hands were on my shoulders, squeezing and massaging them, I couldn't help but close my eyes and tilt my head back.

"Hey Buddy, has it kicked in yet?" Mark asked as he continued to rub my shoulders then let out a little laugh. By my reaction to the sudden shoulder rub, I realized that I was high, the beginning effects of this wondrous euphoria. I tried to answer him but couldn't until *drunk* Nicole responded for me.

"Why don't you ever give me shoulder rubs like that?" My eyes were still closed as those words filled into my head. Mark just laughed and continued to rub my shoulders. Nicole sounded serious, a hint of jealousy. I kept smiling.

"Haha because you're not on Molly," Mark said.

"Oh so I have to be on drugs now for you to want me?" Nicole hissed. I don't know when this turned south, or if she was serious.

"Mark don't stop," I let out, and I quickly bit my tongue. I knew I was only adding fuel to this random fire Nicole decided to start.

"I won't," Mark replied. I heard Nicole storm away, the air still flowing around me. Mark stopped and went after Nicole. I stood there and slowly opened my eyes. The lights were more colorful, and the music even brighter as I slowly began to dance.

I was out of breath from dancing as I stumbled down a long, dimly lit hallway in search of the bathroom. The floor was tiled, and the walls were lined with Garcia's family photos. Monica, when she was born, to her first school photo. The same with Chloe. This light down the end of the wall got my attention more than any of the images did. It was beautiful, It appeared to be trying to communicate with me. It was flickering and dancing as I slowly walked toward it. A door next to it suddenly opens, and stumbling out is Jason Brophy. He had on old cowboy boots, a massive gold belt buckle, and was carrying a beer in one hand and an unlit cigarette in the other. His eyes were bloodshot and glossy.

"What the fuck is this? Who invited you?" Jason said, taking a sip of his beer then placing the cigarette between his lips. I didn't respond as the light behind him was screaming and had my full attention. It was then a ruby reflection on Jason's belt buck glimmered at me, causing me to smile and slightly tilt my head.

"What are you looking at? My dick?" he mumbled with the cigarette between his lips. I kept staring at it, noticing red and white jewels, all cheering my name with excitement. Each gem has its own distinct voice. "What the fuck are you laughing at?" He pulled his cigarette from his mouth, walked toward me and grabbed the back of my neck, pulling my head down toward his belt buckle.

The shimmering jewels quickly vanished. The air suddenly thickened as I found myself on my knees, pulling my head away from Jason's crotch. The left side of my cheek firmly pressed against Jason's gold and silver belt buckle. He opened the door next to us, slapped the back of my head, grabbed my hair, and flung me inside. It was all happening faster than I was able to breathe. The room was completely dark. I could tell the bed I was on was small, a child's twin, unable to move as Jason had to prove he was more powerful. My eyes were closed with my arms tucked under me. I could hear Jason hock a loogie and spit his mucus on my back. Fight or flight reaction kicked in as I became extremely passive. Jason forced two of his fingers inside my mouth, tasting the dirt underneath his fingernails. His callused index as it scratched my tongue. Clockwise then counterclockwise. Then three fingers. I quickly grabbed his wrist, and Jason countered by grabbing my arms, spreading them out like a cross, then squeezing both my triceps. I didn't fight back as he quickly reached one hand under me, unbuttoning my jeans, and sliding the top-down, and hocking another loogie. Instantly feeling cold, wet liquid. He was pouring his beer down my back, down to my jeans. A bead of salt sweat ran down my forehead, enough had collected in my eyebrows that it began to leak into my right eye. Burning them closed. Jason led his head toward mine, breathing down my neck, followed by a tidal wave of burning that only worsened with every move I made.

Stabbing piercing pressure-filled hatred.

"Sssstupid faggot, *is this what you want*?" Jason grunted in my ear.

Across the room, I could hear a whisper, a shimmer, as Chloe's faint night light was trying to get my attention. I painfully opened my eyes —a blue and white light reaching for my hand. I continued to stare directly at the night light without blinking. A tear running down my face as the blue and white light slowly turned into William. Instantly, we were back at our favorite mountain top, the sun was just about to set. He placed his hand under my chin, picked my head up, and said, "everything will be alright, *I promise*."

I lied on the small bed, still staring at the night light for about fifteen minutes after Jason had stopped and finally left. The music was still silent as I opened Chloe's bedroom door. A stranger walked down the hall behind me and asked what I was doing in there? I was caught off guard, not sure what to say, so I didn't say anything. I looked down, and my pants were soaked from his beer and still unbuttoned. The party was still active and full. Ryan was floating around the room, and a few people were wet from the pool. I walked over and felt the jolt of pain as I sat in the dining room, looking down at my red hands and then touching my head where Jason hit me. What was the point of fighting back, just to get punched in the face? I could then hear Mark and Nicole in the next room.

"Jusssssst tell me! Are you gay?" Nicole asked, you could hear the slurred in her 's' you could listen to the whiskey pour out.

"What are you talking about?"

"You were flirting with Tyler! Don't try and ssssay you weren't! You were rubbing hisss back and shoulders right after he took that pill!"

"Friend or flirting?" Mark responded.

"If you are that isss fine, I just need to know, because if you do like guys tttthen we can't date anymore."

"Nicole, what the fuck?"

"I'm being honestly, honest. Tell me righttt now."

It was then that I could feel it, the sting. An emotional pain that complemented my physical one. I continued to sit in the dining room, continuing to have Nicole remind me that I am poison. Then back to Jason's whispering words echoing around in my head like the inside of a dark moist cave,

"This is all you're good for, faggot. This is all you're good for, faggot."

"I don't like guys, Nicole. Also, that is really homophobic. Why would you say all that, like it would make a difference if I was bi or something," Mark said.

"Oh my god, my coussssin is gay, I'm not homophobic, why do you always have to start fights and drama? My cousin is down visiting, and here we are fighting. I just wanted you to be honest with me."

I couldn't take hearing that nonsense any longer. I got up slowly and walked out of the dining room. The fire sensation still fresh. The kitchen was full as I was having an out of body experience looking around at everyone. Two people passed out on the couch, several teens making out in the corner, and Monica sitting on her throne surrounded by her minions. This was not my scene. I don't belong here and look what happened. Someone had spilled a drink all over my jacket. I grabbed a napkin and tried to dry it up. My eyes were still red, the music in my head was still silent.

"Hey Tyler, have you seen Nicole?" Ryan asked as he nearly spilled his drink all over my jacket again.

"Um, yeah, I saw her back over there."

"Thanks. Also, did you pee your pants?" Ryan joked. I just looked up at him, my right eye bloodshot from the sweat. He didn't say anything as he turned around, heading back to the party.

I put my jacket back on and slowly walked home.

JENNIFER HALL

Brian got a little anxious when I told him how often I run and where. He was uncomfortable with the fact I ran alongside the road on the dirt. There really isn't anywhere else to run, the isolated desert scares me. It wouldn't be worrisome if I was on an ATV or bike, but not just running. So I came up with an alternative, I began using the high school track field. I had just finished my sixth lap when I decided to take a break, drink some water and check my phone. I've still been doing early morning runs before work, especially when I have scheduled meetings with parents.

I could tell my face was bright red, lips dry, and heart visibly beating. I try to wake up early and jog before work, a healthy way to energize my mind and body before taking on the day. The mornings have been getting pretty chilly, but after my second lap, my body was warm enough. I tossed my jacket and flapped my wings. Soaring higher and higher into the morning crispy sky. Taking a deep inhale and closing my eyes for just a second. The calm wind blowing against my face as I really stretched my wings. Slowly opening my eyes to be miles above Lincoln, looking down as I slowly exhaled.

Michelle Tuckerman approached me yesterday with concerns about Tyler. He is a sensitive student, one that we monitor and make regular catch-ups with. Still, she mentioned that this past week he has been even more introverted and quiet. I told her that we should meet today and come up with a plan, fill me in on all the small details, and I would also like to take this opportunity to see how she is doing. Dissect if possibly she might be a contributing source, or perhaps his father, Ricky Tuckerman. More often than not, the answers we are seeking are right in front of us.

◆ ◆ ◆

Michelle was taking off her jacket as I gathered my belongings. I still hold the meetings with the parents in my office at the school. I want to maintain consistency, build an environment of trust and openness.

"Where did you get your coffee from?" I asked as I adjusted my glasses and sent a welcome smile.

"I stopped by the Desert Flower. I usually

get coffee at the elementary school when I arrive, but the teacher's lounge was closed when I left, so I stopped there." Michelle answered. She seemed a little off, nervous perhaps. She kept tapping her foot against the floor, but that could just be the coffee. The room had a soft lavender and pine smell. I recently read a post about the calming properties that lavender promotes. I even invested in a white noise machine. Lizzie Chapelton's mom really finds the white noise machine to be helpful. At the same time, Greg Norris' mother refuses to reach out or want any help. They are rumored to be moving before the end of the year. Sadly, some people have forgotten the tragedy of Greg and Lizzie, after Cameron's death. One memorial service pamphlet being replaced by another.

"I'm concerned about Tyler," Michelle began. "He doesn't want to help me grade papers or eat dinner at the table. He didn't even want to go with me to the Lincoln Day Dinner dance at the VFW," she said as she took a sip of her coffee, shaking her head a little. "I was in his bathroom cleaning, and I could hear sad music coming from his room. I walked over and tried to open his door, but it was locked. My heart started pounding. I know he said he wasn't feeling too well, but why lock the door?"

Michelle started to choke up a little, placed one hand over her mouth for just a second.

"As I was walking back to the living room, not sure if my baby was still alive in that room, his door opened, thank heavens, and he walked into the bathroom. Jennifer, I have never been so frightened in my entire life. The possibility that I could have just lost my boy. I need your help."

"I'm sorry you feel that your son has been avoiding you. But, it's perfectly normal for a teenage boy not to want to help grade papers or have dinner at the table. Those aren't caused for concern. But I will say, Tyler locking himself inside his room for hours on end is more problematic."

I didn't mean to dismiss her other concerns, but those are what teenagers do, and she needed to know it's okay. However, the isolation inside a locked room is slightly different.

"I am so glad you came to me." I leaned forward and grabbed Michelle's hands. Her eyes were teary soft. "Tell me every detail you can remember, everything leading to Tyler's sudden change in mood. When he started to severely isolate himself? Did he go to the parade?" I asked, leaning back in my chair.

"Yes, we both did, we had a little group of elementary teachers all watching the parade, collecting candy. He was walking around filming the parade like he always does. That night he just wanted to stay home. The following morning is when he started to lock his bedroom door."

"Was your husband there?"

"No, Ricky hasn't been around the house lately."

"What do you mean?" Now we are getting into the weeds—the dissecting of the problem.

"He has been having an affair. He hasn't told me for certain, but I hear things, people around town see him. This isn't the first time, but this is for sure the longest." Michelle started getting emotional.

"That could very well be the reason for Tyler acting out, being distant and pushing me away," I handed Michelle a tissue.

"He would just rather be at The Saguaro chatting it up with friends and flirting with girls."

I then had flashbacks to when I first moved into town when I first went to The Saguaro, my first time meeting Ricky. He acted in that place as if it was his home, the people he interacted with, and how he interacted with them. This is my bar, and you're all my guests. Yes, even the bar dog ran up to him.

"So Ricky hasn't been around in a month? That alone can cause emotional stress to a teen. Is there anything else you can think of that has suddenly changed?"

"I'm not sure if he's been doing any recent film projects. Football season ended, and I think Coach Roberts is going to ask him if he can film all the basketball games next. He didn't go to his favorite camp this past summer. Welcome to

215

Earth up in northern Arizona. He used to love going there. I don't know what happened. *Why the sudden change?*"

Interesting. Could what Mark Watson was saying about Tyler and William be true? William passed away in the spring, and Tyler did not want to go the upcoming summer. I looked down on my notepad and jotted down:

- *meeting with Tyler tomorrow morning, Wednesday 11/05 - inform his first-period teacher prior*

"I have heard great things about that camp."

"Jennifer, can I ask for a favor?"

"Yes, of course."

"As a mother, I could never live with myself snooping around his stuff, then having my heartbreak if I do find something Indicating he wants to harm himself. Can you peek into his room one night? I'll make sure we are out of the house. Just to see if you could find any signs? Any harmful pictures, or writings, or searches on the internet?" Michelle pleaded.

Absolutely not. It's completely unethical. I am loyal to my students, it's a total invasion of his privacy. Not to mention my reputation would be shot if it ever got out, including my license possibly being revoked. Absolutely not.

"I am sorry, Michelle, but I am going to have to decline. There are other methods of reaching out to Tyler about how he feels, other than me invading his privacy. It is a different story if you look through his room. It is your house, and he is your son. But asking me to do that is an extreme step. Let me schedule a meeting with him tomorrow. I'll fill you in on how it goes."

"Please, Jennifer! I feel like I'm watching a movie, and I know how it's going to end. My son has changed. I want to take the most extreme step. If I don't and I'm the next mom who has to host a funeral service, I will never forgive myself," she cried. "This Thursday is the sports banquet at the high school. I'll bring Tyler along, the whole thing will last about two hours. I will leave the door to my home unlocked. No one will ever know," Michelle begged as she took a sip of her coffee. I have never in my professional career placed in a situation like this.

"I am so sorry, Michelle. I completely understand your concern about taking the most extreme step, but sometimes those don't always yield the best results. Let me meet with Tyler first, get a sense of his headspace," I said. This was such an uncomfortable position to be in. Michelle looked away, then began searching through her purse.

"I'm going to have to up my Xanax prescriptions," Michelle let out. I was a little taken aback, curiosity running through my mind. Was everyone in Lincoln really on some sort of medication?

"How much are you currently taking?"

"About half a bar. I'll probably talk to Dr. Singh up at the clinic about taking a full bar instead. I don't take it every day. Just in times when I'm feeling overwhelmed with anxiety and stress. Like today and the next few days."

"Does Tyler know you are taking this medication? Do you keep it somewhere locked and safe so he cannot get to it and possibly do something irrational?"

"No, I don't think he knows. I keep them in my dresser drawer. The only person who would snag a few is Ricky."

"I have a few colleagues I could recommend that Tyler begins to see. Begin to make recurring meetings, and possibly, if it gets to that point, have Tyler professionally monitored. At the same time, he is prescribed safe dosages to help. They are all located in Phoenix, so this would require you to make trips back and forth." I recommend it. I'm okay with prescription medication, but it has to be monitored by a professional. I don't feel like Dr. Singh at the local clinic is a very reliable source in regards to adolescent development and psychological monitoring.

"Oh that would be great, yes I would love to have a few recommendations. Thank you," Michelle said, folding up a used tissue she found in her purse, wiping below her nose.

♦ ♦ ♦

Brian recently bought a new propane grill he wants to try out. He invited me over for evening burgers and beer, the only way to enjoy the end of a busy day's work. I told him I would bring over some potato salad. I wasted no time getting ready after my meeting with Michelle, which kept my mind racing. I could hear my phone buzz on the other end of the counter, it must be a few texts from Brian.

I stopped by the Coleman Grocery Store to pick up the potato salad and some extra beers, just in case. Trying to decide on a type we both enjoy. I know he likes domestic beers. I don't mind them. It's nice to enjoy an ice-cold beer when you've been on a wine kick. As I was pulling up into Brian's driveway, I saw Nicole taking the trash out, and just like your typical teenage girl doing household chores, she was still in her sweatpants. It appears she quickly threw on her cowgirl boots to venture outside.

I don't think I have ever seen Brian in sandals. He was wearing blue Wrangler jeans, an all-white t-shirt, and black sandals. He stood over the grill, flipping each burger, then pressing down on it. You could hear the sizzle. He then reached over, grabbing his beer. That is probably one of the sexiest things I've seen an adult man do. I brought over the potato salad and set it on the picnic table.

"Those burgers smell amazing," I said, walking over to the grill, Brian turned around giving me a huge smile and leaning in for a kiss.

"This grill is a beauty. You can also light a single stovetop. Over here is a chopping board," Brian said as he began to show me all the cool tricks his new grill can do, like a kid showing me his new toy.

"That is very impressive, it will definitely get the job done. I brought some potato salad."

"Oh wonderful, Nicole loves potato salad, as I do," Brian said as we both sat on the picnic table. He began telling me about his day as Nicole came out to join us. She changed into jeans but with the same cowgirl boots. She and her dad are so Texas, I love it. The burgers were about done as we began to pass plates around and beverages. Nicole opened beers for Brian and me and a soda for her.

"Do you have any fun plans for this upcoming weekend, Nicole?" I asked.

"Just relaxing mostly. Tomorrow I have tutor lessons with Chloe Garcia. After that, we begin swimming lessons.... Which reminds me, I need to find my inflatable arm floaties," Nicole said, quickly pulling out her phone and texting frantically.

"You're tutoring Chloe, that is great! And teaching her to swim, that is an instrumental skill to have." I said, taking a sip of my beer. Nicole was still texting when she finally looked up. Brian began passing the burgers around the table.

"Sorry, yes, I miss being near a pool so much! I text Mark to see if he has any inflatable arm floaties since he has a little sister," Nicole explained, then taking a bite out of her juicy cheeseburger. Ketchup oozing out the sides.

"How is it?" Brian asked, Nicole's mouth full as she tried to answer him, holding one finger up. Brian and I both started laughing.

"Dad, you know your burgers are amazing."

"Good girl!" Brian said as he then took a big bite. Why was my mind racing? Like a brick wall just hit me, it was Michelle's words, asking him to help Tyler.

"Hey, Nicole, I thought you were going to invite some of your friends over for dinner tonight?" I wanted to see if maybe she has heard from Tyler without directly asking her, and not to seem as if I am singling him out in her opinion. I took a bite of my burger, awaiting her response.

"Yeah, I asked Mark, but his mom was making dinner, so he decided to stay home. I tried calling Tyler, but he didn't answer," she said." He's had a pretty bad cold, so he hasn't been to school the last two days, so it's probably for the best he didn't pick up,"

"Was Tyler also out until one o'clock in the morning the night of the Lincoln Day parade like you and your cousin were?" Brian asked. "I wonder if that is where he got that cold from."
Nicole froze, mid-bite. "Ryan called his dad that night," Brian continued, "when he knew he would be out late, just to let him know and not to worry."

"Ummm, so you've known this whole time?" Nicole asked with a surprised 'I can't believe you' look teenage girls radiate.

"Oh yes. It must be nice that a father and son can have such an open-dialogue relationship. I wish a father and daughter could have the same type of relationship. Don't you think that would be great?"

"So Ryan and Tyler both went with you to the party? Do you think they hit it off?" I had to ease the tension, Brian likes to poke at Nicole, his way of suggesting things change is by leading her there with bread crumbs instead of just point-blank asking, it seemed practical.

"Umm, they were friendly to one another. Just because there are only two gays at a party, doesn't mean they're going to run away together," Nicole explained. She had a point. But I wanted to steer the conversation back to Tyler.

"I think Tyler had a great time at the party," she continued. "I actually have never seen him so social, especially in large groups like that. Alcohol surely helps with that. But, toward the end of the night, he seemed a bit down, and Ryan said he saw him leave before any of us did. I wonder if he began to miss William, and felt guilty once he realized he was having fun for the first time since William's death." Nicole took a sip of her soda. "Dad, remember I was telling you about William, that day we took Mark's four-wheelers out for a ride."

"Yeah I remember, he's the boy from Berza County. You showed me his Facebook Memorial Tribute page thing," Brian said as he quickly got up to double-check the propane grill was turned off. "You were telling me that Tyler and William dated, right?"

"Yeah, they met at Welcome to Earth Camp," Nicole said. "Jen, Mark mentioned to me that he told you about that camp and that he sorta knew William. It's still so crazy to me. I couldn't imagine what Tyler must have felt when news broke, or even to this day."

"Death changes people," I responded.

"Which got me thinking. On William's tribute page, I noticed this girl, Hannah Walker, who keeps commenting on it often. I figured she must be William's best friend. So the other day, I reached out to her, a quick Facebook message. Not trying to be creepy. I told her that I'm Tyler's best friend and figured she was William's best friend and that I wanted to do something in William's honor for Tyler." Whenever I think the Clark family cannot surprise me, Nicole does this all on her own." I think it will help him, in some way, work through his grief. I am not sure if he ever got a chance to say goodbye."

"Nicole, I think that is a wonderful idea," I said; honestly, it's rare to find that selfless compassion in teenagers. I knew this town would benefit from having the Clarks.

"That's my girl! Always looking out for others. Alright, we got two burgers left, who wants seconds?"

❖ ❖ ❖

The attic was so dusty with boxes everywhere. Sandy lent me the keys to the storage attic above the cafeteria where the school keeps old files, memorabilia, and the torn used mascot costume. The data were categorized by year. Getting to the 1950s took some digging. I searched James Scotts' records, trying to get to know anything about him, about his story.
Finally, the last box, 1955-56, and the first file in the box was James Scotts'. Inside had only one class photo. It was worn out and trying to make out, but he looked young and innocent. Also inside his file were newspapers clippings from his suicide, why did the school keep those? My

meeting with Tyler is today, I came to school early, before any students arrive. There wasn't much else in James Scotts' file as I searched through papers, covering my mouth and nose with my jacket sleeve. Who knows what kinds of particles are floating around up here.

I eventually made my way back to my office. I took James Scotts' file with me and poured myself a fresh cup of coffee. I told Ms. Johnson to let me know when Tyler arrives for his first class. After what Nicole said about him missing school and not feeling well, I hoped he would show up today.

I never heard from Ms. Johnson. I wondered if she forgot. I got more and more antsy and finally poked my head out of my office.

"Goodmorning, Sandy," I said.

"Oh, good morning, Ms. Hall," Sandy replied, still knitting her orange scarf.

"Have you heard from Tyler Tuckerman today?"

"Yes, his mom called not too long ago and said he would be out sick today."

"Okay, Thanks, Sandy." I slowly closed the door to my office. I heard my phone buzz on my desk next to my keyboard. It was a text from Brian. I always let out a little smile when I get messages from him. He was inviting me over for a movie night with him and Nicole, there was no way I could say no.

♦ ♦ ♦

The moon was full as I headed to Brian's house. It was a sweatpants only attire, with slippers and hot cocoa. Nicole made the cocoa, and I supplied the baby marshmallows. Nicole mentioned how she was going to invite Tyler. Still, considering he didn't come to school today, she figured she best let him rest up. These days keep passing. These vital days, I should be seeing him, investigating his mind, and evaluating his overall well-being.

"So, what movie are we watching?" I asked as Brian and myself got cozy on the couch. Nicole, off to the right of us, was on the large leather recliner.

"One of my favorite rom-com, you're going to love it, Jen. It's called, *And Then There Was Just Us*. This small-town girl moves to the big city, I won't spoil the rest," Nicole replied as she took a sip of her cocoa. I loved Brian's sweats, they had a pine tree pattern and what appeared to be deer.

"Jen, are you going to the sports banquet tomorrow night?" Nicole asked.

"I want to, but I have some work I have to catch up on. I hope Mark gets a few awards, after seeing him play I'm sure he will." I tried to support each student on whichever extracurricular activity they were a part of. I even attended a few rehearsals on the Choir Club. I walked around the art gallery the Art Department put up for display. It was all minimal and only five pieces, but I still wanted to show support. Just as we were about to start the film, Nicole's phone began to ring. She quickly got up and ran to her room.

"I'll be right back, don't start the movie without me!"

"Don't worry, we won't!" I shouted as Nicole ran upstairs. I then looked over at Brian, and we kissed. "Thank you, Brian."

"For what?"

"For everything."

"I should be thanking you, Ms. November 28. Lincoln is thankful to have you. I am thankful to have met you," Brian said as we again leaned in for another kiss. Who would have thought that I would have met such a wonderful man coming out to this remote desert town? I don't like to look too far into the future, but we could have a future.

"My parents are coming down for Thanksgiving," I told him. "Do you and Nicole have any plans?"

"Nothing out of the ordinary. Just cook up a big turkey and mashed potatoes."

"Let's do something together."

"Meeting the folks? That's a big deal. I'm in," Brian said as we again leaned in for a kiss for the third time. We take these little opportunities when we're alone to show our affection.

"How about I host Thanksgiving since your place is so small." Brian offered.

"That would be great. My kitchen is tiny. And I don't know where we would all sit."

"There is plenty of room here."

"Thanks for offering," I said, looking around to make sure Nicole was still out of the room.

"Michelle Tuckerman approached me with concerns about Tyler. She is worried he might do something to harm himself."

"We've had our eye on someone at the Tuckerman residence, we're going to start pressing Billy Porter for answers. We think someone from the Tuckerman family is helping Billy get his hands on prescription drugs he's been selling," Brian said, just as Nicole was coming down the stairs.

"Alright, are we ready to begin this movie?" I asked, but Nicole didn't have a pleasant look on her face. She looked distracted, on her phone, then back to us.

"What's the matter?" Brian asked. "Is everything okay?"

"I just got off the phone with Hannah. She called me after she got my Facebook DM when I told who I was and my plans to do something for Tyler to honor William," Nicole said in a sound of frustration. "I just don't get it."

"Get what?" I asked, placing the cup of hot cocoa on the end table. "What happened, what did she say?"

"She said she and William were *dating*. That they were dating for *a long time*. I asked about his suicide, and she told me he didn't die by Suicide. She said everyone around town thought that at first, but after investigating by the police, it was an accident. He was going elk hunting with his dad and brother. He was cleaning his gun when it accidentally went off. She said they were supposed to hang out that same day after he was done," Nicole said as she sat on the leather recliner, sitting up, alert and confused. I was confused as well. I looked at Brian then back at Nicole.

His death was an accident?

"Did you mention Tyler?" I asked.

"Yes, she said she remembered him when they would go to Welcome To Each camp."

"William's girlfriend?" Brian asked.

"Yes dad, his girlfriend. I don't get it. Why would Tyler tell me he and William were dating?" Nicole said.

That is an excellent question; maybe Willaim was bisexual?

"So does this mean Tyler lied to you about his relationship with William and that William was not gay?" Brian asked. It was apparent this was a foreign topic for Brian. Stuck in the mindset that you are either left-handed or

229

right-handed. Republican or Democrat. I had to interrupt.

"This news about Hannah doesn't necessarily mean William was heterosexual."

"Yeah, Dad. William was probably dating Hannah as a cover. Maybe to hide his sexuality from his friends and family. He probably didn't even tell Tyler about Hannah," Nicole responded, looking back down at her phone, scrolling through Hannah's Facebook page.

"There is a third answer. Maybe, Willaim was bisexual. Out of all the sexual orientations, bisexuality is the least discussed, especially among men. A study was done at Stanford University, citing bisexuals makes up about four-in-ten LGBTQ adults and how they are less likely to be 'out' than the rest. Coming out to friends and family is so complicated. Many bisexuals have stated they haven't come out as they don't feel it was necessary to disclose. It's very possible that William had feelings and relationships with both Tyler *and* Hannah."

"The world we live in," Brian responded, putting his arm around me.

"Are you going to be okay, Nicole?" I asked.

"Yeah. I'll be okay. I just can't get over Hannah, explaining to me that William accidentally shot himself. Like, how does that even happen?"

"You know, statically, you're more likely

to be killed by your own gun, accidentally," Brian said.

Nicole was right; that is concerning that this entire time we were under the particular notion that William died by suicide. I should have driven to Berza County weeks ago like I wanted to. Maybe then I could have made this discovery. Williams' death is not connected to the deaths in Lincoln if it was an accident.

"Okay let's have this movie's magic power of love and comedy to cheer us up," Nicole said as she pressed play on the remote, then back to her phone as Brian and I settled into the couch.

The moon was still brighter than ever as I slowly drove home, silence in my car as I turned off the radio. I was lost in a daydream about what actually happened to William. I am not entirely sold on the notion that it was an accident, even after reading his obituary that did not mention death's cause. After more digging, I didn't find any news reports about suicide, and that perhaps the family hid that fact, or maybe i've been in Lincoln for too long. Do I want his death to be from suicide to stay connected to the deaths in Lincoln?

I was sorting a few things to put away when I noticed a few of Ruby's bottom leaves were brown, dried, and dead. I touched a few, only to have it break off from the vine. My heart broke. I quickly gave her a full glass of water and moved her to the hearest window with a few sprays of water from her bottle. These house plants are supposed to be indestructible, what is happening?

My sweatpants were fresh from the dryer, warm, and clean as I crawled into bed. A text from Brian appeared on my phone asking if I made it home safe, I replied with a smile and a kiss emoji. If the truth eventually came out about the real reason behind William's death, why was Tyler still telling people it was a suicide? He doesn't seem like the attention type, telling people worse case scenarios for shock and awe.

Maybe this was Tyler's way of asking for help. In the same way, many people will be "asking for a friend" when asking about something potentially embarrassing. It is ubiquitous among people considering suicide to talk about it, talk about a friend or loved one who has died by suicide as a way to draw attention without actually being vulnerable.
Was Tyler screaming for help?

More and more red flags are beginning to surface. So much so that It was preventing me from falling asleep. What if Tyler was asking for help right in front of me and I didn't see it. What if I ignore these signs, and he harms himself?

TYLER TUCKERMAN

You could feel the thunder as the goosebumps scatter across your skin like lightning.
Your heart, racing free like wild horses.
Death looks at you like no one has before.
Life reaches for your hand, warm to the touch.
If one could love, if one was capable of love, was it a developed trait, or is one unknowingly blessed with the ability to be overwhelmingly loved?
As I'm falling like orange autumn leaves, it wasn't long for me to discover I didn't possess that ability, that magic power that turns man from beast.

Life's touch became cold as ice.
My goosebumps faded away.
Realizing the numbing pain that the job of letting life go wasn't as difficult as predicted.

My hand was cold to the touch with empty eyes.
A blackhole where life cannot escape.
This was everything they wanted, this is what they live for.
They don't know it yet, *the beauty of death*.
Twisted tales imagined by dark fantasies told by believers.
Make Lincoln believe, but in order to believe, you must first *lie*.

JENNIFER HALL

I was in my office exchanging out the pine-wood air freshener can with a new one. Sandy was kind enough to order me a twelve-pack from Costco on the school's business card. I didn't get much sleep as Hannah and William's latest revelation and his possible accidental death drowned my mind. I already had two cups of coffee, and I was ready for a refill. This morning I had met with Bobby Jones again; he seems to be doing better, well better in the sense that he's not scratching up his arms or coming to school drunk. These kids were slowly making progress.

My third cup of coffee was fresh and warm. As I made my way back to my office, I saw Ms. Johnson was waiting by my office door. She had her bifocals down around her neck with an anxious look on her face.

"Good Morning, Ms. Johnson!"

"Good Morning, Ms. Hall." Her tone was quick and stern, "I am not sure if this is something I should be bothering you with."

"No, tell me, what is it?"

"I wasn't sure if you still needed or wanted to meet with Tyler, or if you had already, but today we did a poem exercise." I looked down, and Ms. Johnson had a piece of paper in her hand.

"Wait, Tyler, came to school today? I haven't met with him, his mother said he's been at homesick," I said as Ms. Johnson handed me the poem. Coffee, in one hand, the poem in the other as I quickly scanned through.

"It's dark," Ms. Johnson said, and she was right. This was the second time she flagged some troubling poem pieces written by Tyler. "I interpret some of those lines to be suicidal thoughts. But I could be over-thinking just given the recent set of events the past few months."

"No, I'm glad you brought this to my attention. You're not over-thinking, some of these lines are cause for alarm," I said as I turned and walked to the copy scanner and made myself a copy. "Sandy, can you look up Tyler's class schedule and phone his teacher, instructing Tyler to come to visit me?" I handed Ms. Johnson the original poem back, "Thank you again, I will meet with him right now."

◆ ◆ ◆

I sat in my office chair and read the poem again and again and again. These are all the concerns that kept me up all night. Tyler subtly screaming for help. I cannot ignore these warning signs any longer. Suddenly, there was then a knock at my door. It was from Tyler.

"Tyler, good morning," I said as he walked into my office. I was surprised by how much different he looked compared to when I saw him last. He appears thinner and paler, and dark bags under his eyes like he hadn't slept. His hair looks greasy, and his shirt wrinkled and dirty, like he hadn't showered. I wonder if it's because of the cold his mother said he had.

"Hello, Ms. Hall. Good morning."

"Come on in. I hope you're feeling better. Your mother mentioned that you were not feeling too well," I said as Tyler walked in and sat on my office couch. He was quiet, more quiet than usual. I shut the door to my office. "Tyler, thank you for meeting with me today. I want to follow up on the meeting we had a few weeks ago. How has everything been? At school? At home? I hear you had a good time at the Lincoln Day parade." I took a sip of my coffee as Tyler stared at me from my office couch.

"Things have been okay, besides the cold I had," Tyler replied.

"Did you film the Lincoln Day parade?"

"I did. Every year the council asks me to film it for them. Did you go?" Tyler asked.

"Yes, I did. I was helping throw out candy with the Police Department," I said. "Now, Tyler,

I want to talk to you about something that was brought to my attention." I didn't want to bring up Hannah as I don't want him to lose confidence in Nicole, I want them to maintain their close friendship. I spun my chair around and handed him a copy of the poem he wrote. His eyebrows formed an almost angry yet surprised look.

"Where did you get that?"

"Tyler, if you're thinking about hurting yourself, you can talk to me, and we can get you help. You don't have to tackle life alone. You don't have to bottle things up. I am here for you. People are here for you."

"That was just a creative writing assignment," Tyler said, handing the poem back to me.

"It's pure fiction. There is no underlying meaning behind it."

"I am just concerned, given the past few months. I just don't want you to think self-harm is the only way to solve any problems you might be dealing with."

"I would never do that. I know how it feels to lose a loved one. I will be okay, Ms. Hall. I always am, *believe me*," Tyler replied, as he then slowly got up, "I have a math exam in ten minutes, may I go?"

"Yes, of course. Tyler don't hesitate to come and talk to me about anything. I am here for you. And good luck on your exam." I said as I opened the door and walked Tyler out.

"Goodbye, Ms. Hall."

That was not the meeting I wanted to have. There are still so many unanswered questions. I was still unsure about his well being. I continued to sit in my office, rereading the poem, then searching for the first poem Ms. Johnson flagged to me, comparing both. Neither of them has a definite undertone or a positive outlook on life. My foot was tapping against the floor. I then decided this escalated step is the risk I am willing to take to help a student. It will be okay, Michelle is giving me permission to come into her home. It's not illegal if she gave me permission. Okay, I am going to do this. I quickly pulled up Tyler's school profile and searched for his mother's number of emergency contact information.

"Hello, this is Michelle."

"Hi, Michelle, this is Jennifer Hall. So tonight is the sports banquet, and I was curious if you're still open to the plan you suggested."

"Jennifer, it's so good to hear from you. Yes, yes, I am." This move was definitely going to unbalance the scales. One extreme step on one side, I just hope that the outcome recenters the levels and renders an absolute resolution.

◆ ◆ ◆

The night was moonless as I drove past

the high school. The parking lot was full as everyone attended the sports banquet, a dinner event where they gave out awards to the players from MVP, to highest points scored, and Player Of The Year. I heard the right amount of people attend the sports banquet. After seeing the parking lot, they were correct. Sandy was telling me that various families come together to cook all the food. Sports being the saving grace, the only thing bringing people together in Lincoln, besides The Saguaro.

Michelle said the front door would be unlocked and that the house would be empty. My role would be to search for any clues that could indicate Tyler might try to take his own life. Anything from a journal, highlighting troubling pages from a dictionary, or even Google searches.

I parked a little up the street and walked over. The streets were dark, with only every other street lamp providing light. I walked along the chain-link fence surrounded by the sound of crickets. The house was small, with an okay-sized front and backyard. The little swing set in the front yard gave me flashbacks to that photo of Emily I have in my office.

I walked up the wooden steps to the front porch and slowly opened the door, developing a spy complex. It's interesting how each home has a distinct smell to it. Michelle told me that Tyler's room is on the left side of the single wide home. I heard a few cracks in the floor as I walked down the narrow hallway to Tyler's room. A few old family portraits of when Tyler was a toddler, nothing recent though, lined the hallway. At the end of the hall, there was only one door that had to be Tyler's room. For a split second, I got a sinister vibe, a feeling that I would walk in to find Tyler hanging from the ceiling. I got goose-bumps.

I opened the door to Tyler's room and flipped the light on. I was surprised at how clean and organized it was. An alphabetized bookshelf contained titles like the entire Harry Potter series, *The Lord of the Rings*, and Plato's *Republic*. His nightstand had an alarm clock, an empty glass of water, and a notebook. After taking a second glance, it was actually a play, one that I recognize—an existential French play I had to do a report on one semester in college. Definitely not your typical casual read for a high schooler, but then again, Tyler is not your average high schooler, as I've recently discovered. The play was twisted yet outstanding. It was about three souls damned to hell, all stuck in the same room together. Various references to *Ontology*. The philosophical study of being, existence, and reality. All three characters performed horrific acts such as murder, adultery, and suicide. As a result, they were sent to the room in hell. Their punishment is each other, never being able to escape, surrounded by the others being and consciousness, forever.

The bed was made well as if I had just entered into a motel room, the sheets tightly tucked and folded. I then opened a few drawers, opening folded pieces of paper, moving pencils and batteries around. Nothing out of the ordinary was standing out. I walked to his closet and slid the door open. All his shirts were neatly hung, below were his shoes lined up against the wall of the closet. I then noticed at the end was a black Nike shoe box. I didn't think much of it, then remember when I was a young girl in middle school I would save letters from school in a pink box similar, I leaned down and picked it up, sitting on his bed with the shoebox on my lap.

I removed the top and glanced inside. This must be stuff Tyler collected from Welcome to Earth Camp. Inside was a whistle, a black wristwatch, a name tag reading William Ackhurst in black ink. This must be where he kept memories of William, where he hid their relationship from everyone. The box also contained dozens and dozens of pictures. I picked up one after another. My heart beating faster and faster with each image I looked at. None of them were of William and Tyler together. Instead, they were all pictures of William, and in each one, he was sound asleep. Each had a date stamp: 07/10/2015, 12/15/2016, 03/01/2016, 07/12/2017, 12/18/2018, 07/15/2018.

I tossed the pictures back into the box, pulled my phone out, and took a picture of the contents, and then closed the lid. Completely perplexed and confused. This is very concerning, especially after the news we got last night from Hannah. I gently placed the black shoe box back in his closet and slid the door shut. I looked behind me and quickly got on my knees and looked under his bed, nothing.

He had a few pictures framed on his wall. None of the people in them looked familiar. Like the pictures in the hallway, they seem to be older pictures, nothing recent. I turned around and noticed a poster on the back of his door of Lady Gaga with bold letters, "Born This Way."

The first thing I did notice when I walked into his room was his computer desk that sat in front of the only window in the room. On the desk were his camera, laptop, papers, and film magazines. His desk didn't have any drawers. It seemed to be more of a table. I picked up his camera. It was fairly dense with lots of buttons and grooves to add on attachments. It was nice.

I sat in his chair and slowly opened his laptop. Just like Michelle told me, it was locked. But being the good mother she is, she made him write down his passwords. I quickly pulled my phone out and scanned through our text messages for the password—capital "S" in Smile123. Instantly a beautiful desktop picture of a lake surrounded by mountains appeared. I scanned for his internet browser and did a b-line for his search history. I didn't want to be on his personal laptop for too long; see if he was searching for anything harmful. I see web results for Google images of Lake Louise Canada, the Facebook tribute page of William Ackhurst, techniques for filming in water, a porn site, the philosophy of *Romeo and Juliet*, Holbrook, Arizona, and a search for my name: Jennifer Hall.

Was *Tyler obsessed with William*? Mark Watson mentioned that Tyler got sad at camp when news broke about William. The shoe box filled with pictures of William asleep, his camp name tag, and now this search history.

I thought of one of the lines in a poem that Tyler wrote: "his Will that he had lost." He didn't mention William when I asked him about the poem or why, when I asked about him using the word, beautiful, to describe the acts in *Romeo and Juliet*. When I was scrolling through William's Facebook tribute page, there were no pictures of them together. This didn't seem like your average crush, it seemed darker.

Tyler, what is wrong?

Looking around at all the notebooks, cords, and camera equipment, I noticed a camera attachment he had on his desk. It was slightly wet and was on top of a kitchen towel. I think I was done for tonight, the only alarming thing was his dark obsession with William. I went to close his laptop when I noticed a folder on his homepage. The folder's name was *11:28*. Those numbers again. My mind going straight to Brian reminded me to remain thankful and count my blessing, not my misfortunes. But I was still overcome with curiosity. Why name a folder those specific numbers? Was it just a coincidence?

Inside the folder, I saw various files. The names on them were pre-edit, music collaboration, raw, photo slideshow, and at the bottom, another folder called *Make Believe*. I double-clicked on the folder and saw only two files: MakeGregandlizziebelieve.m4v, Makecameronbelieve.m4v.

These must be the funeral service videos he made for the families. I wondered why he named the funeral service video, make Cameron believe, believe in what? The same with Greg and Lizzie. I opened Cameron's video. The video began, all black with no music, then bolded white words started to appear on the screen, it was a Bible verse.

"Come to me, all you who are weary and burdened, and I will give you rest"
- Matthew 11:28

The video started with baby videos of Cameron sitting in a highchair with a small red cake in front of him, on his first birthday. He was looking around at all the people, not sure what to do with this thing. His mom kept putting his little hands on the cake, trying to show him he can eat it, and it kind of worked. Halfway through the clip, he started crying.

Then the video cut to Cameron's funeral service starting. A shot at all the beautiful flowers and the service pamphlet, on the cover Cameron's red cheeks and blue braces smiling.

Suddenly, on the screen appeared a white bathtub. *A boy was lying in it.*

Before I could begin to process what I saw, the video changed scenes to people entering the church, greeting the family—each person, one by one, giving Janet a hug. Then footage of Cameron trying to take his first few steps, balancing on both his little feet then gravity taking over as he fell to the side.

Then appeared the bathtub again. The shower was on, and you could hear the water hitting the tub. *It was Cameron.* He was wearing a white button-up shirt, sleeves rolled up, and white underwear. The video slowly began to zoom in. His inner forearms bled black. Black blood running down both sides of his arms and spiraling down into the drain. His lips quivering. The razor blade he used visible on the bathtub ledge, surrounded by black droplets.

A photo slide show began of the family on vacation at the beach, under a giant rainbow umbrella, a lunch basket open surrounded by small sandcastles. Then photos of the day Cameron was born at the hospital, various family members holding him, posing for a picture.

Then back to Cameron's purple face, with birth and death dates in bolded white letters appearing on the screen, Cameron in the background, stiff and cold.

Cameron J. Fulton
2005 - 2019

I slammed the laptop closed, quickly wiping away the tears rolling down my face. Heartbroken and terrified, I just sat there in shock of what I had seen. That couldn't be the actual suicide. No way. In need of reassurance, I quickly re-opened the laptop and double-clicked the next file, Makegregandlizzie-believe.m4v. My adrenalin pulsating. I fast-forwarded a bit. *Pause*. My hand trembling to press it, my fingers softly over the key, afraid to push it. *Play*. The scene came up, the faint outline of a blue vintage mustang hood, engulfed in thick gray smoke—the sound of an engine running with birth and death dates for Greg and Lizzie. I stood up and turned away, placing both hands across my mouth.

Tyler, what have you done?

I frantically pulled my phone out from my pocket, almost dropping it as I tried to unlock it. Try again, try again. Fuck, come on! I quickly called Brian to have it ring and ring and ring, fuck come on, Brian! Finally, he answered, I gasped for my words, but he responded with instant words.

"Jen! We just got a call, get down to the Garcia residence!"

"Brian... Brian..." I couldn't catch my breath to tell him what I'd discovered.

"There was a 911 call, something happened to Chloe Garcia. She might be dead. Meet us there now."

TYLER TUCKERMAN

Nicole and I sat along a brick wall outside the high school cafeteria. I understand why Nicole came, her boyfriend is probably getting a few awards tonight, so she's a supportive girlfriend. The only reason why I am here is that my mother dragged me. Why am I going to a sports awards show? Bored out of my mind. I was barely listening to Nicole rant. I was still processing what had just happened, pause, play, rewind, pause, play, rewind over and over and over. It was exquisite. I want to go home. I wonder if William would have come if I was getting an award?

"Are you feeling better?" Nicole asked.

"Yeah, I'm feeling much better now. Alive again."

"That's good. I wish I was feeling better. Mark just has been a little distant since Monica's party," Nicole explained, scratching her head and skimming through her cell phone erratically. "We did get into a little argument that night, now I feel awful." As you should. She probably doesn't remember the things she said to me that night.

"Have you tried talking to your mom about it?" I suggested.

"What? My mom?"

"Yeah, like what do you think your mom would say?"

"Oh, that I should just apologize and give him space for a little bit."

"And after he wins his awards tonight he will be all happy and forget," I said

"Hey Ty, have you heard of a girl named Hannah?" Nicole asked, but just then a few guys walked outside to shut the doors to the cafeteria, Nicole and I quickly got up and ran inside. Let the show begin.

All the tables were round full three-sixty views of your table audience. Our table sat little toward the back, I was next to my mom, and a few of her teacher friends. A white sheet covered the entire table with two fake flower centerpieces. Across the room is where Nicole and her dad were sitting. In the back was the line for food. A wooden podium with the initials LHS on the front stood at the top of the cafeteria. Well, I better get comfortable, this thing is probably two hour's long. Principal Miller walked up to the podium and cleared his voice.

❖ ❖ ❖

The girls' portion of the awards show was wrapping up, which only took about twenty minutes. Loretta Espi won Player Of The Year, she looks so happy jumping up as they called her name to go collect her glass ball award. After she is handed her prize, they then take some quick photos with the coaches for the school paper and for social media postings. My plate was halfway eaten, I wasn't too hungry, but I was on my fourth glass of sweet tea. Staring forward, I could see that Coach Roberts walk up to the podium, It looks like the guy's portion is about to begin. I scanned the room for Mark to see if he was becoming antsy, as he probably knows he's getting a few awards.

"Tyler, do you play any sports?" Mrs. Rose leaned over and asked me, she works with my mother at the elementary school, I believe it is 2nd grade she teaches or 3rd. Had she gone to any of the games, she would know that, no, I do not play any sports. She is pretty old, so she probably doesn't even know who is playing.

"No I don't Mrs. Rose, I just came to support a few of my friends who play sports, they are all so good, it will be hard to determine who will win Player Of The Year," I lied. It was just so much easier to lie, tell her what she wants to hear, and not tell her that I could care less about it. It was then that I heard it, piercing through my ears like a dog whistle. I quickly picked my head up.

"Tyler, Tuckerman!" It was then followed by clapping. The room lighting up. My eyes widened with shock, my head looking around the room, everyone was looking at me. Coach Roberts started off the guy's portion by presenting me with an Outstanding Film Award. My very own glass ball, for all the filming I did for him at all the games. I couldn't believe what was happening. My heart was pounding. I slowly stood up from my chair and began to walk toward the podium. My mom, shouting, "Yay Tyler!" I looked over, and Nicole was whistling with one hand. I couldn't help but smile; this feeling was incredible.

I was winning an *Oscar* for Outstanding Film, Best Director, and Best Cinematography; my dreams finally came true. I shook Coach Robert's hand as he handed me my very first film award. I turned and faced the crowd, my heart still pounding as I tried to catch my breath. I just smiled and looked back at everyone, and for the first time, I feel like everyone actually saw me, the real me, and not just my silhouette. This was a huge honor, thank you so much, *I couldn't have done this without* Cameron Fulton, Greg Norris, and Lizzie Chapelton, *they were the stars, and this award is for them.*

Everything was in slow motion as I could still hear the clapping in my ears. It was then I saw Jason Brophy. Ten feet away at one of the round tables with a few of his jock buddies. I tried my hardest to avoid eye contact with him. This was the first time I've seen him since Monica's party. I blacked out for five seconds, being transported back to that room, hearing the sound of him grunting, feeling the weight of his body pressure as he pinned me down, feeling him enter me. I turned to face the other side of the room. From the corner of my eye toward the back of the cafeteria, I could see the commotion, one person answering a phone call, then standing up quickly. The school reporter shuffled me next to Coach Roberts and Principal Miller for a picture for the school paper,

"One, Two, Three!" FLASH, when I heard the shrieking sound. It was a horror gasp one produces when given life-shattering news. The commotion in the back of the cafeteria picked up with people running out the door.

"Let's take one more, okay ready; one, two, three!" FLASH, everyone then began to look around, erupting into whispers. One person ran back into the cafeteria, grabbing belongings a few people left behind, then running back outside. Sheriff Clark leaning his ear into his dispatch radio, he had an unpleasant look on his face. He quickly pulled out his phone, got up to leave, kissing Nicole on the forehead, and went.

This was happening faster than I had anticipated. Lincoln won't understand the *art*. They will fear it, instead of embracing it. It's beautiful—an elegant reminder on how life repeats itself, *one breath at a time.*

"Alright, everyone, we are going to continue. Please keep it down. Thank you, Tyler, for all the great filmmaking you're doing. It really helps out. How here is Coach Roberts to continue," Principal Miller said trying to regain control of the room. I slowly walked back to our table, everyone lost to inside conversations, even my mother. Don't you want to see my first film award, Mom? Fuck, I forgot to thank you and Dad up at the podium.

The only person interested in seeing my film award was Mrs. Rose. Probably because she is too old for anyone to whisper with, from what she could see, she really liked the glass ball. I looked across the room, and Mark had his arm around Nicole, who was crying, she must have just heard the news. Guess they are back together again? Leave it to tragedy to bring people together. My mom then began to cry, along with a few others at our table, gentle tears rolling down each respective cheek.

"Darling, what is the matter? Dear Heavens." Mrs. Rose asked the table, realizing sadness as she tried to pass around napkins she pulled from inside her purse to help wipe the tears away. My mother leaned over and grabbed a napkin from Mrs. Rose, answering her.

"They found Chloe Garcia at the bottom of their swimming pool."

◆ ◆ ◆

I walked into the bathroom just south of the cafeteria—a quiet place I often find solace when needing to escape the noises of life. Like a peaceful tomb, I've grown to love with all of its musky, overly bleached aroma I found comfort in. Since the beginning of my freshman year, when I could no longer take all the unfamiliar faces glaring at me, the end stall became my go-to. It was a place where I would sit to escape everything and be with the only pure existing creature, myself.

This time was different, as I could feel all the mourning happening inside the cafeteria. Lincoln still doesn't understand art. I needed to escape, handing my mother my oscar and entering isolation to fully express the magnitude of what I was feeling. I walked up to the oversized mirror, etched with student's names, hearts, a love of drugs, several swastikas, and obscure words.

My pupils were dilated like a black hole —the event horizon swallowing all the matter released by a dying star that had finally met its end. The iris of the universe as I too absorbed the energy they all released, the heart pulsing, full breathtaking matter. A slight smirk slowly began to appear as I drew my hand to my face, tracing down with one finger along my cheek. Imitating the salt tear path that everyone was experiencing. Best actor in a leading role.

I slowly turned the knob on the sink, placed my finger under the cold stream, and then back up to my eye: one drop, two drops, three. My eyebrows curled, and my lip muscles contracted, "Chloe! No, why?" or as my mom repeatedly said, "oh my god, how did this happen?" I ran my finger under the now warm stream and practiced again, but this time with more enthusiasm with both hands covering my face. "No, why god. Why?"

I peeked at my reflection through my fingers, then gently lowered my hand, grinning from ear to ear. Damn, I had talent.

JENNIFER HALL

lashing blue and red lights lit up the night sky as I was approaching the Garcia residence. My hands trembling on the steering wheel, the radio turned off, and tears still rolled down my race. Flashbacks to the footage of Cameron bleeding to death in his bathtub haunting me. Never in a million years would I have predicted this outcome. Reminding me of the depths, one's dark mind is capable of imagining—the monster next door. As soon as I parked, I was too scared to get out. I was scared to face whatever awaited me in the Garcia's house. I closed my eyes and took a deep breath, slowly opening them and the door to my car.

The back doors to a white and red ambulance were open next to the garage. The house sat about half a mile from the main road. Right as you turned off the path you were presented by massive black metal gates, a small nine-digit code box stood before the gate; however, the gates were already open. A string of cactus and pine trees line the driveway to the house, a massive five-bedroom modern desert-themed oasis, one a business and landowner could only afford. An SUV sat on one side of the three-car garage.

As I entered the kitchen, I could hear all the commotion coming from the backyard. Monica is crying in the living room with multiple people around her. I slowly walked outside as everything appeared to go silent. I couldn't hear anything except the sound of my own breathing. Chloe's body was being pulled from the swimming pool. I looked down, and on the glass table was an orange cone marked "Evidence 3." Next to it sat a book. *The Night the Angels Cried.* "Evidence 4" lying next to the book was what appeared to be Chloe's cell phone, in a pink and white case.

I looked up at Brian, he was talking with the paramedics. You could see her small outline inside the adult-sized body bag as the medics began to stroll her away. Everything is still silent. Flashbacks of Emily blinding me. Whipping away the wet hair from my twelve-year-old face as the rain poured down, finding Emily, underwater as her blonde hair floated to the surface.

Myself and Chloe were of the same age. This has to be a coincidence, but I wondered if Tyler was involved? How could he have filmed it if he was at the sports banquet? It was then that I broke down, placing my hand over my mouth. I remembered his camera attachment in his bedroom was slightly wet.

◆ ◆ ◆

Brian walks over and hugs me. When he told me something happened to Chloe, he didn't know the situation. He didn't realize she drowned. Otherwise, he would not have told me to come as he knows about Emily. He whispered his apology repeatedly. He could tell I was shaken, and right now, that's all I want, his embrace. It was calming. Silently standing warm in Brian's arms, he then kissed my forehead. It was then my denial of Chloe's death turned to anger, Brian had his arms around me as I lifted my head up to look at him,

"We need to talk about Tyler Tuckerman," I whispered to him. "More than likely has something to do with Chloe's suicide."

"What makes you say that?" Brian responded, still hugging me.

"Brian, I found video footage of each suicide on Tyler's laptop. He filmed them and stitched together a barbaric storyline. One second you're watching their birth video, the next second you're watching them die."

Brian remained silent. I could feel him hug me tighter. He was taken back to what he just heard. I tried to hold the tears back. "I prayed for it to be fake, I prayed over and over that what I was watching was not real, It was just kids playing pretend, playing make-believe of some sort. Oh my god, the title of those videos was make believe!"

"What? The title is called make believe?" Brian asked, "Do you have his laptop?"

"It's in my car."

"Now if what is on that laptop is true, and they are the actual suicides, then we need to make sure he is locked up. With no hiccups and no loose ends," Brian said, instantly falling back into the role of sheriff. "We need to obtain this piece of evidence lawfully. I didn't want to tell you this, but we got the search warrant pending to search the Tuckerman residence after we got a massive tip from Billy Porter. Billy caved in and told us his accomplice in the drug selling case. When we conduct the search, I'll make sure to grab Tyler's laptop, so it must go back as soon as possible." Brian looked stern, aggravated, upset, angry. "If you have what I think you have, then this will turn into a homicide situation."

"A homicide?"

"Yes! If he has anything to do with her death, then we will approach this as a homicide."

"Billy told you who's been helping him get his hands on the prescription drugs?"

"Yeah, Billy told us. It's Michelle Tuckerman. She was the one selling Billy the drugs. He seemed a bit apprehensive before telling us," Brian said.

Are you fucking kidding me? Michelle fucking Tuckerman was selling the prescription drugs to Billy, who was then selling to the high school kids. Jesus fucking Christ. It's always the last person you expect.

"I'll rush it back the second you're done watching it. Oh god, Brian, those poor kids, those videos. The contribution to the suicides and evidence have all been under the same roof this entire time." Tears began to form, my eyelashes wet and clumped together.

"I'll follow up with the judge on that search warrant."

We then began to walk toward my car. Brian called his sergeant to come along as well to watch.

"Hi Sergeant Ramirez," I said.

"Fucking tragedy. I can't believe it," Ramirez said.

"I know, and I'm sorry, but it's about to get worse, my heart is shattered. Please, both of you get in the back seat." I got in the driver's seat, they both got in the back. I passed them the laptop with the first video ready to go, they pressed play. I took a deep breath and held it.

All black screen with words appearing, *"Come to me, all you who are weary and burdened, and I will give you rest"* - *Matthew 11:28*.

Why is Tyler using that specific Bible verse? There has to be some explanation, perhaps a Bible study group, or maybe a horror film?

Then it hit me, the bookmark in blue pen had the same writing—the same numbers. The book at the Coleman grocery was the property of Lincoln High, was it the same book? The same book that is lying amongst Chloe's crime scene. I had to find out.

"Brian, I'll be right back," I said, but he was too distracted to notice. Behind him, was Cameron's face reflecting off the black back window from the laptop screen. Another wave of coldness erupting into my stomach as the blood rushed to my face.

Flashing red and blue lights still lighting up the sky. The side door to the house seemed heavier to open this time. Obstacles preventing me from arriving at my destination. Life hinting at me to stay away, alerting me that I do not want to know the answer. The sliding glass door outside was still open. Monica's friend came running into the kitchen, grabbing some water bottles and mumbling about how they all have to leave the house.

I placed both my hands together as I stepped outside, the sight of the pool and water haunting to look at. A few police officers were by the end of the pool, talking to each other as I grabbed the book on the glass table. Instantly transporting me back to the Coleman Grocery Store. This once curious, attentive piece of literature, now brings me to my knees. Terrified of what might be inside. I quickly began searching through it until I found the bookmark, but it was different. I skimmed the page real fast, It was still saved on the chapter where the little girl dies, but It wasn't the same bookmark, it was the backside to a polaroid? An all-white backside polaroid.

I turned it over to discover it's the photo I have of Emily in my office, swinging on her swing set.

TYLER TUCKERMAN

I was lying on my bed, staring up, again counting the glueballs that lost their glow in the dark star. My mood was calm. I looked over at the glass ball award sitting on my nightstand, right next to it was my favorite play, written in 1944 by Jean-Paul Sartre, No Exit. It's such a riveting example of life and death, pain and grief, love and solace. My room would be William and me, together forever, finally. I loved the idea of the 'Second Empire' French furniture from the play, so that part can stay. My sweet William is already in our room, waiting for me. Getting everything ready for our eternal honeymoon. I like to believe that everyone has their own room version that they are sent to when they die, it's none of my business to know what they are, or why they are, just to help them get there, "*In Camera.*" I opened to the scene where Garcin, Inès, and Estelle confess their actions. So much beauty, so much rippling effects of that beauty.

I then got a little annoyed as I could see fingerprints all over my glass ball award, I've already had to clean it several times, I whipped my shirt across the front. The beautifully detailed text, "Tyler Tuckerman," "Outstanding Film," "Lincoln High School," "2019."

What a year. This, by far, has to be my best. I can't even begin to describe to you the kind of year it has been. It has been my best and worst, my darkest and lightest. I definitely understand what made this year the worst. That was losing William, my warm blue eyes, my tall, handsome mountain man. Him showing me, guiding me to discover all the beauty this universe has to offer. I know I will see him again. But I want to see him now. He was the most beautiful creature I had ever seen. I know when he killed himself, he let that beauty out into the world. He released himself free. He went to our *room*.

I had my journal next to me on my bed, split open with one pencil and one pen laying in the crease. I had just finished my current piece, I was doodling a sunset, one that I always draw, the top of the mountain where William and I would always go. Inside the sun were my warm blue eyes looking over me. Above the sunset, up into space weren't stars, but instead bubbles. Small bubbles and big bubbles racing to the surface of the universe. But which way is up? Below the sunset, below the horizon wasn't land, but instead water. Clear as water can be with murky vision. Light shading and dark shading. Pencil and Pen. Only right after you look, squint your eyes tightly to the point they nearly close you can see it. You can read it, deep under the water, the words floating to one side, "makechloebelieve."

Voices were coming in from outside. A few of my mother's friends all decided to come over after the sports banquet to hash out what just happened to Chloe. My mother was already pretty drunk and was the loudest. I hate attention, intense social interaction, both from people I know and don't know—more than one pair of eyes on me. My winning tonight was the most I've had people stare at me, which will be my last time. Don't look at me.

That reason alone, the attention, is why I don't tell people I was there. I was present in the room when the transitions occurred. The beautiful reverse transition from life to death, then experiencing the release, like a dying star. My heart is racing. I got up and grabbed my laptop and camera off my desk and jumped back on my bed. Tonight was the perfect night to begin working on Chloe's video. The surge of inspiration after winning my outstanding film award. I plugged in my camera and began to transport the video onto my laptop. Full-screen HD. *Pause. Play*.

Chloe was dancing about the ledge of the pool. Nervous. All she needed was a little *push*, and in she went. Water splashing about the pool's surface with only her fingers visible, they appeared to be reaching for the moonless night sky as she slowly sunk. My underwater attachment became so useful for this scene. The splashing subsided. Chloe's fingers no longer visible as I submerged my camera into the pool. A faint stream of blood slowly emerged from her nose and mouth, like diluted carmine watercolors, a painter's dream. I had to witness it again, Chloe's transition, her release. You could feel the matter; you could see the ripples through the eye of the lens only. Very similar to the feeling I got at Monica's party after taking that pill. Once the video was over, I immediately rewound the footage, watched it again, and again.

I don't tell people because I don't want attention. They would never understand art. They don't understand and will never understand that just like giving life, the inverse, it is just as beautiful. I will lie by omission, if that is what is required to make everyone believe, someday, believe in the beauty. They will all come around eventually.

I know William thought of me the second he closed his eyes and pulled the trigger.

"You cannot tell me that you honestly believe her father was around, enough to see his family?" my mother ranted. Our single wide walls were pretty thin, you could hear the cracks in the wood of the porch as they walked around. "He is never there, never!" she continued. It sounds like my father.

"They are both always out of town, oh my god, it's unbelievable, someone should have been at that house, and that poor little girl wouldn't have drowned," Susan replied. I could then hear her set her glass drink down on the table. "Why would you get a pool if your kids don't know how to swim? They should be held liable somehow!"

"Exactly, install the pool after you teach your children to swim, not before, fucking idiots," a mysterious third voice said.

"I just don't get how no one was home while this was all happening?" my mother continued. "None of this feels real still like it's a dream, we all saw her at school yesterday, and she just looked so happy."

"Who found her again?" Susan asked.

"Carlos, he's a guy who works for Louie out on the farms, he helps manage a few. I guess he was putting some stuff in the garage, you know their massive work garage, and as he was leaving, he found her at the bottom," my mother said as she began to choke up.

"They should just drain that fucking pool, I know I would," Susan replied.

They are all so riled up, so full of questions and wild theories. I continued to lay on my bed, admiring my newest drawing. I honestly think William would have loved my beautiful tributes. I flipped back to the beginning page.

Slowly scrolling through, page by page at all my months of creative wonder. It was mostly all about William, well about *us*.

I could see it from the corner of my eye— a glimpse. A tantalizing rainbow faintly dancing about the wall of my room. The colliding colors are beautiful and totally random, the blue reminded me of William. I had a small collection of markers lying on my bed, different shades of blue, black, and gray. Thanks to the rainbow, I got a surge of motivation. I felt like William was telling me to do this through the dancing colors. With the light blue marker in my right hand, and gently, patiently wrote our numbers on my inside left wrist *11:28*. Blew gently on the fresh ink, soaking into my skin, then leaning in, kissing my new tattoo. The rainbow of colors kept getting brighter and brighter until my room was lit up with blue and red lights. Brighter and brighter. They are coming from my bedroom window. I looked out my window to see five police cars outside our front yard, all on the road. I stood there, watching a sea of police officers walk into our yard, and up to our porch.

"Michelle Tuckerman!" a man's voice thundered, "we were approved for a search warrant by the county judge to search your residence. We received a massive tip on the current prescription drug problem that invaded Lincoln." The voice sounded like Sheriff Clark.

"Excuse me? Who tipped you off about

what? You're not going inside my house. You do not have the right to enter my home without my permission, you hear me?" my mother yelled.

"Ma'am, we have a legal search warrant to search your entire residence," the man said again as I could then hear our front door open. I could listen to them enter our house.

"Get the fuck out of there!" my mother yelled.

They sounded like they were going through all my mom's belongings as I slowly tip-toed down the hallway, unsure of what to do. I kept having the same feeling of when Jason Brophy forced himself on me, unsure how to react. I just stood in the hallway.

"This is all your fault, you bitch! You fucking little cunt. I trusted you to come into my home, and this is what you do? You have the police investigate me because you're too inadequate to help these kids! You have your little boyfriend come into my home? You were supposed to help my son! Is this how you help people? By having their parents arrested?" I heard my mother shout out, who was she yelling at? "Get the fuck off my property, Jennifer, I never want to see you again!"

Jennifer Hall is here? My high school counselor, my holier-than-thou school counselor, always puts herself in places she doesn't belong to. It was then I leaned over down the end of the hallway and saw Sheriff Clark walk out the door, he was holding a bag of something. A clear ziplock bag was full of small orange containers—prescription bottles.

"Michelle Tuckerman, you're going to come with us. You have the right to remain silent, anything you say can and will be used against you in a court of law."

"You bitch, get your fucking hands off of me, this is ridiculous. Susan call my lawyer! Get John Ludlow on the phone now! John Ludlow! I have a legal prescription to be taking those medications!"

"You have the right to an attorney, If you cannot afford an attorney, one will be provided for you." Office Clark kept reading my mother her rights. *Lub-dub*. What was happening? What did they find in my mother's room that was so alarming? I'm scared. Just then a blinding light hit me directly in the eyes, I squinted and looked away. I could still feel the piercing sun.

"Hi, son, you're going to have to come with us," an officer said as he put his arms on my shoulders and led me down the hallway. Two more walks past us and into my bedroom. What was happening? Everything was beginning to go silent. I could hear a ringing deep, deep in my ear, deep in my skull.

JENNIFER HALL

The entire town of Lincoln was lit up. Within hours it became a circus—a dark, grim malevolent spectacle. Residents were driving by one by one to crack a glimpse of what was going on everywhere. Snowbirds walked out of their houses and RVs parked in empty lots to understand the severity. They were all still unaware of the tragedies. Life shifting as life always does, significant shifts, in my past experiences, the big changes have always been for the worst.

I was walking back to my car outside the Tuckerman residence. Michelle's acid tongue replaying over and over.

"I trusted you!" "This is how you help the kids?" "You fucking cunt!" "You, you, you."

The feeling of being misunderstood, being labeled a character you're not, and knowing you probably couldn't change it anymore. I sat in my car silently. I placed both my hands on my face, then racing them through my hair, taking a deep inhale. I couldn't think I couldn't ponder or process what was happening at this very moment.

I looked over, and they were walking Michelle to an SUV sheriff patrol car. She still seemed to be hissing back at the officers. It was just yesterday we had such a productive talk. Only then, right behind them, an officer was walking with Tyler. My stomach dropped at the sight of him. It was like watching a stranger, a stranger you've never met, but somehow, you feel like you might have somewhere deep in your memory. Like a frightened cat focused on potential danger, I couldn't look away. I watched as the officer took him to the patrol car.

I realized I was experiencing terror, I was afraid of Tyler. If he was behind that photo of Emily inside the book at Chloe's crime scene, was he also behind that morbid single sentence letter I received about Emily killing herself? Was I being targeted? Why was he trying to bring me so much pain? Tears slowly emerged. It was then a wave of emotions began to hurtling back in, my throat drying up. My stomach went ice cold, and at that moment I did the only thing I knew, the only thing that would help me was that I pulled my phone out of my jacket pocket and called my mom.

Brian suggested I stay over at his place, he

knew I didn't want to be alone, and I don't think he wanted to be alone. I was going to his home right after I stopped by my place for clothes. I was in no mindset to be picking out attire, so I grabbed whatever. As I was leaving, I noticed Ruby, wilted, and dead on the window ledge. Her years of vine growth gone. I picked her up, tears pouring down. I placed her in the kitchen with some water and a few ice cubs. My life was in freefall, the scales so badly skewed I feared it might be broken beyond repair.

Nicole was more than likely asleep by now, so I used the spare key they kept hidden under a fake rock and crawled into his massive bed. The sheets are warm, and the pillows smelled like him, it was comforting. It was hard trying to fall asleep, as my mind kept racing. Crime scene, after crime scene, after crime scene. Purple faces, black blood, smokey garages, and blonde hair floating in the water. I could then hear creaks in the ceiling, sounds like Nicole walking around, the poor thing probably can't sleep either. I pondered about going upstairs to talk to her until I heard a guy's voice. It sounded like Mark. That's good, she doesn't need to be alone right now. I wish Brian were here, he wasn't sure what time he would be getting off work, especially considering what they found in Tyler's room. I continued to lay there in a fetal position under his thick brown bed sheets. I could finally feel drifting, my mind drifting, my heartbeat relaxing, and my body going weight-less.

I was back home, running down our carpeted stairs to beat Emily to the living room. The sister who wins the race every year gets to open the first Christmas present. I am the champion three years in a row. The smell of freshly brewed coffee filled the living room. Frank ran down the stairs behind Emily, heavily panting with his tongue nearly touching the carpet. Christmas mornings are my all-time favorite mornings. Dad makes his signature bacon avocado omelet for breakfast and Mom, helping us open and assemble our new toys. The second I found out I got an Easy Bake Oven, I started screaming! I wanted to start making desserts for everyone, but after breakfast, Mom said.

Then Dad comes barging into the living room, shouting, "Girls! Girls! Girls! Santa left something outback! Come look!" Emily and I looked at each other, then again, raced to the backyard door. I couldn't believe it, as we both looked out the back door, face firmly pressed against the door window. It was already assembled and put together perfectly, a swing set! Our very own swing set! Emily and I opened the door and ran outside, totally forgetting about all our other presents. Mom coming out, snapping pictures. I grabbed the camera and took a snap of Emily as she began to swing higher and higher. Her blonde hair and a bright smile radiating toward me.

The sound of Brian's door as it creaked open woke me up, slowly bringing me back into reality. I looked over at his nightstand clock, 2:00. I could hear him quietly taking off his uniform. The velcro coming apart, unbuttoning his holster, untying his boots, laying his badge on his dresser, and the slight screech of his metal safe door closing, a safe place he stores his gun. I could then feel him quietly slide into bed, coming up right behind me as he brings one arm around me, squeezes tightly once, then releases but keeps holding me. The safest place I've ever felt.

◆ ◆ ◆

I walked back into Brian's room with two cups of coffee and pajama pants on with puffy eyes. I think neither of us got much sleep and as hectic as last night was, I believe today was going to be as hectic. We dealt with the same situation, just now with the sun out, with more people pulled in, an anxious town, and hundreds of unanswered questions. This morning I prayed that I woke up to proof that this was all just a dream.

Steam engulfed the bedroom as Brian

walked out of his bathroom, hair wet with a blue towel tightly wrapped around his waist. He smelled of Old Spice and pine. I gave him a smile as I handed him his fresh cup. Taking a quick few sips then ran his dry hand through his wet hair. There was something I needed to tell him, but I didn't want to worry him or add any more to the stress. I was supposed to go to work. But, something was preventing me from leaving. I had to tell Brian.

"So, I know where that photo of Emily found inside that book at Chloe's crime scene came from," I said as I looked over at Brian. He was halfway putting his pants on when he stopped and faced me.

"Where is it from?"

"It's the exact same one I have in my office at school." There was an instant silence, "I have that same picture framed on my desk." Flashbacks of last night began storming back in. I took a sip of my coffee.

"Then it looks like we're heading straight to your office this morning." Brian said, buttoning up his uniform.

"Okay, There is also something I want to show you, but it's at my house. I'm going to shower and change. I'll call you when I leave," I said, walking toward him. We looked at each other for a few seconds, gave the, we're in this together look as he then leaned in and kissed me goodbye.

We both walked into the front office of the school at the same time. The feel of the cold air conditioning gives me slight goosebumps. To no surprise, the front office was quieter today. Sandy was in the back making copies, while Principal Miller was on the phone in his office. But that was it. No students patiently waiting to call their parents. No teachers buzzing in the teacher's lounge. Even the front office phone took the day off. The horrors of the night patiently wait for us to wake up, it craves our attention—no matter where we go or what we do. The fears are now with us, in pure daylight, and there is no single person in sight.

I opened the door and flipped the light on, and they're sitting on my desk was the picture, still in the frame. Neatly standing.

"Is that the picture?" Brian asked.

"Yes, yes, it is." But something was off after I had stared at it for a while. The positioning was off, as I would always use the empty space next to it to stack files. I knew not to put the frame that far over. "Wait, Brian, that frame has been moved. I can tell, that is not where I had it."

"Alright, grab your laptop and some essential stuff, we're going to dust this room. It will then be closed off as it is now a part of a crime scene," Brian said. I tried to process what he just said about my office being a part of a crime scene and trying to think which essential files I would need as I unplugged my laptop. Brian walked out the door, instructing dispatch to send officers and a crime scene technician to the high school.

"I was not expecting any of this to happen." I shut my office door and walked toward Brian, laptop, and files inside my leather tote. "There is still something I want to show you. At first, I just chalked it up to someone playing a sick joke, to realizing what transpired last night" I set my leather tote on the table next to us, and began searching through my purse. Brian was patiently waiting.

"What do you have?"

"Here, I found this in the outside crease of my door a few weeks ago." I said as I handed Brian the evil letter I received, about Emily.

I took over one of the study rooms inside the library as my temporary office. I still wanted to remain connected and accessible to the students or parents. They are going to spend the weekend dusting my office. The morbid letter and the book, *The Night the Angels Cried*, to see if they could find a consistent print: Tyler's, or a mysterious third party. I still don't understand how he could have snuck into my office and swiped that picture? He must have made a copy then put the original back. After I showed Brian the letter I received, it was apparent I was being

targeted, but why? Brian got extremely protective and escalated the investigation. He didn't
want me to be alone. Insisted I stay at his house,
and instructed the department to begin monitoring my calls. The concern was if Tyler was
working alone or had an accomplice that is still
at large.

Brian had to head back to the station
while he let the technician continue to photo-
graph my office. Principal Miller called a Friday
half-day for student and faculty bereavement.
The halls were full of whispers, even in the
teacher's lounge, gossip not only about Chloe
but also about Michelle and Tyler. Word began
to spread that Tyler is with Child Protective
Services because police arrested his mother and
were unable to locate his father. I was trying to
be productive today, but my mind was in ten
different places. My mom said they were going
to come down and stay for a little bit, which
is probably the best thing for me right now, be
around family. She promised to bring the dogs.

Brian and I talked throughout the day, he
said they found a journal in Tyler's room full of
mystic drawings of each suicide, short stories,
and poems. He said they also collected the black
Nike shoe box. I told Brian I would stop by the
station after work. I sent a few texts to Nicole,
checking in. She is beating herself up pretty bad
over Chloe. She blames herself as she was teaching her to swim. I should stop by the house

first before heading to the station, see how she is going. I then heard a knock on my temporary office door, it was Sandy.

"Hello, dear, I just wanted to let you know they are about to send the kids home."

"Okay that's good. They should really be at home and with family. When you take into account these last few months, it's been a lot on them."

"I know. For all of us. Even you. How are you holding up?"

"I'm trying to remain strong for the kids, be here to help them, guide them through this troubling time. It's never easy, losing a friend, a classmate, a sister. That stuff follows you. But you cannot let it control and define you, for the worst."

"Bless you, Jennifer. Well, Eddie is about to pick me up. Is there anything you need before I go?"

"No, you try and enjoy the rest of your day, thanks for checking in, Sandy."

"Of course. We have to look out for each other. If you're not doing anything later, my dear friend Eleanor is coming over to bake and watch television if you would like to join us," Sandy offered.

"Thank you, Sandy, that's a kind offer. I'll call you if I find myself in need of girl time." Sandy then walked into my office and gave me a hug.

◆ ◆ ◆

The station was chilly, I don't know why they keep it so cold. I saw a few familiar faces around the station, like Deputy Gomez and Deputy Flynn. They, too, looked exhausted. Brian was just finishing up some reports, so Deputy Gomez showed me to his office. I could wait. His desk was messy with papers and a few photos of him and Nicole.

I sat behind his desk and picked up his red and blue stress ball, Emerald Texas County Sheriff's Department. I gave it a few squeezes.

"Hey Jen, how's that stress ball?" Brian asked with a smile.

"It's actually just making my muscles sore, probably adding to the stress." I tossed the ball on his desk, he walked over and kissed me

"I stopped by your house to check on Nicole," I said.

"Thank You. How is she doing? I wanted to stop by for lunch, but the day gets ahead of me."

"She seems to be doing better, she was cuddled up on the couch watching her favorite romcom. She said Mark was coming over when school was let out. Do you know he stayed the night last night?"

"He what?"

"It's okay, it's okay, she didn't need to be alone. She has been beating herself up over Chloe's death. I think it's good for her to be around people, and not be alone," Brian then walked over and sat in the chair in front of his desk. "This fucking kid, this fucking psychopath. Just bringing pain and destruction to everyone and everything," Brian said as he began to pull some items out of a bag labeled EVIDENCE. "Here, check this out." I leaned my hand over and grabbed color copies of Tyler's journal. "We sent the journal for evidence processing. This was all premeditated. Tyler knew what was going to happen. Hell, he probably encouraged it, set the whole scene for them. I will see to it that that fucking psychopath is locked up. It fucking pisses me off how close he was to Nicole, the thought of how he could have encouraged her to hurt herself."

I looked at Brian with soft eyes, understanding his pain and frustration. It was then that there was a knock at the door, it was Deputy Flynn, he popped his head in real quick,

"Sorry to interrupt, Sheriff, but you have a call about that domestic abuse case from last week."

"Alright. Thanks, Flynn. I'll be right back." Brian said to me. I looked back down at the journal. A stack of copies stapled together. The outside copy made it appear brand new, no writing or drawings until I opened it up. These stories sound like him and William making some hike, *The Shepherd's Trail*?

Title: *SUMMER of 2015* written at the top. I scanned through the story, he was so infatuated with William. A few lines from his story stood out to me; he wrote in here that William was 'confused' and also interested in him in a romantic way.

"I felt like there was something invisible between us, an un-foreseeable being pulling and twisting us together."
"A playful flirt."
"A milli-second laps in time, I was in his arms, and exactly three heartbeats later, we kissed."

I kept flipping the pages. One was completely gray. Gray pencil from top to bottom, and in the center, faint words in pen spelling out something, hard to read until I got really close, "MakeGregandlizziebelieve."

Shit. Fucking shit. The pencil shading looked like a garage filled with smoke. This was so difficult to see, knowing everything from the very beginning. Having talked to the parents, hearing their grief and pain, now seeing all this. All these signs are pointing to several mental disorders, his inability to feel remorse, compassion for other people. I thought how during our meetings, he about must have pretended to be showing remorse for his fellow classmates. He was lying to me from the very beginning. He knew it all. I still don't understand why with all the names he writes, Make so and so believe, in what? In his psychotic reasoning? In his fucked up way, he views human life? This doesn't make sense.

I was addicted to what I was reading, what I was seeing. Tyler's journal dates back to when he first went to camp. That must have been when he first saw and met William. Another story title read: *WINTER of 2017.*

"This has been our fourth time doing this hike."
"It became a flow, a routine of intertwining each other into one another. Reading the other, gentle observations fueling the ever-expanding idea of us."
"he grabbed the back of my neck, leaning me in for a kiss."

I cannot believe this, and there, those numbers again, 11:28. It says he writes as if it's their two favorite numbers? How could he know William's favorite number? Then it hit me, the Bible verse he used at the beginning of those terrifying, disturbing videos. Matthew 11:28. That Bible verse has to be the real meaning behind those numbers.

"So every night our watches go off at 11:28, it was my idea, I thought of it last winter."

The next page was all red. A red marker that seemed to be running down the entire page, slowly running down like spilled paint, and along the legs to the far left, "makecameronbelieve."

Goosebumps raced down my arms, starting from my shoulders, quick flashes of Cameron bleeding to death in his own bathtub. It was literally his entire inner forearms. His left side was worse than his right, making me wonder if Cameron didn't have the strength to continue on his right arm as he began to lose consciousness. I remember from the video his right cut mark was half the length of his left. I still don't understand how he convinced three of his classmates to take their own life. It was then another story.

Title: *SPRING of 2019*, that's the same time that William accidentally shot himself. I could feel the pain, I could feel Tyler trying to process what had just happened, and maybe, possibly, the beginning to all of this in Lincoln.

"I leaned my head over and cried myself to sleep."
"Down the side of my neck is where I would feel his warm breaths go."
"The alarm on *William's black wristwatch was going off.*"

At the bottom of the page, he wrote on all caps: "EVERYTHING HE DID WAS BEAUTIFUL."
It was then Brian came back into his office, I was so focused on this journal the door opening startled me, I jumped.

"Brian this journal is intense and insane. This explains so much. Tyler has a serious mental health problem. He believes his own lies and the stories he tells. He shows zero signs of remorse or empathy. Except to a boy with whom he never dated but claims they were in love." I slowly closed the journal and set it back on Brian's desk.

"You mean William Ackhurst?"

"Yeah," I scratched the back of my head, pondering my thoughts. "A part of me thinks Tyler wanted me gone, out of Lincoln, I honestly believe he wanted me to stop trying to help at the school."

"Well he couldn't get rid of ya. That's for sure," Brian said, trying to make me feel better. "He's going to be tried and convicted for all the fucked up shit he did, I can guarantee that. Mental health issues or not, the state of Arizona does not have an insanity defense. He's going away for a long time."

"We also obtained unedited footage of each suicide from various tapes he had, it's fucked up. All the shit he pulled, after watching the unedited footage, you can definitely tell his intentions were for them to die."

"So you're saying Greg, Lizzie, Cameron, and Chloe did not want to die?" I asked.

"Not according to the unedited footage we obtained. Tyler would talk to the victims a little before, ensuring them it was all for a scene for a film project. With Greg and Lizzie, you can hear that Tyler will open the garage door once the scene is done. They thought they were making a modern-day *Romeo and Juliet*. Tyler said in the footage how he wanted the garage to get really smokey for effect, but he never opened the garage door."

"Brian, where is Tyler right now?" I asked

"He is here. In one of the cells. We are moving him to Berza County Jail tomorrow. Michelle is here too. She has been meeting with a lawyer all day. It turns out her husband Ricky was the one supplying the dealer with the drugs. We are going after Billy Porter for lying to authorities."

"Are you serious?"

"Yeah, it's a mess. We took K-9 Freedom around the Tuckerman house last night and found where Ricky was stashing the pills. He hid them under their single-wide home. Two five-gallon buckets were full of Xanax and Oxy. Who knows how long he ran this operation for. He got in with a big drug dealer, and Michelle says he used his semi-truck to transport the drugs. Once Michelle found out he was involved in mass distribution, she kicked him out. The pills we found in her room were part of her actual prescription. She didn't know he was still storing buckets under her single-wide," Brian said.

"Where is Ricky?"

"We're looking for Ricky. We didn't tell Michelle the case against Tyler. Our fear is after we tell her, she might not help us with the case against Ricky. Like it said, it's a mess. The state sent out a guardian ad litem for Tyler. She arrived a few hours ago."

"Ad litem?"

"Guardian ad litem, they don't have custody over the minor but instead help the judge determine what is in the child's best interest. In Arizona, they are required for foster care cases, a child in juvenile court, or neglect cases. Never requested one for an underaged serial killer before."

"You mentioned Tyler was here?"

"He's meeting with his guardian ad litem now. I think they said her name was Amanda." Brian replied. I then had an idea.

"Can I ask for a favor?"

"Yeah, of course."

"This may sound weird, and totally out of protocol, but can I meet with Tyler before he is sent to Berza County? I need to try and understand why he did what he did. I was targeted, He reminded me of my little sister's death: the letter, the photo, and Chloe. Please, Brian, I need to know for me. Let me talk with him, I'll approach it as a counseling session." I grabbed both my hands and placed it on his desk, looking up at him, my eyes were wide and soft, but my heart was red, hot, and ready for combat.

"Let me talk with Sergeant Ramierz and see what we can do. But you know Amanda will have to sit in on the meeting."

"I understand. That's okay."

"Alright, I'll see what we can do," Brian

said as he again got up and left his office. I hope this works out. I need to understand why he did it. I started getting a few docs ready and started jotting down ideas and possible arguments I would make, especially if Tyler denies the whole thing, then what? Just call him a liar and leave the room? I need him to confess.

◆ ◆ ◆

Sergeant Ramirez walked me down a long hallway, white flooring with long fluorescent bulbs lined the ceiling. The station only has one interrogation room. It's mostly used for the storage of old files and office furniture. As we approached the door, my heart started to pick up, the feeling you get right before you have to go on stage and speak in front of an audience. Tyler was in the room, waiting.

A short blonde lady stood outside the room. She was wearing a black blazer with black slacks and two-inch black heels, she looked our way and smiled.

"My name is Amanda Gregson. I'm Tyler's guardian ad litem."

"Amanda hello, I'm Jennifer Hall. I was Tyler's mental health counselor at the high school."

"Hello Jennifer. Sergeant Ramirez was

telling me you wished to see Tyler? May I ask what it is regarding first?"

"Our session yesterday was cut short. I want to finish where we left off. Give Tyler the opportunity to finish telling me what he wanted to tell me. Be ears for him."

"I completely understand." Amanda replied as she placed both her hands together. "I'll have my chair in the back corner of the room."
I walked in to see Tyler on the other side of the table. There was one light above our heads, your stereotypical interrogation style room. Amanda sat in the corner behind Tyler.

"Ms. Hall? I am so glad to see you." Why am I here? Can I go home? Where is my mom? What is going on?" Tyler frantically said. He had dark circles under his eyes.

"Tyler, your mom is doing fine. I am not here to get you out, I just want to talk. Would you like some water?" I then got up and tapped on the door, asking Sergeant Ramirez if he would fetch us some water.

"Talk about what? Ms. Hall, why am I here? I want to go home. My dad will be worried if my mom and I are not home. I'm sure he is already stressing." He did look worried, confused, but he has to know the reason why he is here.

"Tyler, do you honestly not know why you're here?" He has to know but just doesn't want to tell me. He has been lying to me the second I moved to Lincoln. He keeps looking down, barely keeping eye contact.

"I honestly don't know why I am here, please let me go home," Tyler said, still looking down, he then started scratching his eyes. Was he trying to make it appear like he was crying?

"Are you religious at all, Ty?" I asked, just then a knock at the door, Sergeant Ramirez was back with two cups of water.

"Thanks, Gabe," I said, grabbing both cups and sliding one over to Tyler.

"Not really," Tyler said, taking another sip. "Why are you asking me that? When I first came out to my mom, I was forced to go to the East Side Church every Sunday. The great Lord could save me, the ever-loving Lord, who loves all his children as they say, but not enough to love me. I am not religious." Tyler is still barely making any eye contact.

"I am sorry that your mother and society were not accepting at the time. Things are changing, society is changing for the better, they will accept." Then that got me thinking if Tyler was trying to play the sympathy card, my fondness for helping people was leaning into what he was saying if it was true or not.

"Why are you asking me if i'm religious? Are you religious?"

"To some degree, yes. I believe the ones we love remain with us, through our love for them. Have you heard of the Bible verse, Matthew 11:28? If you haven't I can recite it for you."

Tyler remained quiet. Taking a sip of his water.

"It sounds familiar," Tyler replied.

"Tyler, are you still not going to tell me why you think you're in here?"

"They found some stuff in my mom's room. I saw Sheriff Clark walk out of my mom's room with a bag of orange bottles. That could be why. Maybe they think I was helping her sell them? Which I wasn't and why you need to help me get out. This is all a misunderstanding, you have to believe me, Ms. Hall."

"They found the video footage of each suicide on your laptop in your bedroom."

I didn't want to be so blunt, but I needed to drop the bomb. I then got extremely nervous, fuck, I forgot for a split second that Amanda was still in the back corner. I am not sure if I was allowed to tell Tyler that? She hasn't said anything to me yet. Tyler then slowly picked his head up and looked at me directly in the eyes.

TYLER TUCKERMAN

They fucking went snooping through my bedroom? I knew it. I knew they would never understand art, never understand beauty. I just kept staring at Ms. Hall, I felt her line of questioning, asking over and over, why I thought I was here. How could I be here for that? Releasing people free, deep down, they all wanted it, Greg, Lizzie, Cameron, and Chloe. We all got something out of it. I got to experience a beautiful transition, and they were set free. It was a win-win. I was no longer going to cooperate with this bitch. My mom was right, she is a fucking cunt.

"They asked me to film it."

"You're saying each student individually approached you and asked you to film their deaths?" Ms. Hall asked as if she didn't just hear what I said. "Why would they want you to film it?"

"Yes, and I don't know. I was just willing to help." Damn, should I spell it out for her?

Them all asking me wasn't exactly right, but she doesn't need to know that she doesn't deserve to know my creative process, how it took weeks of planning. Greg and Lizzie were probably the easiest to convince. I didn't exactly tell them they would be set free; everyone loves surprises. I am sure they are both in their eternal *room* together, just like in my favorite Jean-Paul Sarte play. Ms. Johnson recently had us read *Romeo and Juliet*. I was always obsessed with that play. True love. I approached Greg and Lizzie, who was already dating for a while about doing a film project. They were totally on board. "Adversity's sweet milk, philosophy" I needed it to be authentic. Be real.

We decided to film the death scene the same night as graduation, they had the idea to wear a cap and gown. They first wanted to use a fog machine, but I insisted on the real thing. I also may have promised to quickly open the garage door after twenty seconds of filming. To make sure they didn't get up and open the garage door themselves, I snuck a few of my mom's Xanax and oxy to help them relax. I read movie stars do it all the time. They were both pretty tipsy before filming, so that probably sped things up. After I got my scene, I left. Completely blown away and star-struck by watching their release. All I could think of was, Woah, this happened to William.

"Why didn't you try and help them? Not help them kill themselves, but help them seek professional help?" Ms. Hall asked. She just doesn't get it, she never will get it. I didn't know about the beauty of suicide until my sweet William led me there. Everything he did was beautiful, and so I had to witness it first hand, I was instantly hooked, like a drug. It was the first time I felt genuinely connected to William since he died.

"But I did help them, Ms. Hall. I helped them get what they wanted."

"Tyler, helping your classmates die by suicide is not helping them. Do you understand what I am saying?"

"Ms. Hall, I don't think you understand what I am saying. You have your own way of helping people, and I have mine. We are clearly two different people. I like to help people the same way you do, just different philosophies."
It was then Amanda cleared her throat and chimed in. I actually forgot she was in the room.

"Tyler, you have the power to leave this room if you wish."

Maybe I should. Just get up and leave, have Jennifer hanging with the thought of how I just compared us to helping people. None of my searches on Jennifer yielded anything unusual about her. Old. Single. Christian. Until I learned why the family never went on another camping trip again. Until I learned what happened to her when she was twelve-years-old. I actually got somewhat jealous, that must have been a flawless transition to witness.

JENNIFER HALL

"Okay, thanks, Amanda. I think we're wrapping up here shortly," Tyler said.

He is never going to tell me the truth. He is never going to say to me that he forced these suicides, that Tyler coaxed them into dying just so he could get off on his sick fantasy.

"We don't know why people are led to commit such terrible acts, anyone could later be drawn to take their own life, which makes me wonder, given the trendiness of it. Do you think if Emily still had consciousness, she would have eventually killed herself?" Tyler asked.

My stomach going ice-cold; it was him. He was behind that mysterious letter I found outside my place. This monster was so incredibly calculating that you have no idea how bad I wanted to reach over this table and punch him across the face. How dare he? I wasn't going to get anywhere, he would just continue to lie to me. He doesn't trust me, it was then that I knew what I had to do, play fire with fire. I had to *Make Tyler Believe*, believe that we are the same, only then would he open up to me. This was going to be the most challenging thing I've ever had to do. Forgive me, Emily, as I now have to lie to make him be*lie*ve.

"You don't know the full story of what happened to my little sister?"

"I have internet access. She fell into a lake and drowned while you and your parents were camping," Tyler said.

"That is true, we were all camping. I was twelve, and Emily was eight. I've never told anyone this, but she didn't fall by accident. I pushed her into the lake, knowing she couldn't swim." I was trying so hard to hold back tears, that was so incredibly difficult to say out loud. I am so sorry, Emily. Tyler looked up at me with a devilish grin, and then with curiosity. "Wow, yeah, I never told anyone that. She always got all the attention, all the love from both our parents, and I was pushed out, forgotten." I even pretended to choke up, "I wanted things to go back to the way they were. Before Emily was born, where I got all the love. Where I was an only child. No, Tyler, I don't think you deserve to be here because you helped people die. After all, I did it too, I killed my little sister." You could tell Tyler was enjoying this conversation now, his posture changed, he was more attentive, I hope it was working. Please be working, so those words I just said weren't for nothing.

"Tyler, I think we should leave," Amanda

said as she stood up.

"Wait, not yet, Amanda. What did you feel as you watched her drown?" Tyler asked, then taking a sip of his water.

"Alive, it was such a rush." I decided to use a few lines from his journal, a way in which he would be able to understand. "I could feel her release, her transition. It was an amazing feeling."

"Right!" and right then is when the first smile erupted on his face.

"To make my conscious feel better, I became a counselor to help kids. But I want to feel that release again, watch another transition."

"I felt the same way after Greg and Lizzie! Watching Cameron's transition was so much more fulfilling. His was even easier to make happen. I gave him a few of my mom's Xanax and oxy until he became loopy, then I walked him to his bathtub, fed him more, and more until he fell asleep. I forgot how incredibly sharp a razor blade is and how fragile your skin is, it was like slicing butter."

I cannot believe what I am hearing, Cameron never died by suicide, I knew it, I just knew it.

"I did a little on the right then really went for it on the left arm. Turned the shower on, then quickly ran behind my camera and began filming. Ms. Hall, we have so much in common. I underestimated you. However, no matter how many transitions I watch, they will never compare to the feeling I got when I looked into William's warm blue eyes."

It worked! He told me the truth about how the suicides occurred, or I should say murders. Right when I think he couldn't be more sick and twisted, he says all that. I have to keep this going.

"You mean William Ackhurst?"

"Yes. My sweet William. I miss him every day."

"I am so sorry for your loss, Tyler. The police found photographs of him in your room. Inside your shoebox."

"My memory box," Tyler said softly.

"Why is every picture of William taken while he was asleep?"

"He was a beautiful sleeper."

"Would you ever sleep in his bed?" I remembered a few lines from his journal, detailing the way Williams bed smelled and felt.

"Sometimes." I wonder when he would, "I sometimes would when William would sneak out, crawl into his bed just for a bit. I was keeping it warm for him."

So what he wrote in his journal was right, he would sleep in William's bed. I just like to hope the masturbation in William's bed part he wrote was fiction.

"So he doesn't know you took these photographs?"

"I was going to tell him, surprise him with

something. Until he decided to set himself free."

"The transition," I replied. I don't think anyone has told Tyler that William's death was an accident. William did not die by suicide. And I think just the thought of it though, was Tyler's favorite part. "Hey Ty, I'm curious, how did the transition feel with Chloe?" I asked him. Tyler was admiring his wrist, running his finger over it, where a watch would be.

"Oh even better than Cameron's. They keep getting better and better. The feeling more intense. I used the same trick, snuck some Xanax, and oxy. I told Chloe we were shooting a music video. Then just like what you did to Emily, I pushed her in," Tyler said as he eventually looked up at me. I was holding my breath as he described every detail.

"And you left that book and a photo of my sister at the scene?"

"That was before I knew we were the same. I was trying to scare you so you would leave town. After I read a few articles online about what had happened to your family, the next transition I wanted to witness would involve water. Your story inspired me. Water is a very tricky thing to film. But my underwater attachment became so helpful."

My face was becoming red hot, I couldn't lose my composure, I just stared directly at him, without blinking. One Mississippi. Two Mississippi. Three Mississippi. Four Mississippi. I was interviewing a monster. In the presence of evil. Pure evil.

"How did you get that photo?"

"I went to high school with my mom one Saturday morning. She was getting stuff ready for a board meeting. I snuck into your office and made a copy of the picture." Keep the truths rolling in you little shit.

"And why did you choose, *The Night the Angels Cried*?"

"Because the little girl dies. Killed by someone in her own family. I didn't realize how accurate it was going to be. See, everything happens for a reason."

I took a sip of my water, then another, then another, until my cup was empty.

"Everything happens for a reason," I told him. "You're right about that. And I must say, that verse you used before each video was so beautiful, so meaningful. But, if you're not religious, why use Matthew 11:28?"

"If I was religious, I would gravitate to the Old Testament. I feel that God would understand me more. More than this New Testament God, that is all about love."

"You read the Old Testament?"

"Yeah. Holy shit, it was long," Tyler laughed. "Get it? Holy shit. While I was reading, I felt like that God was similar to me. He enjoys witnessing the transitions—so much death in the Old Testament, especially the death of children.

I didn't know what to say, but I had to say something, direct the conversation. I was trying to figure out, from Tyler's fucked up perspective, why he chose Matthew 11:28, I don't even think it's in the Old Testament.

"So, why that particular verse?"

"Because I am giving them rest. Greg, Lizzie, Cameron, Chloe. I knew deep down they were weary and burdened, so they came to me, and I gave them rest," Tyler said. To think when I thought he couldn't sound anymore crazy, he rationalizes his murders with Bible verses. I watched as Tyler took the last sip of his water, his eyes were closed and mine wide open, glaring directly at him. "And I'll repeat it, I am sorry I lied to you, I just had to so you would believe me. Because you can't spell 'believe' without, *lie*," Tyler joked.

For years there has always been the argument of nature versus nurture. Are human behaviors determined by genes or by the environment? There is no doubt that Tyler suffers from a chemical imbalance, a few receptors turned off. A poisonous mind. But what about if nurture exacerbates nature? Accelerating cancer spreading inside him.

Tyler being gay, came to define him in the eyes of others but was not how he identified himself. The plans his parents had for him were cut short, their expectations ruined. Many teens have physical aftermaths upon coming out: kicked out of homes, violence, cut off from families, their past shunning them. But with Tyler, he got nothing. He wasn't hugged by his mother or drunkenly punched by his father. He was the only one among his peers, and not a single one embraced him. I believe that the world of isolation caused him to live too much in his own head, and in the world, he saw through his camera lens. He told the world who he was. He put it out there, and all he found was an emptiness.

"I can forgive you for lying, but that's it. You are right, Tyler, you cannot spell believe without, lie," I grabbed my empty cup, stood up, leaned over, and grabbed Tyler's empty cup. "Thanks for the chat Tyler, I sincerely hope that one day you find rest, genuine rest of your soul. Where you look at yourself and everything that has happened. Use your curiosity for philosophical reasoning to fully comprehend the existential crisis you're going through, and discover compassion. As Voltaire once said, 'Every man is guilty of all the good he didn't do.' You also cannot spell 'believe' without '*be evil*'." I pushed my chair in and turned around for the door.

"Wait, wait, Ms.Hall, We're the same, remember? You're going to help me get out, right?" I opened the door and turned to look at Tyler, answering him.

"No."

♦ ♦ ♦

I walked back to Brian's office and gave him a huge hug. We stood there for a few seconds, processing what just happened.

"That was more difficult than I thought it was going to be," I said as Brian unclipped this small black box from the back of my jeans, untapped the chord that ran up my side and clipped to my bra.

"Did we get it?" Brian asked.

"We got him. Confession to four counts of murder in the first degree," I said.

"I'm so proud of you, Jen. You should consider applying for the force," Brian joked. "Your parents just arrived. Your Dad called not too long ago."

"Thank heavens, I miss them so much."

"Let's go take them to lunch," Brian suggested.

"Where should we go?" I asked.

"Well, there aren't too many options. We could go to the Desert Flower Cafe? Tell them this was the place of our first date."

"Perfect! I'm so excited to see them, we can take my car."

PART THREE: WILL THE KIDS BE ALRIGHT

TYLER TUCKERMAN

So much metal, steel, and iron surrounds me every day and every night. Large bolts pounded into the iron to support the stairs, railings, and doors. My floor is bare concrete, cold and unwanted like so many that surround me. The tables with attached chairs are silver polished. Permanently installed fixture scattered about the main living area, where all the exceedingly offensive and strangely foul juveniles hangout. This all feels like a dream. I have been here for a few weeks. Which may as well be a few years. I know that I am going to wake up any minute, wake up in my cozy bed, and in the arms of my warm blue eyes. The first thing I see when I wake up every morning is bricks, pale cheap white bricks, not my warm blue eyes, not my little nightstand or bookshelf, but fucking bricks.

◆ ◆ ◆

I hate the damn morning rituals. Every

morning at precisely 7 AM, they round us up and make us stand in line like a bunch of dairy cattle. We all have the same oversized onesies. White with black stripes, or black with white strips? Like I said, dairy cows that had gastric bypass. I had on black rubber flip-flops trying to walk directly on the yellow line on the ground, the yellow line directing us all to the showers. I wish this were the line for the gas chambers instead. Just put me out of my misery.

You could hear shouting, whistling, and catcalls erupting from the showers, fucking juveniles. They give you exactly five minutes to lather, rinse, and repeat here at Berza County Detention Center for Juveniles. The water is reasonably hot, but we're all packed into a shared shower room. I'm still extremely uncomfortable getting naked in front of the other inmates. Everyone is all so rowdy. It reminds me of the football locker room back at school. I hated walking in there when Coach asked me to go into his office to hand over the game footage.

SLAP! Ugh, also, you're continually being smacked by wet towels as the guys swing it over their shoulders to scrub their backs. I always try to get the shower done as quickly as possible, then head back to change and eat breakfast before a colossal line forms. I'm not one to engage in conversations, I try to keep to myself. Usually, that means sitting alone and not making eye contact. Everyone here is fucking dumb, the way they talk and what they talk about. Ugh. The only thing I know for sure is the exact time, right on the dot when I wake up, eat breakfast, lunch, and dinner, and what time I will go to bed. So strictly regimented.

I got my small tray of eggs and what looks like slop, swine slop that's a mixture of various foods, and one carton of milk. I usually try to eat alone, the sad cafeteria is always so full, this place seemed a little crowded. My cellmate, Jordan West, sat down next to me. He is gaunt and annoying, I think he's fifteen or sixteen, but the way he talks he might as well be twelve. He has a few tattoos on his arms and legs. I have no idea what the significance of those is.

"Sup cuz, aye this fuckin soup is bomb man," Jordan said as he sat next to me, I wish he hadn't. I think he is going through some identity issues. He talks as if he's some cool thug when he's probably the whitest guy here.

"I'll trade your milk for my slop," I suggested.

"Alright, cuz. Bring your tray over and pour it on mine."

"Here, you just do it."

"Thanks cuz. Aye, you want to go hang on the quad when we're done? Maybe play some ball?"

"No, I have a meeting," I lied. I try to spend most of my days in the small library they have. It's a sad excuse for one, but I'll take it. Jordan appears to be halfway done, slurping the slop down, so gross. He's not the brightest juvenile. Not too long ago, he was arrested for grand theft auto. He did manage to steal the car, as well as a one-year-old strapped in the back seat, so they got him for kidnapping as well. They caught him as he tried to flee to Mexico, he set the car seat with the baby strapped in on the sidewalk once he discovered a stowaway, dumbass. I guess he was pretty close to the border, a coward trying to escape his punishment.

"Aye, I'm gonna head out to the quad, cuz. Hit me up if you decide to go out there." Jordan said as he got up and put his tray away. I just smiled and nodded, I was not going out there. A fight always breaks out on the quad, these fucking juveniles try to act as if they are in a real, thug infested, gang dominated prison. I need my Wiliam here with me, I need my warm blue eyes to be looking at me, telling me everything will be okay. Just then, a detention guard came up and told me I had a visitor. I quickly got up, and he escorted me to the visitation room. A few people scattered about small two-seater tables, a few tears, a few laughs echoed around the room.

It was my mom. I walked up, and I gave her a huge hug. This is only the second time she has visited me. She looked tired, exhausted. Her makeup glanced done as if she had done it in the car once she arrived. We sat at the table.

"Did you bring it? Did you bring what I asked?"

"Yes Ty, I gave it to the guards, and they said they will take it to your room." Last time I mentioned to my mom how the library here sucks and how I wanted my favorite play to read, my journal to doodle, and to marvelously creative poems as an outlet. I am so happy to hear that you agreed and let me hand them over to me.

"Yes, they technically considered it a donation to a particular cell. So Ty, how have you been? You look thin, are you eating enough? Are they feeding you properly?"

"Yes I'm eating, when it's appealing and not slop. Mom, I want to leave this place. Why do I have to stay here until my trial? I hate it here."

"Ty we talked about this. You were denied bail. So until your trial, you have to remain here. Be happy they agreed to keep you in this juvenile facility and not at an adult prison. Don't worry, the lawyer who helped me also said he can take your case, he's good."

"The same lawyer who pinned the drug sales on Dad?"

"Now you listen, your father was not so innocent," she paused, took a slight exhale. "Ty let's not get into that."

"Were you also able to bring my camera?"

"No, they would not allow that, sorry, son." Well fuck. I miss filming. I miss playing make-believe and witnessing the world through my lens, seeing my world. I just remained quiet, arms folded, and leaned back into my seat.

"Ty, don't get mad, you will have your play and journal. Are you making any friends here? It might take some time, remember a few years ago when I first took you to summer camp, you hated it. You refused to go and labeled it a prison. But then what happened? You made friends and wanted to go every chance you could."

Did she really just compare the two? And why would she bring up William? I'm over this conversation. I wonder if she lost her job as a result of the arrest?

"How's work going?" my turn to twist the knife.

"I'm still on leave. Ty just so you know, I'm selling the house. I cannot afford to live there. I've been staying with Susan." She is selling my home, the only place I've ever known to feel pain and be okay with it. I didn't want to respond. Everything in the outside world was changing, and not for the better. I know she traveled far to see me, but I'm over this conversation.

"I think I'm going to hit the library and read my favorite play or draw. Thanks for coming to visit. See you next weekend?"

"Probably not next weekend. It's expensive driving all the way up here. You probably won't see me for a while, Ty."

This was her way of getting rid of me, I knew it, she was just like everyone else. I decided to rip the bandage off, I stood up and gave her a hug and had the detention guard escort me back inside hell.

◆ ◆ ◆

I was sitting at a desk in the library, reading one of the few novels they have. I decided to stop here before heading back to my cell, where my items my mom brought me were. The majority of the books are self-help, personal development style writing, not my style. Still, I understand why they offer them, these juveniles could really use some personal development. I was deep in this crappy novel when I felt a presence walk by, I looked over, and it was Darnell Thompson. He's the third kid in my cell. Due to overcrowding, they stack three people in a battery, they are relatively large, but damn, three people.

Darnell looked at me and gave a slight head nod. He was tall, black, and in pretty good shape as he had been in this detention center since he was thirteen-years-old. His stepdad was abusive, especially toward his mom. One night, Darnell shot him, one shot in the back right after abusing his her. It makes sense; he was defending his mother. The kid was probably terrified and quickly grew up and became a man that night. They both asked me what I was in for, I told them I was an artist who was caught with unlawful creative pieces, they just assumed I robbed an art gallery.

A few kids were in the room, playing cards and board games. They keep a selection of activities to do on the weekend and after hours. During the week, since we're all juveniles, we have to attend "school" aka pack up all in a few rooms and call it school, a sad excuse for one. I rarely pay attention as all the stuff they are teaching is irrelevant to me. I've learned that already, my journal will come in handy, doodle all day as they teach us 1 + 1 = 2.

As I was walking back to our cell, I could hear Darnell yelling from inside our room.

"What the fuck bro, where the fuck is my ramen noodles, bro! I'm going to whoop some ass, what the fuck!" He sounded like he was throwing things around, really upset he couldn't find his noodles. I totally get it; from what I've found out, those things are a hot commodity. This is the second time his noodles have gone missing and a few of his cigarettes. I decided to not go into our room and headed back to the library. I don't think Darnell likes Jordan very much, Darnell is surely a homophobe, which is why I try to avoid him and remain quiet around him as possible.

My mom has been putting some money in my account here to buy basic necessities like soap, shampoo, toothpaste, and on occasion, ramen noodles. For a few days I've been saving, I stopped buying a few things. I usually purchase ramen every day, but I was saving. I wanted to buy an assortment of colorful markers, so I could continue to doodle after my mom bought me a new journal. Write and tell stories about William and I. Get my mind off these bare white brick walls and out into the world, wherever we wanted to go.

On some day's time moves reasonably quickly, we had already eaten dinner, and I was in our cell lying down. I have the top bunk as that is the least desired, and I'm at the bottom of the totem pole. Jordan had his bed under-mine, and Darnell has his own separate bed with no top bunk, as he was the alpha of the room. I was lying on my thin, sad excuse for a mattress looking up at the white ceiling—the play *No Exit* on my stomach and my new journal by my side. Darnell was doing pushups close to the cell door, and Jordan was retaking a shit. I hate it here.

It hit me that reality has a funny way

of circling back, making you live through the things you love, dear. I was in shock, the kind of excitement where I slightly laughed to one-self. The universe was punishing me, making me live through my favorite play, *No Exit*. Here I was trapped for eternity in this room with two other souls, always surrounded by other people. Constantly surrounded by and in the presence of their consciousness. I can never close my eyes, I can never sleep as their being, their presence was noticeable, and just feet away. So then who were we from the play? Jordan was definitely Joseph from the play, as they both cowardly tried to flee after committing their crimes. Ines was a man-hating lesbian, and Darnell is a homophobe, so those two could go hand and hand.

The only one left was Estelle, who would be me. By default, of course, and not because in the play, she drowned her own son, similarly to how I let Chloe sink, oh, and also because her lover died by Suicide, just like my William. Dar-nell kept making grunting noises as his pushups became more and more intense. Jordan would fart every once and a while, god that smelled. Wow, the universe was crazy, I had to admit, he was right. Jean-Paul Sarte was right, "*hell is other people.*"

JENNIFER HALL

I was just about done cleaning my home office and tidying up. Stacking files, collecting pencils, paper clips, and sticky notes so I could dust down the tabletop, then noticing the dust collection on the ceiling fan's blades. Just as I was finished cleaning the fan, I looked over at my reading lamp, it was covered. My place was pretty dusty. There have been a few consecutive days in which I stayed over at Brian's. Especially the week following the arrest. We've been supporting each other, to listen, to talk, and to console. Like this, all still feels like a dream. My mother FaceTimes me once a day, usually in the evening. On the weekends, they are often during lunch.

It was so good seeing both my parents. Having them come all the way down to Lincoln to support me, distract my mind. I missed my dad's laugh, it's so contagious it can overtake any room. I think he said something about them coming down every other weekend. I missed my mom's cooking. We took a trip to Coleman Grocery Store and got mom whatever she needed to make a favorite recipe. She made sure I ate at least three times a day. Seven o'clock breakfast around the table. Lunch in town. Then dinner at eight o'clock. A routine we still try and stay on, even after they've left. I believe a reliable method is what we all need right now, healthy healing.

❖ ❖ ❖

I had just arrived at Brian's to pick up Nicole. A routine that we recently started was to jog around the track field at the high school. Evening jogs when the sky is slightly changing, and the weather is absolutely perfect. We average eight to ten laps—a healthy release. We also started a thing where we both wear baseball caps while we jog, caps of our favorite sports teams. This week the sport is college football. Nicole came running out of the house in black shoes and shorts while sporting a maroon and white Texas A&M ball cap.

We stopped by the Coleman Grocery Store to pick up some lemon-lime Gatorade and chocolate chip granola bars. After every two laps, we get a reward. I usually then end up having three entire bars. Jog, eat, jog, eat. Nicole also needed to pick up a new phone charger. I think a cute gift would be to get her a portable charger, I think it would be useful. Just big enough to fit in her purse.

The store was calm as I walked down the granola aisle, comparing the various brands. It was then Michelle Tuckerman's cart began sliding down the aisle toward me. I turned my head and gave a slight smile. Behind Michelle was Susan. She stopped her cart next to me.

"Guess where I was the other day?" Michelle asked. I looked down into her cart: beer, whiskey, and steaks.

"Hello, Michelle." This was extremely uncomfortable. I quickly glanced over at Susan, who also seemed nervous.

"I was visiting my son. My son the one you got locked up in some juvenile detention center surrounded by animals. The poor thing is even thinner now than he was. You caused pain to my family and our closest friends!" Michelle hissed, the same tone she used when the officers arrested her, and she banned me from her property. I didn't know what to say. She was speaking as if the evidence against her son was not specific. He did it. He murdered those innocent kids. Why is she blaming me? She is in the worst stage of denial.

"Michelle, we should just keep moving," Susan said. "She is not worth our time, come on."

"It doesn't matter anymore. What is done is done. My boy is gone. My husband is behind bars, I'm alone. Just what you wanted, isn't it Ms.

Hall? Well, I guess we better let you go, you have a sheriff to get home to." Susan gave Michelle a nudge.

"Come on, let's go." Michelle then finally turned and continued on. She was in so much pain, her entire life was turned upside down, but I don't regret turning Tyler in. Just then Susan walked back down the aisle, what does she want now?

"Jennifer, I am so sorry. We are all trying to help Michelle. Poor thing has lost everything and will not accept the truth," Susan said, putting her hand on my shoulder. She ran her finger below her right eye. "This whole town thanks you, Jennifer. Any of our kids could have been next." Susan gave a smile, "I'll let you be, enjoy the rest of your day."

"You too, Susan, and thank you for that."

I met Nicole by the checkout line. I was keeping my composure pretty well, but hearing and seeing Michelle's pain unsettled me. It did actually happen. People are forever changed. Life reminds me that nightmares don't just happen in dreams.

"This charger is $20." Nicole joked.

"Oh, wow, desperate times." I looked down at the newsstand as we waited in line. I quickly pulled out my wallet and handed Nicole my debit card. "Hey, can you go fill up the car, and I'll buy the granola, Gatorade, and your charger?"

"Really? Okay. Thanks! But how would you pay for this?"

"I have cash and thank you. You can fill it all the way up." Nicole smiled as she enthusiastically grabbed my card and walked out the door. I then looked back down at the newsstand. They must have just come in—new issues. I did not want Nicole to see these, I mean she probably will, but not right now. Every day I'm reminded, in some way, that it was all true. Followed by a rapid moist crime scene slideshow.

Phoenix Tribute: Arizona teen filmed classmates' deaths and made it appear as a suicide.
People Magazine: Tyler Tuckerman: Arizona teen murdered classmates and filmed it (their death).
The Berza County Sun: Lincoln teen accused of filming friends' suicides.

TYLER TUCKERMAN

T
he same routine day in and day out: Wake up, shower, eat breakfast, read, eat lunch, doodle in my journal, eat dinner, explore the library, then bedtime. On days and times that we don't have school, we have to work, either outside, as everyone calls the "chain gang" or laundry, washing, drying, and folding everyone's towels and clothes. I hated both, but at least with laundry I wasn't outside whacking weeds or digging holes. I have become on such a strict regimen I could do it with my eyes closed. I've been doing an excellent job at keeping a low profile, the quiet art gallery robber, as a few would describe me. I mindlessly walked to our cell to relax and daydream about William when I could hear them from inside. It was Jordan and Darnell arguing. I stopped dead in my tracks just a few feet from the door to our cell, trying to make out what they are explaining about, I think I might know.

"Bro! Who the fuck keeps stealing my noodles?" Darnell shouted.

"Yo, don't look my way, It wasn't me, Yo!"

Jordan replied you could hear the worry in his voice as Darnell was a lot bigger.

"Bro, don't fucking play me, bro!" It sounded like Darnell was starting to catch on, my plan was working.

Dinner was okay and mediocre at best. I think I've had the same dinner at least four times now, they should really mix up their menu. Afterward, I decided to come out of my shell a little and play a card game with a few juveniles younger than me. I taught them Goldfish, 21, and Egyptian Rat Screw, disclaimer I didn't know the exact rules, so I had to improvise on a few parts. They didn't see the difference, I nearly won every game, damn I should have played for money, or other high priced items in hell, like stamps.

They were about to sound the bell for bedtime when I decided to walk back to our cell. I was humming a song to myself, "*Iris*" by the GooGoo Dolls. Just to have Darnell walk up behind me.

"Sup, Bro?"

"Oh, hey, Darnell. Damn, we better not have eggs and slop again for breakfast tomorrow."

"I feel ya. Yo, so have you seen Jordan around my stuff?"

"Yeah I have, I didn't want to get in the middle, but try looking under his mattress,

I think you might find some interesting stuff under there."

"His mattress, yo?"

"Yeah, I didn't see him stuff anything under there, but that's always a good place to start. I didn't want to tell you this, but if he did steal your stuff, it wouldn't surprise me."

"Brah, what do you mean? Did he say some shit, Bro?"

"Well, just the other day, he said how your mother deserved what she got when your dad was beating her. I told him not to talk like that." I could see Darnell's eyes turn red, he bit his bottom lip and clenched his fists as we approached our cell. "Please don't tell him I told you, I don't want to start anything." but Darnell remained quiet the angry silent type.

We walked into our cell to find it empty. I quickly jumped up to my bunk and watched as Darnell ransacked through Jordan's belongings. There, under his mattress, were Darnells missing items, and in Jordans shoe box were Darnell's noodles. My goodness, I wonder how those got there, I smiled internally.

"Bro, this fucking kid is going to get it. He is going to fucking get it. That fucking white cracker piece of shit. Bro, you have to keep a watch out."

"Okay," I said just as a guard walked by, I think that might be the last round they do before bed. I was getting antsy, like a child trying to sleep on Christmas Eve. Jordan needs to hurry up. Darnell kept pacing. He, too, was getting antsy until he finally stopped and sat on his bed, patiently waiting.

Finally, it was showtime as Jordan walked into the cell. He seemed to be chatting with other guys as he entered laughing and pointing. Darnell didn't even look at him.

"Yo, that new kid is fucking funny, yo!" Jordan said as he plopped down on his bed. I didn't say anything, just peacefully waiting.

"Fucking cracker, you want to explain why I found all my stolen shit hidden in your fucking shit?" Darnell picked his head up, just then, the cell door was shut, and you could hear the bolt lock shut. Showtime.

"What yo? I didn't steal none of your shit," Jordan said. Still, Darnell was not convinced, he quickly got up and opened Jordans shoe box and flung Jordan off his bed to lift up his mattress, exposing a few items.

"Yo, Wh..what the fuck, I...I didn't put those their!" Jordan began stuttering. Darnell's eyes were red again, I could feel his anger.

"And you fucking think my mom deserved to be hit? Deserved to be smacked around? I'll show you what it feels like to be hit!" Darnell yelled as she slowly walked toward Jordan.

"Yo I don't know what your..." Jordan was interrupted by Darnell, punching his across the face, he fell to the ground. My eyes widened with shock, a slight grin appeared. Jordan has a bloody nose as he lay on the ground, both his arms were up.

"Man, I didn't do anything, man!" Jordan squealed. Darnell sat on top of Jordan's chest, his arms pinned under Darnells legs, unable to move. Darnell put his hands around Jordan's neck and began choking him. I quickly jumped down off my bed and got on my hands and knees.

"Fuck you, bro! Fuck you, bro! Fuck you, bro!" Darnell kept shouting. After each chant, he squeezed tighter and tighter and tighter around Jordan's thin long neck, his face turning red, his eyes bulging and watery. It was happening; the *transition was approaching*.

"Keep going, Darnell, he's almost there! he's almost there!" I said encouragingly as I put my face closer to Jordan's blood, bursting eyes, not blinking as I stared at him. I was beginning to feel it again, and this time without my camera, it was possible to witness the transitions without the lens. It was aesthetically marvelous. Almost there as Jordan's eyes were on the brink of bleeding, Darnell biting his lower lip as all those push-ups were put to good use. "Almost there, Darnell, remember he said your mom deserved to be hit!"

"What the fuck is going on!" A guard yelled out, quickly unlocking our cell door, running in and grabbing Darnell. I instantly crawled back to the toilet as more and more guards ran into the room, restraining Darnell and checking Jordan's vitals.

"We still have a pulse, quick call medical!" A guard shouted.

"Fuck you, bro!" Darnell, still shouting as a guard, was putting him in handcuffs.

"We need medics in cell 3, I repeat we need medics in cell 3 NOW!" A female guard said into her dispatch radio. I was still on the ground against the wall, appearing distraught and scared, but inside I was alive again.

I was asked to give a statement on what just transpired. Jordan was taken to the medical wing, and Darnell was born to a solitary cell where I'm sure they would add more time to his sentence. I was alone, I had the entire room all to myself. I could dance, joke, and do whatever I wished. My eternal *room* changed, I like this *room* a lot better. Just me, my journal, and my favorite play. My first night alone was so cozy, I wasn't awakened by Darnell's snoring, or Jordan taking midnight shits. It was peaceful.

I awoke the next morning to my regular routine. There was whisper around the facility within the juveniles on what happened last night in cell 3. I kept getting asked over and over and over again, but it was just your standard cell fight, nothing more. Many of the other juveniles knew Darnell had a temper, so hearing the news was no surprise. After the hell shower and breakfast, I pranced back to my penthouse cell to find a guard standing between the doorway. What the? Please don't tell me they are both back, my alone time was short-lived.

"Tuckerman, you have a new cellmate," the big beardly detention guard said as I approached. A new cellmate? I walked in to be greeted by a tall, handsome guy, oh my, I tried not to blush, "Tuckerman this is Jackson. Jackson, this is Tuckerman," the guard quickly introduced us.

"Hi, I'm Tyler. Tyler Tuckerman," I reached my hand out, excellent grip. His hair was brunette and buzzed short, and *those eyes, so vivid.*

"Hey Tyler, my name is Gavin, Gavin Jackson," he let out a slight grin and then continued to put a few things away as the guard left. I was nervous. I just stood there.

"You can have whichever bed you want, I don't think the other two will be back anytime soon," I said. Gavin laughed.

"This one will do just fine." He picked Darnells' bed. I wasn't too fond of climbing up and down regularly, so I took over Jordan's bed.

I pulled out a book I borrowed from the library pretending to read, but I couldn't take my eyes off this magnificent creature. Gavin kept asking me questions and wanting to have a conversation. I told him the same story about how I was caught with illegal art pieces, and he confessed that he was involved in selling drugs.

"Yeah, it was mostly weed and Molly. When I was caught, I had ten pills on me. Fuck, I wish I didn't go to that party. Have you ever tried Molly?"

"Yeah. Once at a party."

"It's the best, the best feeling. Hey, don't' rat me out, but I'll see if I can somehow sneak us some. I know a few guys."

"That would be awesome, I remember when I took it, everything felt amazing," I said. Then realizing what also happened that night, fucking closet case Jason Brophy.

"Yeah, I get super touchy-feely, and I laugh a lot," Gavid said. I was still in shock on how yesterday I was in hell, now, the universe has brought me to heaven. My eternal room changed from hell is other people; to heaven is other people.

◆ ◆ ◆

A few days passed, and I forgot I was in juvenile detention. I forgot I was being punished for my art, as I now never want to leave this room. Gavin was so understanding, well-read, intelligent, and devilishly handsome. He understood and knew many of my favorite novelists and philosophers. He also read all of Tolkien's magical masterpieces and knew of Jean-Paul Sartre.

He would always ask what I was writing in my journal and said he would write as an outlet. I was shy to show him any of my workings, becoming completely vulnerable.

"Come on, Tuckerman, finally show me what one of your writings?" Gavin asked as he leaned over and grabbed his book and glasses. "Just let me read a small bit," he laughed. I just smiled back, not the exciting bright smile, but the smile you give when a cute boy in glasses is winning in the argument. The smile that if he says one more word, I'm caving in. "Okay, how about this. I'll draw you something if you let me read something you wrote."

"Okay. Sounds like a good barter," I replied, still smiling as I looked through a few of my things. A white, folded piece of paper I use as a bookmark. An origami bookmark that softly hugs the corners of your pages.

"Sweet! Maybe I can draw us a window for this room, what should our view be?" I looked up at him. That was the cutest sentence. But, I'm not sure what our view should be.

"Maybe, someplace we've never been?" I suggested.

"Great Idea. Maybe our room is on the 54th floor in New York City! Now that would be a view!"

"I would love to go to New York." and then finally, I found it. My bookmark, I wrote it when I lived alone in our cell. I got nervous just as I handed Gavin the folded piece of paper. He slowly began unfolding, rearranging, and rotating. Destroying my poor origami.

"I'm going to read it out loud, okay?"

"Outloud?" Okay, I did not agree on that.

"Yeah, it will be fine." Gavin adjusted his glasses. "Who is, He?" Gavin read the title, his voice rippling through the air, gently running up my arms, giving me goosebumps.

He had to rebel against his dynasty because he kissed a boy and liked it.
He unknowingly disrupted the expectations set before him.
A disappointment.
Hetero, Homo, *Being and Nothingness.*
A place where opportunistic potential and inescapable inabilities meet.
That fine release line.
So delicate.
Fulfilled or empty.
Life or death.
Untitled (Black on Grey)

There was silence after Gavin was done. I held my breath throughout the entire reading. Gavin was still looking at the paper, as if he was re-reading it, to himself.

"Wow, Tyler, that was really good. Thank you for letting me read it. There are days when I feel all of these you wrote out, positives, and the negatives. Question though is the Untitled (Black on Grey)."

"A Mark Rothko painting, yeah." we got closer just now, maybe not physically, but connected. Gavin is the first guy I showed my personal writings to. The ones were written in complete darkness. He is the first guy I let see a part of me, which could only be felt. He felt me while reading. What made him understand it even better was that he knew he just wanted to confirm if I was referring to a painting. Goodjob Gavin. A pure masterpiece.

Gavin was telling me when he was younger, he wanted to be an artist. He said that dream only lasted about a year until he then wanted to be a rock star, which then changed a year later to an engineer, then again, and again. He's a man who tries many things and is hugely open-minded, and down to earth, he's a good influence on me. My inspiration that I was lost without.

❖ ❖ ❖

They kept us in the same cell, that number; it became my *favorite number*. It reminds me of everything possible in this world, it told me that I could be loved and that I possessed that magic ability that turns man from beast. Three. All the good and wonder that exists, all the possibilities of happiness that I only dreamt about. That I am alive, I was seen and heard through all the bullshit noise of the world. Three. Taking off my weighted vest and removing the tape across my mouth. I think his spirit animal would be a horse, a silky American Quarter as he was so strong, yet so gentle and patient. Every time I hear it or see it. The number, three. It reminds me of *him*.

I looked over, and Gavin was reading *The Silmarillion*. He looked so beautiful in his reading glasses, my nerd in shining armor. I grabbed my pencil and went back to my *journal,* smiling at every sentence.

JENNIFER HALL

I arrived back at Brian's place with all the missing items we needed for Thanksgiving dinner. It was still pretty early. Nicole was still sleeping, and Brian was out on his morning run. I began unpacking and getting a few things ready—a quick trip to Coleman and grab last-minute essentials, like orange juice. I heard a few cracks up above, Nicole must be awake.

I headed upstairs to check on Nicole. I heard a few things move around, so it's safe to assume she was awake and dressed. I grabbed her folded sweater sitting on the counter to toss aside when I felt something flat inside. I unfolded the bottom and reached my hand up, pulling out what felt like a magazine. I turned it over, it was the *People Magazine* issue about Tyler, his full name written across the cover. Followed by the words "murdered classmates." The four souls smiling back at you. Chloe, Cameron, Greg, and Lizzie. I blinked a few times, then placed the magazine back inside her sweater and slowly walked up the stairs.

Her door was slightly open as I gently

gave it two knocks. She politely invited me in as she brushed her hair, still in her pajamas, the same pattern as her father's. Her room was clean and well decorated. Then it hit me, this was the first time I was in her room. This was the first time I was invited into her world. I could see all her awards and trophies stacked neatly on her shelves and dressers. A well-used metal softball bat leaning against her table. A picture of Nicole and her mother neatly displayed in a handmade frame. Her bed was made, she must have developed that, make your bed every morning habit from her father. I was still at the entryway of her room, making my way inside.

"Wow, look at all of these awards and medals. I have to say, this is the first time I've been inside your bedroom and how impressive it is." I said, but Nicole was unfazed as she continued to brush her hair in the mirror. "May I sit on your bed?"

"Yeah," Nicole replied. She was in pain, an incredible amount of pain for a teenage girl to have to go through. How can you heal when you're constantly reminded of the nightmares thanks to news outlets and magazines. I didn't want to mention that I found her *People magazine* about Tyler. I slowly sat on her well-made bed, blue bed sheets on a wood frame, cute. I looked over, and she was still brushing her hair, not acknowledging me at all.

"Nicole, I am so, so sorry, for everything.

You do NOT deserve any of the crazy shit that has happened here. You moved to this new town with your dad to start a new life, new friends, achieve new awards for your already many collections. This was not supposed to happen. A joyful, inspirational girl like yourself should not have gone through what you did, and I am sorry for that. I know you probably think I'm just some school counselor talking you up to make you feel better. Still, just like yourself, I understand loss, I understand pain at a younger age. Do you remember our first meeting at school and saw a picture of Emily in my office, and you asked if she was my daughter and I told you she was my little sister. Our meeting was cut short, so I couldn't tell you she passed away and how when I was twelve years old, and to this day, I still blame myself. It was my idea to go out into the woods to play make-believe in our princess costumes. It was my idea we split up and fight the imaginary villains, only to have her slip off the muddy ledge and into the lake, alone." One tear fell off my left eye, then two more on my right, "I convinced her to stop eating lunch at our campsite and go play with me in the woods, not realizing she would never be coming back." Nicole stopped brushing her hair, "Then, seeing what happened to Chloe, witnessing it again, those nightmares, that guilt came hurtling back in." Tears rolling from both my eyes, I couldn't stop, the dam was broken. "I'm not telling you this, so you feel sorry for me, or think I'm trying to beat your pain with mine, but instead know, I feel your pain because I too live with it every day." Nicole turned around, eyes filled with tears as she ran and hugged me.

"Jen I am so sorry. I just want my mom back. I want my mom back so bad. This isn't fair. Why am I being punished? Why does everyone I care for end up leaving me? I am always alone!" Nicole sobbed.

I couldn't talk as my throat was dry and tears covering my face. We both sat on her bed, holding each other, we were there for one other as we were both broken souls just trying to make our way in the world. I slowly looked at Nicole, wiping away her tears from her red cheeks and dirty blonde hair.

"Listen to me. You are a strong and beautiful woman who takes her pain and manifests it into beauty. Whether it be sports, or art, or poems, or whatever, you know how to use that pain and learn from it. I know because I see a lot of myself in you. I see a lot of your father in you, and I know you're a fighter. You're strong, and I know your mother was a fighter as well! Remember our first meeting, I told you I believe the ones we love, continue on through our love for them, your mother is still alive in you. She has never been prouder on how strong you have become!" I softly said, trying to keep my composure. Nicole just continued to hug me. "You are beautiful, you are strong, you are a Clark!" I said, as Nicole let out a slight chuckle, the room became light. We looked at one another, both eyes wet, red, and puffy.

"Thank You, Jen. I'm thankful for you, I'm thankful that my dad and I met you. I don't know what we would do in Lincoln without you."

"I promise I will never replace your mother, but I really care about your father. He's a good man."

"I think he really likes you too," Nicole said, using her long sleeve t-shirt to wipe tears away. I leaned in and gave her a hug.

"Let's go downstairs and have a mimosa, one won't hurt. Don't tell your father." I winked.

"Deal! I'm just going to jump in the shower real fast." Nicole said as she began to search through her dresser drawers. "I cannot wait to eat!"

I set up a little prep station next to the cooking station, followed by the eating station. I stood over the sink, washing bright orange carrots, Idaho potatoes, and fresh green beans. The living room was empty and quiet.

"Alexa, play top country hits!" I yelled with both my hands deep in the sink. I waited a few seconds, but she never responded. "Alexa, play top country hits!" I said again while taking a step back, drying the inside of my palms against my jeans, walking toward the living room. Then in the corner of my eye, the side living room window, a teenage boy in all black flashed across. I instantly froze in my tracks. Tyler filled my mind. I couldn't breathe, and could only hear the ambient sound of the sink faucet running. Tyler is here. The backdoor slowly began to open, the darkroom getting brighter. Then I heard him.

"And that is why the Cowboys haven't won a Super Bowl since 1996!" Mark joked while carrying two pies, and behind him, taunting away was brian. He just got back from his morning run. He looked cute in white basketball shorts and a grey tank top. I walked over and turned the sink faucet off. "Happy Thanksgiving, Ms. Hall!" I dried my hands and took both the pies from Mark.

"Happy Thanksgiving, Mark! These pies look delicious, is this one Cheesecake and this looks like Pumpkin Pie?" I sat them both down on the kitchen table, walking over and giving Brian a kiss.

"Oh wow, you're good," Mark said as Nicole came down the stairs, she walked up and gave Mark a kiss. "You look cute." Nicole smiled back at him.

"Jen I can help you prep food."

"Thanks, Nicole. I just finished washing the veggies. We can start chopping up the potatoes and carrots." Brian walked into the living room and turned the sports channel on, Mark grabbed a soda and sat on the leather recliner.

"Jen, you said your folks were bringing the turkey?" Brian asked from the living room, remote in hand as he stood watching sports recaps.

"Yeah, she called three hours ago, so they are probably close, I'll send her a text." Nicole and I were chopping when I nudged her elbow, then pointed with my eyes at the other end of the sink, there stood two tasteful poured orange mimosas. Next to them, a slight flash of green got my attention. Ruby was coming back to life! Fresh vines with baby leaves peeking out from behind the brown and dried leaves. I got so excited, I quickly stopped chopping and placed a few ice cubes on her soil bed. I moved a few of the dead pieces around to reveal the stunning green—a new chapter.

◆ ◆ ◆

I've missed the Thanksgiving aroma that fills and lingers. A turkey that was based for hours slowly roasting in the oven. Fresh garlic and butter from the mashed potatoes. Tarty cranberries combined with steaming corn on the cob. Is it possible to get full from the smells?

"Looks like we have one more hour until the turkey is done," My dad said as he looked at his phone then placed it back down on the living room table.

"Oh perfect, we should be done by then." I replied, reaching my hand in the bag to pull out a random tile. As we all waited for the food to finish cooking, it was a Hall family tradition to play board games in the living room. We split into teams and played Scrabble. It was Nicole and Mark's turn as I looked at mine and Brian's tiles, we don't have the best, not a single vowel. The game was getting pretty competitive between the three generations sitting around this table. My mom and dad felt they had to win as the wise elders, whereas Nicole and Mark wanted to be known as the underdogs, thus strived for victory. Brian and I knew what we could accomplish when we put our minds together, and so we had nothing to worry about.

We have all come such a long way, we all grew immensely the past few months, for many of us, the day began when we moved to Lincoln. We are all on our own healing path, taking that process one day at a time. We all have our own unique Tyler-inflicted wounds that need time to heal. As I look around, I know the process is working, as I hear the laughs, I know the steps we're taking are working. With the love of family, you can tackle almost anything. All because we have each other, and the love and support of friends. At the end of the day, that's all that matters.

TYLER TUCKERMAN

Journal Entry: SPRING of 2020

We had just moved into our new two-story cookie-cutter home near the big city. Our two golden retrievers, Rusty and Trixie, were all wet as I had just given them a warm bath. They were drying off, shaking their bodies then running down the hallway to the stairs, then out into the backyard. The smell of burgers on the grill overcame me as I too walked down the stairs. I could hear Gavin shout from outside, "Babe, bring some paper plates, the burgers are about done!" Thank goodness, I was starving. Just as I was about to search for the paper plates, our front doorbell rang. Our neighbors had arrived for the BBQ, fresh potato salad in hand accompanied by their golden retriever, Max. We all walked out to our porch, the sun was warm and not a cloud in the sky. I watched as Gavin was putting the patties on the plate, turning off the grill, then playing fetch with the dogs. I walked over and handed him a beer. He leaned in and gave me a kiss, then another, and one more. I just continued to stare back. Admiring him, and those *vivid green eyes*.

PRAISE FOR AUTHOR

A focused, impressively nuanced tale about teen-agers, drugs, lies, and the terror of hidden enemies.

- KIRKUS REVIEW

Touching on painfully relevant subjects of depression, teen suicide, drug abuse, social alienation and collective grief, this is a blunt story that doesn't shy away from uncomfortable themes. The multiple narrative voices make the story more complete, bridging the perspective gap between adults and children, broadening the narrative arc, as well as the book's potential readership. Regardless of your age or personal experience with trauma, this hard-hitting novel is an unpredictable, heart-wrenching, and timely read.

- SPR

Cory Wolfe's MAKE BELIEVE is an intriguing

psychological thriller fir for young adult and adult audiences.

- INDIEREADER

This is a queer psychological thriller that really kept me gripped till the end! And remember, not everything is as it seems.

- VIC AT LGBTQIA+ BOOK REVIEW

Readers will devour this captivating story in one sitting and be blown away by the twist at the end of the book.

- ELITE CHOICE AWARDS

The way the author seamlessly weaves in foreshadowing and background plot points is just amazing. I can't recommend this enough!

- A. MESSINA

ACKNOWLEDGEMENT

A LOT, a lot, a lot of walking and daydreaming took place that conjured the necessary environments for this story to take shape. I first want to say THANK YOU to my editor, Kevin Callahan, for your editorial assessment and impactful feedback. I will always remember the first line in your email after finishing Make Beleive, "Well, I must say, you surprised the hell out of me." And to the platform Reedsy for providing the marketplace for authors and editors to meet. This story isn't full of bright lights and heart-bursting love; it's on the opposite end, the side of darkness and pain. With that, I made it through, with my sanity intact, thanks to a few of my closest friends and family! Thank you for all the love, support, and real-time feedback. My wonderful school teaching aunt, Christy Carter, and my kickass superintendent aunt, Gloria Dean. Thank you to my childhood best friend (and first girlfriend in 5th grade), Cinthia Ruiz. A huge thank you to a few sisters I never had, Heather Healy, Ginny Hicks, and Sam Battis! And lastly, a huge thank you to my audio team, Zane Boyer and Stacey Rae Allen, for delivering a fantastic performance throughout the audiobook. As well as Carlos Santana, with Prosantana Studios on your collaboration for the Jennifer Hall narratives.

CRISIS HOTLINES

If you or someone you know is battling with suicidal thoughts, drug abuse, or trouble with sexual orientation or sexual identity, please utilize the below resources.

National Suicide Prevention Lifeline: (800)-273-8255

The Trevor Project: (866)-488-7386

LGBT National Hotline: (888)-843-4564

Crisis Text Line: Text START to 741-741

The National Runaway Safeline: (800)-786-2929

SAMHSA's National Hotline: (800)-622-4357

American Addiction Center: (866)-723-2194

UPCOMING BOOK BY CORY WOLFE

Sullivan Young, a novel

Dear Theodore Sullivan,

We are so very excited to have you begin our 4-week orientation training within the Private Wealth Investments team here at Kauffman Schwartz. Throughout this orientation, you will be equipped with the necessary tools, resources, and mentors to successfully begin your career. Inside, you will find your daily schedule, filled with KS seminars, functional training, team meet and greets, and fun gatherings. Along with training material for your Series 7 and Series 63 exams. Your hall buddy is - Isa Kraus. Please review the hall buddy best practices on the KS policy & procedures tab. If you have any questions or concerns, please contact your designated New Hire Coordinator.

We look forward to having you be a part of the team!

Audrey Stone
Managing Director
Private Wealth Investments
Kauffman Schwartz

Made in the USA
Monee, IL
18 January 2021